Keeper of the I

1 of *The Keeper Tr*

By Alyssa Laus

This is a work of fiction. Similarities to real people, places, or events are entirely coincidental.

KEEPER OF THE FALLEN

First edition. June 10, 2021.

Written by Alyssa Lauseng.

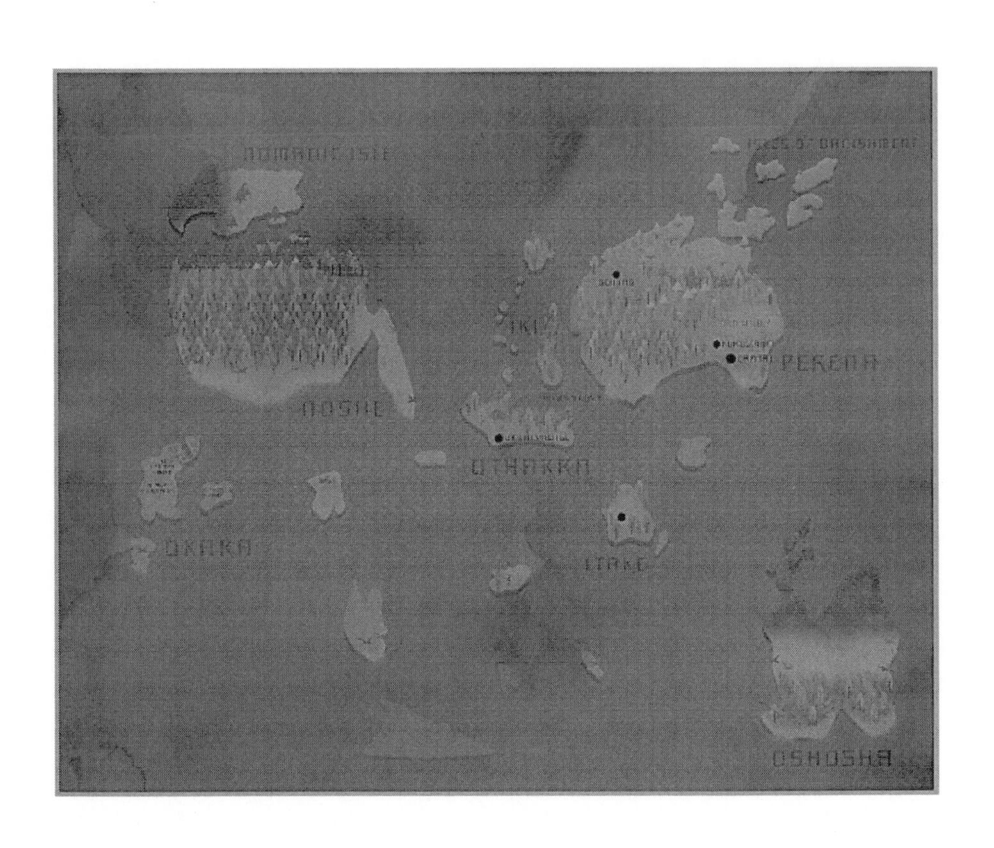
NOMADIC ISLE
PERENA
OKARA
OSHOSHA

One: The Guidance of the Fallen

"Then it's settled," Lord Minoru's golden eyes looked up to meet the solemn gaze of his successor. "The Giahatian troops will be arriving on their ship soon. They will meet with me tonight, sign a treaty for peace, and tomorrow you will be writing to the Noshians to share the good news."

Takeo's expression turned dubious. He shook his head, letting frustration and concern overtake his features. "Lord Minoru, I know you've worked tirelessly to reach this point and have continued to do so since I took over, and I know I said that I wouldn't interfere, but...the Winds are telling me that something isn't right. We've resisted the Giahatian Empire's advances on our territories for ages. Why are they suddenly willing to stand down and make peace with us? This is beyond the temporary cease-fires they've called for in the past; Emperor Akuwara isn't exactly famous for being merciful."

"Your instincts are rarely wrong—you *are* Lord Kohaku's true descendant, after all—but this may be our last chance to garner more reasonable negotiations with the Empire. We can't afford any further losses to battle with them; you know how that turned out for the true-blooded Perenins." Lord Minoru pinched the bridge of his nose with a sigh. "Enough talk about bloodshed. For now, lad, go and find your daughter. I hear she's gotten quite talented with shuriken lately. Perhaps she'll become a Guardian just as you once were."

Takeo studied Lord Minoru carefully for a long moment before he finally complied with the veiled order. Whether or not he was now the one they called Lord Okami, he still respected the former Alpha's commands. Outside of the council room where he had met with Lord Minoru, the isle of Othakra was as beautiful as ever in the glow of a warm summer afternoon. Like many generations of Okami before him, Takeo believed it to be his duty to protect the land, which provided so generously for the tribe. The Giahatio, however, sought to exploit Othakra's resources rather than nurturing them, to own the island instead of praising it. The land owned itself. The wolf people who lived on it only borrowed.

Takeo's daughter Sonika, whom Lord Minoru had sent him to find, loved the forest, and so he made his way there to search for her. Sonika had just entered her eighth summer, already proving to be an excellent student to her father and their people's practices. Though her fierceness and temperament were similar to his, the traits she exhibited of her own made Takeo confident that, one day, she would become a strong and courageous leader. She could already coax the spirits of the land into speaking with her, the earth especially, and she easily picked up the training that provided the Okami with a developed means of defense. It was taught to everyone from as early of an age as possible, and how they, so far, had fended off the onslaught of Giahatian attacks occurring throughout written Okami history.

He came upon Sonika near a creek, where she was sitting on a large boulder enjoying the sunlight as it cast warm rays between the leaves above her. Upon hearing him approach, she turned to him with a grin that resembled his own. The low branches hanging from a nearby tree appeared to bow and sway in a greeting toward him. That was the way of any forest, Takeo thought. When it liked who entered, it showed its approval.

"What did Elder Minoru want, Papa?" Sonika asked, her golden gaze becoming deeply curious and breaking Takeo from his brief reverie.

"He would sit on you if he heard you call him 'Elder,' young lady." Takeo chuckled, patting her hair, which was the same color as her mother's had been—only a few shades lighter than black. "He said that the Giahatians will be here shortly and that once negotiations are finished, we can celebrate peace just like we celebrate during our moon festivals."

Sonika beamed. The full moon festivals were especially exciting to her and the other children. They stayed up late with the adults to enjoy singing, dancing, drums, stories, and all sorts of delicious food around a massive fire in the center of the village. Takeo felt his face fall a little; it was one of their many traditions that spurned the Giahatians into calling them savages. Doubt toward the peace treaty curled his insides, but Takeo cleared his throat so that Sonika wouldn't be able to dwell on his sudden pause.

"Now, then, how about some training before we have to make ourselves presentable as Lord Okami and his daughter?" Takeo grinned as Sonika's eyes brightened.

A leather case he kept strapped to his right leg stored Takeo's kunai and shuriken, the preferred weapons of the Okami arsenal, then he presented Sonika with one of her own. As she secured the case, an abrupt silence fell over the forest. Sonika's gaze went to the treetops where birds should have been singing—even the creek beside them seemed to have lost its voice in the sudden heaviness. Takeo's eyes followed hers, an uneasy feeling clawing at him, though he would never show such concern to his daughter. They turned to one another for a long, wordless moment.

"Are they here?" Sonika whispered; Othakra was as living and breathing as the Okami, and the island always tensed in such a manner when the Giahatians landed on it.

Takeo nodded. A pair of squirrels jumped in the branches over their heads and he felt a small amount of relief as the woods began steadily returning to life once more.

When they returned to the village a little over an hour later, Sonika paused briefly to look at the black sails of the Giahatian vessel, which were visible from the small port before they continued toward their home. A group of dressed dancers stopped in their festival preparations to greet Takeo as he passed by. He did not need to demand respect from his people, as they offered it to him quite freely, even Lord Minoru. Takeo had led a few different factions of scouts and warriors from when he was a young teenager until two years prior when he had been named Alpha. He had always taken great care of those he was responsible for, and he was no different as Lord Okami. Sonika was proud to call him her father.

Takeo froze, and Sonika did the same. It was as if the earth had again stopped beneath their feet. One by one, those bustling through the village did the same, then turned toward the council house. An uneasy breeze swept through Othakra's grass, and Takeo felt a chill down his spine. Sonika's eyes raked over the worried expressions exchanged between those who were nearest to one another before that same emotion began to pull at her.

"Papa," she tried, but Takeo put his hand up to keep her quiet while he studied his environment.

Takeo glanced in several different directions, able to detect the scents and blades of Giahatian soldiers and assassins alike. There were many. Through the network of pack communication, he touched at everyone's consciousness. He sent out the resounding message for the warriors to prepare, but to do so as discreetly as possible, then breathed deeply before setting off in a run toward the council house. Sonika hesitated briefly and went after her father; she didn't want to be alone with the heaviness in the air as people nervously followed Takeo's order. They trusted him and his decisions, which made his visible concern worse to witness.

When Takeo reached the base of the stairs to the council house, the doors flew open and Nobu, an advisor to the two living Okami Lords, came thundering down the stairs, his breathing labored and panicked as he tried to speak. Nobu had a shallow cut on his forehead. Before Takeo could react, an ominous feeling enclosed him, his eyes once again drawn toward the stairs, where a Giahatian commander loomed at the top in the lengthening shadows of evening. Sonika was at Takeo's heels, just in time to hear an awful growl rip from her father's throat as he exposed his canine fangs to the enemy. She shrank away at the sound. The commander looked into his hands and played with something between his fingers that gleamed against the fading sun. A cruel smirk pulled at his lips when he threw it to Takeo's feet. Nobu inhaled sharply, Takeo ordered him back.

"I was made to believe that you have one of those, as well." The man sneered. Sonika peered around her father's leg to see the golden pendant of Lord Minoru's necklace soaked in blood, forming a pool around where it had fallen to the ground. The commander chuckled darkly as he circled his hand in the air above his head. "So now, Lord Takeo, you can be buried with both of them."

The Giahatians materialized from the shadows. Just as Takeo began to send out an alert for the warriors to act, two of the soldiers leapt and attacked him from behind. Takeo used his sheer mass to throw them off him and gave his full order through the special Okami power of Mindspeak. Though the time he'd spent defending himself had already proven dire as Giahatian blades stained with red, the Okami warriors flooded into the battlegrounds that were once their village. Sonika crouched fearfully, trying to stay near her father while dodging around his movements as he pushed back another assailant. She fell back. Amid the chaos, Takeo's closest friend and current second-in-command Kinta appeared, scooping Sonika from the ground and shoving her toward her father.

"Lord Takeo!" Kinta panted. "You and your daughter need to get out of here, *now.* Take Sonika and retreat!"

They stared one another down for what felt like an eternity to Sonika. She watched their exchange from the safety of her father's arms, unable to fathom the silent words spoken between them, only able to hear the firm beating of Takeo's heart against her ear. At last, Takeo nodded curtly and fled, the path soon becoming a blur to Sonika's eyes as he ran. When he set her down again, they were outside of their home.

Sonika shook with a terror she had never known before. Her world felt like it was beginning to collapse all around. The only thing she could focus on was how Takeo held her tightly, a safety soon shattered when his hands went over her ears to block out the surrounding noises of death. He repeatedly whispered for her to calm herself, until finally, he gently pushed on her mind with his, forcing her to reflect the calmness he needed from her the most. It was one of the many things Takeo was capable of that had allowed the Alpha's title to return to Lord Kohaku's bloodline after years of being hidden away from the Giahatio's eyes.

"I need you to listen to me," Takeo's voice rumbled like distant thunder, and every syllable betrayed the pain in his heart. "I believe there may be too many Giahatians for us to fight off this time. They've brought everyone, even their assassins."

Sonika worriedly examined her father's face as the weight of his words sank into her. "But—"

"I don't know how many of us are going to survive, but you *will* be one of those survivors, Sonika. Under the floorboards beneath our table, I've stored a pack of supplies and your mother's medicines for this very situation. Once you have those, go to the beach, get into our fishing canoe, and leave the island."

"Papa," Sonika breathed. The Okami never left Othakra. Feeling haunted by the unknown that lay ahead, she hugged her father's neck, and they held each other close once more. Takeo was trembling. Sonika had never seen her father like this.

"Keep running, keep fighting, and never forget who you are as Okami. No matter what, I will always be with you." Takeo kissed her forehead and released her before quickly wiping at his eyes. He opened their front door for her. "Now, go."

Sonika bit her lip as tears welled in her eyes when Takeo turned toward the battle once again. She breathed deeply and swallowed her emotions as he marched away—it was time to be brave. With her father's courage guiding her, she started following through on the instructions he'd given her. She initially struggled to tear up the loosened floorboard until it gave away with a reverberating *crack*, and she was able to reach in and find the elk-skin bag of supplies. Sonika exited the house, unsure if it would be the last time or if she would eventually return. As she stepped over the threshold, a slain Imperial soldier fell from the roof. Startled, Sonika backed away from the dead man's empty gaze, running in the opposite direction of the path she should have taken.

As Sonika ran through the village, her eyes fell on the horror of scattered corpses and tall flames, which engulfed the buildings. She forced herself to continue, eyes always on the watch for approaching enemies. However, when she came upon the demolished council house, she stopped dead in her tracks. She covered her mouth to stifle the outcry of shock erupting from her lungs as her legs gave out underneath her.

Takeo lay on his side, a long gash across his neck, blood still ebbing from the open wound. Helpless, tears rolling down her cheeks, she crawled toward her father and curled up beside him with her head on his chest as her sobs continued. His warmth was fading fast. She desperately tried to remember the funeral chant to the Earth spirits so that he could lay in peace, but her mind was blank.

When tears would no longer come forth and her breathing was only a tremble, Sonika forced herself up once more and, wobbling, started toward the shore, not wanting her father's sacrifice to be for nothing. She hugged herself for security as she walked along paths lined by destroyed residences. Everything had gone silent save for the roaring of the fires, and she felt increasingly exposed. She turned down a side street with homes that were no longer recognizable.

From above the oppressive smoke burning at her eyes and nose, the familiar scents of other Okami came to her, and she followed their traces until she came to a lean-to. She peered in, and twenty pairs of glowing, golden eyes stared anxiously back at her from the safety of the woodpiles stacked inside.

"Sonika!" a voice urgently whispered.

"Riku?" Sonika tilted her head as Riku struggled to dislodge himself from his hiding place. She glanced over her shoulder worriedly as she helped her friend down. "Riku, we need to get out of here."

"Where can we go?" Riku's eyes were red—whether from the smoke or from crying, Sonika couldn't say, though it was likely both; she knew she looked the same way. The other children were peering out from the shadows behind Riku, and Sonika waved them forward.

"The woods," A boy, no older than eleven, said definitively as he helped a younger child down from where they had climbed up to the top of a wood stack. "Mama always told me that the forest would keep us safe if we went far enough."

"The Giahatians also don't know it like we do. If we run for it, we can all make it." The boy's twin brother piped up as he also clamored out of the shed.

"Are you sure we'll be safe? None of us are old enough for our other forms yet." Riku whimpered.

Sonika looked around at the other frightened faces surrounding her. "We have to try."

They all agreed to the plan before letting the oldest two lead the march toward the forest. They went slowly at first, all looking out for Giahatian soldiers, but it soon changed into a run. Sonika and Riku were at the back of the makeshift formation to help herd the younger ones in the right direction. The majority of the group crossed into the shelter of the trees without incident, but Sonika felt anxiety building in her chest as she passed a little one over to the twins. Riku disappeared into the trees from beside her, and she heard the rustle of leaves and branches, which meant they were continuing to retreat into the forest's depths.

A strange scent drifted toward Sonika with the wind as she stepped toward the forest. She swallowed, terrified; she was the last one out in the open. Though the others were far back, she could see them waiting for her in the deepening darkness. She shook her head mutely to tell them to go as she heard footsteps in the dirt behind her. Her eyes went wide with horror.

She turned to run away from the forest, but a blade penetrated the skin on her back, narrowly missing her spine. The attack's force pushed her face-first into the ground, muffling the scream of agony as it burst from her throat. She weakly turned to look at the forest, barely focusing on the gleaming of golden Okami eyes in the distance, which were now rapidly disappearing from view. She could hear men trampling over bushes as they went into the forest to chase down the others, though it sounded as if she were listening from underwater. Heavy footfalls approached her, followed by excruciating pain rippling throughout her back as the weapon dislodged. Sonika's world went unbearably bright and then began to fade toward darkness.

The misty figure of a white wolf appeared before her just as her eyes threatened to close all the way, and she wondered if it was the death she had always heard the warriors worry over.

However, the wolf spoke with what precious little she could remember of her mother's voice. *"The Giahatians are only looking away for now, young one. That will change soon. Come, the pain will pass. I know it hurts, but there is no time to feel it here."*

Sonika forced herself upward at the spirit's command, her entire body trembling and convulsing; she couldn't bear to think about the warm sensation seeping from the wound to her skin. Adrenaline hindering pain, Sonika rose to her feet and followed the spirit. She stumbled through the bushes and brambles at the edge of the forest until she finally reached the shore. As she came to the canoe her father had mentioned, men's shouts reached her ears. She shoved the boat away from the wet sand. Knives sailed toward her through the air and splashed into the ocean around her. Weeping, Sonika collapsed onto the bottom of the canoe, praying to whichever spirits were listening that she would survive.

"Please, Water spirits," she raspingly begged. Waves caressed the hull of the canoe and carried it away.

• • • •

KULAKO AWOKE FROM FITFUL sleep with a start, finding that he had rolled out of his cot and onto the cool stone floor. His muscles sore from the day's training, he was slow to sit up as he tried to calm his racing heart and rapid breathing. Kulako typically had nightmares, but none with the depth of reality like the one he had just witnessed. He looked over to his snoring roommates as he wiped a thin layer of sweat from his forehead, relieved that the other four boys hadn't been disturbed and happy to avoid the expected result of hostility. He pulled his knees up to his chest and rested his back against the wall, staring at the ceiling, wondering where such a dream could have possibly come from. He was exhausted, and hoped that it would be gone for the night.

"Come run with us." The firm but soothing voice of a woman came to him, sending chills down his spine. A mysterious howl rode in on the night's breeze through the small, high window carved into the wall above him. Unable to contain his curiosity, Kulako took advantage of his remarkable stealth, successfully leaving the tiny room and then the building, unnoticed by the nighttime guards.

Kulako studied the empty training grounds in the moonlight for a few moments to ensure that he wasn't being watched. There was a blind spot over his left shoulder, but he didn't feel the need to be concerned with it—he could hear the guards snoring from where they kept watch on walkways attached to the walls surrounding Kurushima's grounds. Kulako picked up a rock near his feet and tossed it at the longhouse next to his. When the noise it made settled and no voices were on the way to investigate, he began to move once more. A gust of wind tugged him to the right.

He found himself at a small foxhole beneath the iron fence that surrounded the training grounds. Again, the wind beckoned to him from the footpath that lay before him on the other side. Kulako hesitated. It wasn't in his nature to follow impulses, but the one to pursue the voice of the woman was too relentless to ignore. The visions Kulako had seen of fires danced before his eyes again. He dug the cavity out further, just enough to squeeze through and set down the trail at a run.

He stopped when he came to a hill where the track ended. The mountains stood in stoic silence in the distance while the moon cast its white light over the open land. Kulako wondered if he had placed too much confidence in his strange dream. The sudden cawing of two ravens alerted him as they swooped down overhead, one touching the tips of his hair with long talons. Kulako shivered when he realized he hadn't felt the wind that should have been beneath the birds' wings. It was as if they were only shadows. He turned to follow them but met instead with two pairs of glowing golden eyes. Kulako jumped back, frightened by what he saw.

One wolf's fur was paler than the moon, and the other darker than the night. The black wolf began to approach, and Kulako could only stare in captivated terror when the white one did the same. The black wolf's gaze was stern and unbreakable as it watched the boy of ten, while the white wolf's eyes reflected the bottomless depths of the ocean. The black wolf's lips peeled back to reveal deadly teeth as it growled lowly at him. The white wolf nudged the black wolf, and the snarling ceased.

"You have seen the fate of our people, young one." The black wolf *spoke* with the powerful voice of a man in Kulako's mind, and his heart pounded against his ribcage from the shock. *"The Giahatio, the very people* you *serve, have destroyed our home and torn us from our land; the entire Okami way of life has been shattered. It exists no more."*

"Kulako," The voice of the woman who had called to him came from the white wolf. He apprehensively turned his head toward her, startled that she had spoken his name. Kulako's initial fears washed away for reasons he could not explain, as if she had somehow lulled his emotions into calmness. He sat down before the two large canines, sensing that they would not harm him and for once, trusting that instinct. The wolves mimicked his motions. Kulako couldn't tear his eyes away from theirs. *"The spirits have placed a very important task in your hands, young one. They want you to protect those of us who remain and repair the damage that has been done to us—this, in the end, is how you will repent for your life here with the Giahatio, and how you will find peace and forgiveness within yourself one day."*

Kulako waited in disbelief in front of the two wolves. He opened his mouth to say something, anything, but found that he was incapable of words. The black wolf met his eyes, and the images from his nightmare flashed before him.

"Protect our fallen." He commanded the young boy. *"You will know what I speak of when the time is right. If you are ever lost, we will be along to guide you. This, Kulako, is your destiny."*

Wishing he could explain why, he reached up and touched the dark fur on the wolf's neck. The two wolves exchanged sidelong glances and the white wolf nodded at her counterpart. They rose to all four paws, fur rustling as the wind began to twist through it. Kulako also stood, wanting more answers, though no words came. They tilted their heads back, and from their throats came the music of a wolf's song. Kulako shivered at the haunted, longing sound of it. As their song faded, the wind carried their spirits off through the still darkness of the hour once more, leaving Kulako staring after them in amazement in the lonely midnight.

Two: The Pariah

Kulako's consciousness met with a strange feeling when morning rose. It was almost like what the older boys would describe as being hungover. He couldn't remember how or when he had returned to the cramped room; maybe he hadn't even left it at all. He kept his eyes closed to center himself after a night of swirling dreams. When he heard the other boys beginning to move around, he stirred but continued to feign sleep. Instead, he shifted so that he could reach under the straw block that made up his pillow and hooked a finger through a loop in the pommel of a knife he kept there. However, unlike with most mornings, his roommates left without kicking, threatening, or shoving either him or one another.

Kulako sat up when he was sure that they had gone and sighed in relief. He knew that he was forbidden from keeping the kunai outside of training times, but being able to defend oneself at all times was a necessity. He stretched and pushed back the rough blanket that covered him. The previous night's encounter had been nothing more than an extremely vivid dream, and he refused to accept a different answer. Kulako was nowhere near daring enough to be out of bed in the first place—stowing a knife away was at least practical, and worth the risk of a beating when caught if it meant he could protect his life otherwise.

He shook the shaggy hair from his eyes once he had dressed and set to making his bed, taking extra care to place the kunai away in an inner fold of his shirt. Today was a rare day for Kurushima, as the training grounds and halls would be empty, but he knew the masters would perform room inspections like they did every day. Kulako had been brought to Kurushima four years prior and remembered only a handful of days where training was dismissed entirely. He had not voluntarily come here, very few did, but Kulako was sure he would never return to the slave island of Okara where he had been born, nor did he want to.

Once outside, Kulako habitually checked his surroundings before cautiously turning the corner around the long building, which was one of several that housed the boys who, if they could live long enough, would become assassins under the orders of the empire that called itself the Giahatio. The practices used in Kurushima's training process were grueling, cruel, and designed to create the world's most cold-blooded killers who would roam the shadows at night at the Emperor's direction. Kulako had seen those men before when they visited the masters at Kurushima. They feared nothing, not even death, and certainly lived up to their reputations of cruelty. Kulako hoped that if he did survive, he wouldn't become like them.

Given the cuts and bruises which constantly littered Kulako's body, it was no wonder how they came to be that way. The boys were beaten, flogged, and even branded for disobedience or showing weakness or hesitation. The training masters ran them through drills with kunai, katana, and hand-to-hand combat until bones cracked. Training also consisted of making poisons and occasional dosages with them to test immunity. Reeds whipped the bottoms of bare feet if the boys were not stealthy enough, and the training masters regularly pitted them against one another to the death in contests of strength. These rituals were endured from the age of seven years old—Kulako had been only six—until at the youngest sixteen, but most didn't graduate until the ages of nineteen or twenty. Those who could not survive were weak. The Empire had no place in its ranks for those it considered weak.

Kulako was still distracted as he decided it was safe for him to round the side of the building.

"Akahana!" he heard what served as his last name harshly called out from one of the masters. A slaveborn didn't have an actual surname, rather their families were named after the regions their ancestors had been taken from.

Kulako turned in time to meet with the back of the man's fist hitting him across the mouth. The master shoved him against the building's outer wall and grabbed him. Kulako coughed and spit blood as his last loose tooth fell to the ground at the master's feet. His head rang like the bells they used to announce morning training.

The master bared his yellowed teeth and slammed Kulako against the wall again, holding him by the hair. Kulako cringed as he looked into the master's flat black eyes. "What the hell do you think you were doing out of bed last night?"

Kulako swallowed nervously. It had only been a dream. "I-I wasn't—"

"Don't play stupid with me. Teiji said he saw you sneaking back into your building," The master glared again. Kulako was finally able to focus on which master it was. He groaned as he registered Hoji's face. "He told me that he got up to take a piss and saw you right by this corner here, looking as if you'd just seen a damned ghost."

Kulako's eyes darted over to the longhouse that lay only paces away from the one he lived in and quickly looked back at Master Hoji. How had he not noticed Teiji? His voice froze in his throat before he weakly lied, "Teiji couldn't have known who that was."

"Horse shit. Let's pretend there wasn't a full moon last night: you seen or know any other of you little red-haired bastards around here that are still alive?" Hoji pushed Kulako down, his expression etched with disgust as the boy landed hard on the ground.

Kulako cowered against the wall. Other boys who had shared common traits of his heritage had come to Kurushima along with him, but the foreign diseases of Perena or a predisposition for not being suited for combat often took their lives before they were even given much of a chance at survival. Kulako had recently wondered if most of them were brought into the iron gates as bait for those who could survive. Finally, Kulako dumbly shook his head in response to the master.

"I could have you flogged for this," Hoji seethed as he kicked Kulako in the stomach. "But I'm damn tired of whipping you, boy."

Kulako gasped for air as he reeled from the blow, but he really only comprehended the fact that he was not going to endure further punishment. The wounds on his back from the last flogging had only healed over a few days earlier.

"You ought to consider yourself lucky, and by Hikari's Light, I hope you do. This is your only warning." Hoji spat at Kulako as he began to walk away, catching him on the shoulder.

Kulako scowled at the master's back before he wiped off the saliva on the building. He checked his surroundings once more and made his way toward the dining hall. Kulako held back his internal disgust like he always did as the same ladleful of gray gruel was slopped into a bowl for him over rice. It never tasted good, but was enough to get him through his days and slightly better than what he had eaten before as a slaveborn. He washed his dishes in the scullery and placed them back on a shelf among neat rows of other returned utensils.

Kulako spent as much of his sparse free time as far out of the way as possible and decided that, with how well morning had started, he should keep to this habit by staying out of sight. He felt better when left alone as it was. His foreign appearance, which came from the Nomadic Plains far northwest of Perena, automatically made him an outsider. It was rare to find the Nomads in their homeland due to the prevalence of the slave trade where Kulako's life and his older brother's life had begun. His red hair, violet eyes, and pale skin marked his differences from the Giahatian and Perenin boys, and they and the masters made sure he was aware of it. Being an outsider was dangerous at Kurushima. Because of that, Kulako made survival his first priority, which meant training even when it was not required.

He found the secluded area he usually sought out after rummaging around for knives in one of the weapons sheds. Kulako's accuracy had significantly improved over the past year, but speed was still his best asset. He did not have the same power as the others who were already growing to be much taller and bulkier than he ever would, and that meant his lethality would always depend on how quickly and how precisely he could attack an opponent. Kulako shuddered. He hated killing, whether he was watching it or thinking of it so casually as he just had, but there was no way around murder in this life. He supposed he would have to adapt eventually.

The air suddenly grew cold around him as he trained, and he paused as he grabbed a kunai by the handle to pull it from the poor tree he'd been using for target practice. It was the middle of summer, yet a shiver still crawled across his skin. Everything felt heavy. Kulako released the knife and turned.

Standing only several feet away was the same large, black wolf he had seen the night before, his fierce golden eyes intense as he watched the boy. Kulako inhaled sharply and froze.

It was just a dream. He reminded himself in a panic as the wolf pulled his lips back and revealed long white fangs, growling thunderously. Kulako realized that the wolf was not looking at him, but past him, and turned to see the long shadows of other trainees approaching. Swearing, he cleaned up his knives, hoping to avoid a confrontation. The wolf's snarling became deeper. Kulako looked at him out of desperation.

"I'm trying," he hissed at the massive canine, though he wasn't sure why he had spoken to him.

The wolf disappeared as a hand came down between his shoulder blades and sent him to the ground. The kunai scattered across the dirt and grass.

"Not fast enough." Teiji's taunting voice sneered from behind him. Kulako groaned, and the older boy shoved his face back into the soil. "What game are we playing today, Kulako?"

Muffled, Kulako replied, "The one where you leave me alone."

"No, I don't like that game." Teiji mused as he allowed Kulako up. "Think of a different one."

Kulako glared at him as he sat up, trying to rub the dirt off his face with his sleeve. There were two other boys with Teiji named Sota and Haru. The three were mostly harmless when separated, but together they were a nightmare, and Sota was the most reserved of the group. Kulako was determined that they wouldn't be confident in pushing him around for much longer.

Haru broadly grinned as he crouched down beside Kulako and Teiji. He poked Kulako's forehead with such force that Kulako was sure there would be a red mark there later. Haru picked up one of the scattered knives. "Maybe we should play kunai-dodge."

"No, he's gotten good at that one," Sota said, trying to sound as intimidating as his companions. When Kulako responded by glowering at Sota, the other boy silenced.

"Not when we're this close, he hasn't." Teiji offered as he also picked up one of the kunai from the ground. He stood fluidly, pulling Kulako up by his arm and released him.

"Teiji, don't," Kulako retreated by a step. He couldn't tell if he was pleading or making an attempt to warn the older boys as they all held knives in the air.

Teiji stabbed straight for Kulako's stomach, and Kulako brought his forearm up against Teiji's to block the attack before he made his fingers into a spear and hit him in the throat. Haru was immediately on his right where he slashed for Kulako's head. Kulako ducked between Haru's legs and twisted around to use Haru's imbalanced stance to grab onto the cuffs of his pants and pull his feet out from underneath him. Sota glanced at the knife he was holding before he dropped it in surrender and then rushed to check on the other two. Kulako didn't bother to look at the aftermath as he fled.

Kulako slowed as he came upon a real game taking place in the main training area. He was still breathing heavily from the incident with the other three trainees, praying to an entity he didn't believe in that nothing would come of it. Suddenly, he felt a hand clap him on the shoulder. He cringed as he looked up and met Teiji's unimpressed expression.

"Fine. We'll play this game instead. You damned coward." Teiji grumbled, still rubbing at his throat. He looked away from Kulako, trying to appear nonchalant. "By the way, you hit like a girl, but I guess even a girl can break Haru's nose with a dirty trick like the one you used."

Kulako felt uneasy as a smirk crossed Teiji's features, though such a change in demeanor typically meant that his less favorable antics were over for the day. Kulako thought of Master Hoji's earlier threat. "How much trouble do you think that means?"

Teiji laughed. "Shut up, Kulako. Do you really think he's going to report to one of the masters that he got taken down by *you*? Besides, no *real* assassin fights fair all of the time. Now come on. They're calling for substitutes."

Teiji was neither friend nor foe, though his attitude depended on his mood. Kulako didn't like it, but he didn't have to; it was one of those things that he accepted and adapted to. He'd seen Teiji fight in the sparring rings on occasion and knew it was in his best interests to keep in good standing with the other boy as much as possible.

Several days later, when the sun was still low on the horizon and beginning to stain the skies in hues of red and gold, Kulako was lined up for the usual morning formation where the trainees stood until they were given daily training assignments. While he was busily hoping he wouldn't be assigned to poisons, the masters who usually paced through the attendance lines were even more preoccupied. There was an unspoken tension in the air, which effectively distracted Kulako from his thoughts. He watched the masters intently as they gathered at the front.

The headmaster limped to the front of the lines after what felt like an eternity, holding a rolled piece of parchment. It was rare that assassins lived to be as old as he was. Unless they became masters at Kurushima, it was rare that they survived through their twenties. The headmaster cleared his throat. Kulako leaned to his right, barely enough to see between those in front of him, making sure he wasn't noticeably out of place. The lines were organized by age with the youngest ones at the back, which meant that without a master directly beside his row, he would be able to get by without being at full attention.

"We have received a report from the troops," The headmaster began in a dusty voice while pulling at his silvery beard. Attentive silence filled the air while he coughed to clear his throat once more. He unrolled the parchment. "As of the last week of the full moon of the eighth month, we are fully in control of Othakra. The tribe that called itself the Okami resisted Imperial rule for the final time, and therefore our soldiers slaughtered them all. There are no more Wolves of Othakra. Our armies will now be able to begin their advancement on Noshe with Othakra as a midpoint and, eventually, a settlement. Today, boys, we celebrate a victory. Feel pride in knowing that one day, you will join these ranks of brave men. As a gesture of solidarity, I have decided you shall be rewarded with an easy afternoon of reading and writing."

"To the Empire!" one of the other masters shouted with his right arm crossed over his heart.

"To the Empire!" came forth the collective echoing bellow from the gathered ranks as they made the same salute. Kulako had only been able to repeat it in an unconvinced voice, thankful that it had gone unnoticed by those who were in line beside him. Kulako felt as if his entire body rattled as the call rumbled through the air.

Kulako tried to straighten so that he looked more proud of the accomplishment, more like everyone else, but a heavy pit dropped into his stomach with such suddenness that he instead thought he might be sick. He swallowed. The night the Okami would have been slaughtered was the same night that he had seen the wolves. After spending the week denying that the strange incident occurred to begin with, he now felt that he could no longer do so.

Gods, all of them? Kulako glanced to his left this time, attempting to hide the way his expression betrayed the horror he felt at such news. The training grounds were in plain view past the raised arms of others in his row. The eruption of cheers and curses at the Okami name faded into the background.

The black wolf's yellow eyes were locked with his.

Three: A Survivor

Sonika's eyes slowly opened to the painfully bright light of the sun. She could barely lift her tired arms to shield her face from it. Her ears were ringing, her mouth was dry, and she felt completely disoriented. Warm ocean water washed over her feet, reminding her of the shore she had struggled to swim up after her canoe crashed into jagged rocks not far out from where she now was. A pained whine pushed up from her throat. She shifted from her back to her stomach and tried to crawl away from the tides. However, that one movement must have been all that remained in her reserves of strength, as she could go no further. The wound on her back was not healing properly. Sonika wondered if she would die from it. She had seen it happen multiple times to warriors after suffering from injuries inflicted during the Giahatian attacks.

She put her left arm out to fumble around for the elk-skin bag containing her mother's medicines and the rations of jerky and dried fruit Takeo saved for her. She pulled it as close to her as she could manage; it had barely survived along with her. Sonika felt numb to the things she had witnessed on the night of the Okami slaughter, though there was a constant pressure in the back of her throat when the image of her dead father crossed her vision. The bag felt like her last connection to a land she may never see again.

Sonika closed her eyes. Perhaps she would see it in death if death came. She thought of the stories the Elders used to tell; they had said that in death, the spirit of the person who passed became attached to the spirits residing over the isle, but the Elders never said if those guides could reach beyond the shores of Othakra. Sonika chose to cling to the belief that they did. With her father's agreement, Sonika was confident that her mother had become a Wind spirit to guide lost souls. She hoped that her father had become an Earth spirit to protect those who needed it most. She felt comforted by the familiarity of her people's beliefs as the sound of waves filled her ears and lulled her.

"Mother," she whispered to the Winds in a dry voice as her consciousness began to slip away, her body no longer able to bear the condition it was in. "Where am I?"

• • • •

MAKOTO ENJOYED HIS daily morning walks. They refreshed his soul after years spent serving a faction of the Giahatio's intelligence agency. Such seemed to be the price to pay for being inclined toward academics and history. Though the Giahatio reviled information unfiltered through by its own officials, Emperor Akuwara was well aware that his allies could not only be made of assassins and soldiers who could barely read, let alone speak peaceably for negotiations. Makoto dismissed these thoughts. His time was once spent studying the people native to the islands that were about to meet with the Empire's expansion. Now he spent his time gathering pretty rocks and seashells along the beach as gifts to his wife. He loved every moment of his peaceful retirement away from politics. The Giahatio had constructed the town he called home a mere five years ago, but citizens rarely spoke of the Giahatian government in public.

Makoto paused midstride when he looked out toward the water; there was debris floating by the jagged rocks that marked the island's north side. Curious, he shifted his eyes toward the shore, wondering if he could find his answer. He sharply sucked air between his teeth when he saw a distant figure on the beach. He rushed forward, dropping the pouch of shells into the wet sand. His heart sank into his stomach as he realized the figure to be that of a small child, but his curiosity only grew when he recognized her dark hair and light brown skin. He looked over to the floating debris once again and concluded that it had been a vessel of some sort. Her clothing was unusual (a dark blue shirt, probably tied at the front somehow, and black shorts), as was the leather case attached to her right leg.

Makoto slowly approached her and crouched into the sand. He called out softly, "Young lady? Miss, are you hurt? Where are your parents?"

The child moaned with discomfort as she opened her eyes and looked at him. Makoto involuntarily retracted as the incoherent gaze of a wolf fell on him. She snarled at him when he reached out to her once more, though it seemed she could not focus well on where his hand was. Makoto inhaled deeply, his heart wrenching as he carefully placed his arms around her to pull her out of the sand. She yelped when he touched her back, which was when he understood she was injured. Makoto knew she needed a medic's attention immediately; her body was trembling from how much pain she must be in, too weak to attempt fighting against him.

She looked up at him with a little more clarity as he placed her small pack on her to carry them both back to town. Her face was fierce, but her eyes were full of sadness and haunted by horror. Not knowing what else to do, he smiled at her in an attempt to comfort her.

"My name is Makoto. You look like you've seen trouble, but there's no need to be afraid of me. I'll take you to see my wife, Aimi. She's the older sister of our town's medic. We'll help you."

Her eyes rolled back before they closed again.

• • • •

"ARE YOU SURE SHE'S Okami?" Aimi whispered incredulously, watching her brother Shika's hands as they cleansed the girl's injuries. Makoto nodded solemnly but remained silent. Aimi pressed, "You said they never left their isle."

"You don't need to whisper, Aimi." Shika chuckled at his sister, glancing up from his work briefly to grin at her teasingly.

Aimi spoke naturally after giving her brother a rather indignant look. "Why would she have come here in nothing but a little boat and almost no supplies?"

"Say what you want about her supplies," Shika interjected again, holding up a jar containing a medicine he concocted from the list that they found in her bag. "Okami women are incredible medics. Many of us have tried to copy their methods, but they always limited their contact with outside cultures, so it's been nearly impossible. This ointment here may have stopped the bleeding and prevented her wound from becoming too infected. It's most likely saved her life at this point."

Makoto looked at the medicine for a moment before turning his attention back to Aimi, relieved that he had another chance to speak. He thought that trying to talk between his wife and brother-in-law was a genuinely impossible task. "The Okami never *did* leave their isle, but there was a rumble just before I retired among the Giahatian ranks about how His Highness

Akuwara was growing impatient with their resistance to Imperial advancement."

"What are you saying?" Shika asked without glancing up from the process of applying bandages that he had begun.

Makoto sighed deeply and pinched the bridge of his nose, as he now grasped the sadness he had seen in the child's eyes. He recalled a conversation during a night of drinking with a General he worked closely with, who had told him that the Giahatio had one last push against the Okami defenses they planned on using, though they weren't sure when they would deploy the method. If their last strategy failed, only then would they agree to working real peace with the tribe. He found it abhorrent then, but foolishly believed that it would never come to fruition. Makoto had thought it to be a game of chance, a gamble Emperor Akuwara was unable to afford.

He looked at his wife with uncommon firmness and did the same to her brother. "We may very well be harboring a little fugitive. That injury looks to be from a chained scythe, and kama are only used by high ranking assassins and soldiers."

"She's only a child—a child can't be a fugitive, of all things," Aimi's eyes widened with horror, and she looked down at the girl who was now on her side; her face relaxed when she finally settled into a peaceful slumber as the pain was lifted from her body. Aimi delicately brushed the long strands of hair away from her face. "How could anyone have done this to her?"

Shika looked to Makoto before he stood from where he had knelt beside his patient's cot. His face adopted a more serious expression, as it normally did when dealing with this side of his work. "Well, you won't know anything for sure until she wakes up. Let her rest, and get me when she finally does come around. She's absolutely exhausted, so it could be a while yet. Chained scythe or not, that injury is in a precarious place, and we'll need to make sure she can still walk and move properly."

"You're sure she'll survive?" Makoto asked sternly, trying to ignore the worry in Aimi's face, but unable to disregard that he had the same feelings.

Shika looked at the child for a long moment, calculating. "If she's lived long enough to get here, she's stronger than she looks. You always said the Okami were a tough bunch when you were studying them. However, it's not her physical condition that worries me at this point; her breathing and her heart sound fine."

"Then what does?" Aimi ran her fingers through the girl's hair again, as if trying to soothe her while she slept.

"If what Makoto is implying is true, I don't want or even think that I *can* imagine the emotional toll of what's been done to her," Shika said earnestly after a moment, searching for the right words. "She needs you two."

• • • •

IT WAS SILENT WHEN Sonika awoke once more. She yawned and stretched, the action agitating the injury on her back, causing her to recoil with a roll onto her stomach. She turned her head, taking in her surroundings: a small room darkened by a drawn shade where she'd been placed on a healer's cot. Her top half had been left exposed, save for the bandage wrap meant to keep the wound closed off. She found her shirt draped across a chair to her right. Sonika could see the repaired tear from where the weapon struck her. She shifted so that she could stand, meeting with resistance from her tired muscles and pain along her spine, but she found the drive to pull her shirt from it and dress herself. She rested against the chair, unable to sit, unable to stand to her full height as of yet. She could smell food from another room in the house; her empty stomach loudly complained at her for its lack of sustenance.

"Stop that," she whispered to it as she straightened as much as possible. "We don't even know where we are."

She anxiously tugged at a lock of her hair while she struggled with the decision of what to do next. Fear told her to try climbing out of the window in the room to run away, but she knew that was impossible in her current state. Sonika's willpower crumbled as hunger gripped her again. She could only ambulate stiffly and slowly, but she thought that perhaps the forced caution was better. There was no way of telling what was beyond that room's door. When she came to the threshold between the living area and the kitchen, she froze, shrinking against the frame. Her eyes fell upon a man sitting with his back to her as he ate. He glanced over his shoulder at her. Sonika thought she should run, though she knew she could not.

"I was wondering how much longer you thought you could sleep for. It's been two days." He told her with a kind smile. Sonika looked away for a second, thinking he meant to address someone else. He chuckled a little. "Come sit, child."

Sonika hesitated before going forward. Her heart was in her throat when she stood beside him, but her concerns eased slightly as he helped her to the floor to sit.

He asked her, "What is your name?"

"Sonika," she answered apprehensively, trying to cross her legs and giving up about halfway through due to the protest in her back.

"Eat well, Sonika. It's just rice and vegetables, I'm afraid; the wife's out buying some meat for supper." He said, giving her another kind smile as he passed it to her. She cautiously thanked him, innocuously sniffing at the meal he had given her to see if she recognized the scent of any poisons she had become familiar with. The older man laughed again, the sound letting Sonika relax enough to eat.

While Sonika ate—he reminded her not to risk making herself ill by scarfing it down—the man introduced himself as Makoto once again and explained how he had found her on the beach. He told her how his wife Aimi would be thrilled to see her finally moving around and that while he and Aimi had no children of their own for her to befriend, their busy town was sure to have a group of playmates for her to attach to. Sonika liked his optimistic words and thought he seemed trustworthy, but knowing that her former life lay in ruins sat heavily upon her heart. Makoto stopped talking when he noticed the sadness darken her eyes once more.

"Child," he said quietly, carefully placing a hand on her shoulder. When she jumped at his touch, he retracted and instead wrung his hands together for a moment while he chose the phrasing of his next question. "Do you wish to tell me about what happened to you?"

Sonika set her bowl down on the table and placed her hands in her lap, looking at the way the afternoon's light through the windows glimmered against her skin in sunny and shadowy patterns from the trees outside. She nodded slowly, her jaw clenched so tightly one of her sharp canines cut into her lip.

"My father—" she could feel tears in her eyes and a sob swelling in her chest. She was unable to control the weight of her emotions as all that had happened crashed down like a tidal wave. Sonika buried her face in her hands and cried. She mourned for Takeo, traditions that would never be celebrated again, songs no one would be there to sing, the friends who she could only pray survived, those who had not, and the pristine lands that were set ablaze.

Makoto found himself struggling to comfort the young girl. When Aimi entered the house once more, thankfully only seconds later, he looked to his wife helplessly. Aimi unhesitatingly sat beside Sonika and took her into her arms. Eventually, Sonika's tears stopped, soothed by the words Aimi sang to her softly while stroking her hair.

Sonika wiped her eyes with her arm, but didn't uncover her face otherwise to look at either Makoto or Aimi. Her chest heaved as she stuttered, "I-I'm sorry,"

"All wounds, no matter how big or small, visible or invisible, need time to heal," Aimi told her gently, taking Sonika's arm away from her face.

Later in the evening, Sonika thoroughly explained what had happened to her people while she sat still for the medic to examine her wound. The medic shifted her arms to test her range of motion, and though she winced when they were brought to their full extension, either inward or outward, up or down, he seemed confident that it was an issue that would pass with time and rehabilitation. However, Shika was quick to warn her that the pain might never completely fade away due to the injury's delicate location.

Though the three adults listened intently while she spoke, even when discomfort from Shika's examination interrupted her, Sonika thought that Makoto looked as if he had been making a calculation the entire time.

"When can she begin training again?" he asked the medic once he was finished with the examination. Shika raised his eyebrows, taken aback by the question.

"She'll need more time to recover first, but likely within the month." Shika's concern reflected in his countenance as he answered Makoto hesitantly. He shook his head in disbelief. "Makoto, you never were a military man. How do you expect to help her?"

"Makoto studied the Okami for years for the Giahatio. He wrote down everything he could about their practices both on and off the battlefield." Aimi reminded her brother. Makoto nodded his agreement to what had been said, then looked at Sonika again as Shika helped her back into her shirt.

Makoto and Sonika exchanged a long, wordless gaze until finally, he told her, "Rest for a few days more, child, and then we'll begin with what you already know—don't look so surprised, you had kunai and shuriken on you when we found you. Oddly enough, in a world where they wish for there to be no more Okami, being Okami is exactly what will help you survive."

Four: Changing Winds

The last month of summer on Perena was unbearable; Kulako was dripping with sweat in the oppressive heat. He wanted this sparring match over as soon as possible, looking forward to when, after, he would find a barrel of water to put his head in. He charged at his opponent. The blade of Kulako's sword locked with the one held defensively against him. They struggled against one another briefly before he quickly turned and slashed the other boy's thigh open from the side. A master appeared from the cloud of dust, waving his hands in a call for the sparring match to end as the boy fell to the ground and gripped his bleeding leg. Kulako watched apprehensively as two other masters came to the first man's aide to wrap the boy's open wound before carrying him off for evaluation.

"Kulako!" Master Hoji's voice reached his ears from behind. "Now!"

Kulako cringed while he sheathed his katana, ignoring the murmurs floating through the crowd gathered by the ring he had been assigned to for the day. His feet felt like lead as he made his way toward the edge of the makeshift arena, where he could see Master Hoji's disapproving gaze bearing down on him. Master Hoji said nothing when Kulako reached him but gestured with a tilt of his head for Kulako to follow along.

They walked in tense silence until they came to the masters' building, where Hoji grabbed Kulako by the collar and shoved him inside. Master Sheng was waiting in the main hallway, looking at Hoji gravely before his eyes wandered toward Kulako. Kulako swallowed nervously as Hoji held his arms behind his back, ensuring that they were immobile with a painful jerk upward. Kulako thought he was about to be branded. He hadn't been told to kill his sparring partner, but he had hesitated when presented with the opportunity for it.

Is that even worth being branded over? Kulako hoped neither master noticed his worried expression.

"First to land a strike again, was he?" Master Sheng's voice was indifferent as he stooped down to loosen the hanging cord of the katana from Kulako's belt before he pulled the weapon away. Sheng held the katana level in his palms. Kulako wondered if he was about to be killed.

"Third time this week, at least," Hoji confirmed. Kulako didn't recognize the tones with which either master was speaking. It was strange for them both. Sheng was never so detached, and Hoji never sounded interested in anything unless he was screaming insults during drills.

"We knew what we could have been asking for when we placed him with the older ones after he killed that other boy a few years back." Sheng tilted his head in curiosity as he looked at Kulako directly. "Unless you ask the masters at Genjing, eleven is too young to be given one's own katana. I'm personally of the opinion that the *normal* years of training are not enough for one to be trusted with it, but then again, I suppose you've already had five, haven't you, Kulako? Do you still share space with any others?"

Kulako dumbly shook his head, not sure what the relevance of the question was. There was one who had moved into the longhouse where the older boys lived not long ago, but the other three were dead; one from failing a contest of strength, the other two from a master's beating after they had been caught stealing bread the previous winter.

Hoji sighed heavily, annoyance thickly coating the air as he exhaled and released Kulako. "Give him the katana, Sheng. It would only be another year before he could receive one, anyway."

Sheng held the katana out for Kulako to take, but Kulako only looked up at the master, not trusting the situation. Kulako was beginning to develop a good sense of when to disengage, but he could not tell for certain if this was one such moment; he felt it more likely than not that he was about to be killed or suffer physically in some manner. Sheng's eyes suddenly fell on the ground and then shot back up to Kulako's face.

"You're forgetting to kneel," he whispered.

Shaking, Kulako complied with the order. He lowered his head and extended his arms as he had seen done before, though those times had been in a much more ceremonious fashion. He felt the katana land in his palms, and he thought his heart stopped. He looked up in surprise. Hoji was now standing beside Sheng, and both were looking at him sternly.

"As far as the headmaster can tell, and we agree, your skill has advanced far enough for this. Since you came here at age six rather than seven, you've served your required years to earn a live blade." Hoji told him. "However, if you go and start to fuck up, I will slit your throat with it without hesitation, boy."

Kulako stood and tucked the katana behind his left arm. He bowed at the waist. "Thank you, masters."

"Dismissed." Hoji growled. Kulako quickly obeyed.

When Kulako was alone later in the evening, he couldn't help but to marvel at the katana the masters were allowing him to keep as his own. The swords received at Kurushima were handed down from previous students or working assassins who had died. Trainees rarely attained newly crafted swords. The weathering on the cord wrap proved that it was undoubtedly from a previous owner, but the blade looked as if it had never been used.

It was far too nice for a slaveborn or any other Kurushima student. Still, he would no longer have to rummage around in the weapons sheds and hope for the best—this was now his until he died, no matter when that death came, and though the design of it made it appear common, the craft was something extraordinary. The handle fit his hands perfectly, the blade moved precisely, and as he tied the hanging cord to his belt, it felt as if it belonged at his hip. There was an odd emotion building in his chest. He felt proud that he had been able to make it this far.

This feeling, however, swept away when he remembered the three other trainees he had killed this year alone. Kulako feared that he was becoming one of the real assassins he used to dread. His stealth was only improving, which allowed him to move among the shadows with ease, his speed and accuracy with the kunai knives had increased, and his most prominent skill was with the katana. Now that he had his own, it would likely become his primary weapon. Despite the pang of guilt in his stomach, it all seemed a testament to the bruises and concussions he received from practice swords, the scars from defensive wounds that littered his forearms, and every aching muscle he had ever experienced.

In the first few months of training, hatred and anger drove him to survive. As he grew older, he suppressed those emotions, only accessing them when he needed to, mostly to kill. Kulako still hated killing, which once again made him the outlier from his comrades, who seemed to enjoy and take pride in it, but he didn't fault them for it. Their sense of mercy had been beaten out of them just as their intolerance to pain. Kulako had eventually decided that numb was best; numb was less emotion than anger, but still enough awareness to survive.

Even numb could be difficult to maintain at times.

Kulako pulled the katana from its sheath once more, pausing when he caught his reflection in the blade. He sighed deeply. If he could survive five more years and prove himself worthy, there was a chance the masters would grant him early release from Kurushima at the age of sixteen rather than nineteen or twenty.

• • • •

IT WAS THREE YEARS later when the black wolf visited Kulako in his dreams again. They met in the clearing of a large forest with a bright white moon overhead. Calmed by the presence, Kulako smiled at the wolf's familiar figure, whose eyes settled on him in the same unrelenting manner as always. He placed his hand in his companion's thick ebony fur, gripping it for reassurance, knowing that the wolf's appearance meant that something was changing; Kulako never dreamed unless it was a nightmare or something more serious was about to take place. The wolf leaned against his leg before he began down an unmarked trail, guiding Kulako along the way.

There was an odd buzz of curiosity and excitement rumbling through the air during afternoon formations the following day. Before dismissing morning formations, the masters had said that they would be making a significant announcement. Now they were pacing anxiously at the front of the lines. Kulako watched them tensely. He had never seen this sort of display from them. Master Hoji stood among those at the front, his hair now flecked with silver from age and the stress of his position.

Briefly, Kulako wondered—and hoped—if that meant he would be bound for retirement soon.

Hoji wasn't different in cruelty from the other masters when he chose to dole out his punishments. Kulako knew, though, that decreasing their numbers was a good sign. It meant a more unequal dispersion of their attention between the students they trained until officials could find a qualified assassin to fill in the rank. The fewer masters walking about meant more peace for Kulako.

Finally, one of the masters spoke. "How many of you useless dogs have trained with chained scythes?"

Most of the older boys and a few around Kulako's age raised their hands. A vexed curse came from his mouth. He broadly motioned to Master Hoji, silently instructing him to take over. Master Hoji gave a rather unforgiving gesture of annoyance to the other master before turning to the formations. Kulako's brows knitted with curiosity—the masters were never so open toward either their students or one another with any sense of emotion.

"All of you with chained scythes will bring them to me." Master Hoji commanded with finality.

"Master Hoji, can we ask why?" Kulako heard Teiji's voice rise from the crowd; his tone dripped with smugness. Kulako glanced over at the other boy briefly before turning his attention back to the masters.

Master Hoji glared. "Kurimo, if it was your damned business, I'd tell you. You're sixteen now. You know better than to ask stupid questions."

A third master elbowed Hoji out of the way; his hand raised as if he planned to stop the animosity floating through the breeze. "We have received word from His Highness, Emperor Akuwara, that all kama are to be melted down and eliminated from training altogether. The same message has been sent to Genjing."

"All for a fucking hoax." Master Hoji interrupted. From where Kulako was, he thought he could see the veins on Hoji's neck bulging. It was actually somewhat impressive to see him so livid yet so helpless against what angered him. Again, the third master raised his hand to encourage calmness.

"What Master Hoji is trying to convey is that His Highness fears they may not be as effective as they were once thought to be." A restrained smile touched his lips. "Please report to the smithy with your scythes before supper is served tonight. A group of you will be assigned to clear out the weapon sheds of those that remain afterward."

"Dismissed, you bilge-rats." Hoji snarled, and the formation broke and dispersed. Some went straight towards the smithy to surrender their weapons as instructed, others stood about in small groups to discuss what had just occurred in low whispers. However, their conversations quickly ceased when the masters walked by and hit them for insolence.

Kulako watched the friction between the various groups for a moment, then went back to where he now regularly practiced on the rotting carcasses of diseased swine. The masters rightfully claimed it was the most similar to cutting human flesh—the smell was awful, but the flies were worse. It was obvious that the masters were hiding something, but he could not place exactly what. He decided to dismiss it for the time being, knowing that eventually, someone would let the smallest hint of information slip, which would allow him to piece a few things together.

Instead, he decided to focus on the type of strike he had been working on—one which would allow an opponent to fall with one blow. A few others, usually younger ones, sometimes watched while he trained alone, but they rarely approached him during such moments. Finally, at fourteen, he was beginning to gain a little edge over the others, something that had been an ongoing struggle since the first day of training. Kulako could sense that they were starting to get a healthy dose of fear for what he was becoming.

It was a relief they stayed back, as Kulako secretly held that same fear.

Five: Run Away

Sonika kept herself busy. In the mornings, Makoto trained her from a blue leather-bound book he'd saved from his time studying the Okami, her afternoons were spent running with a group of children she had befriended, and in the evenings, Aimi would teach her how to cook and sew. Aimi and Makoto taught her to read and write with the insistence both would be necessary tools, especially if she planned to be a woman of medicine. When Shika was available, he worked with her to teach her how to correctly measure and blend the ingredients in her mother's medicines. He would volunteer some of his own invaluable knowledge of what poisons he could identify along with their antidotes.

Though the decimation of her tribe and the ways of her people haunted her daily, Sonika was able to wash away the hurt in her heart by recognizing the second chance she had been given at life. She thanked the spirits for it when she could. There was comfort in knowing that her father's spirit was watching; he must have been relieved to see her taken in by such good people, familiar with the Okami ways. It seemed to her as if fate brought her here purposely, although Sonika wasn't entirely sure how much she believed her own theory.

The nightmares of the death and destruction she had witnessed were slowly fading. When they did appear, they were always warded off by the glowing images of the white wolf who spoke with the firm calmness of her mother's voice and the black wolf whose gaze held the depth and sternness of her father's eyes. The iridescent forms of the wolves chased away the demons in the form of the soldiers and assassins who had reigned down such terror and violence before leading her into a serene meadow dotted with wildflowers. The dream usually ended there, and Sonika was able to wake in peace, the music of a wolf's song softly lingering in her mind.

By the time she was twelve, the pack of young ones Sonika befriended gradually became more aware of her Okami heritage, but Sonika much more quickly learned what it meant if anyone else found out. Makoto had sternly warned them not to say a word once he heard of a reward offered by Emperor Akuwara if she were reported alive and soldiers could retrieve her. Her friends all agreed, though, that they would not tell their families what they knew about her. She was still the strange girl Aimi and Makoto had adopted from seemingly nowhere, and Sonika was thankful for it. She was terrified of the Capital. Now and then, her friends would ask Makoto to sit with him and watch while Sonika practiced the forms passed down through generations of Okami. A boy once asked to spar with her, but the match was over when Sonika threw a swift fist into his eye. He was content to sit with the others after that.

When Sonika set into these routines, all else faded out, and she could feel the power in her blood rise. She hoped that someday she could be as formidable of a warrior as her father had been. Though she was proud of her progress, it also hurt her heart—she could have been striving to be a leader among her people rather than whispering their songs or practicing their dances when no one else could see. Her senses were growing as strong as an adult's would have been—her eyes could easily pierce through the night, she could effortlessly track scents and sounds, and when she moved, at times it felt as if the earth moved with her. Makoto claimed that her kunai and shuriken skills were as accurate and fast as a Giahatian soldier's was. When she did get to practice hand-to-hand combat, it rounded out her fighting prowess perfectly.

However, Sonika was well aware that without Makoto and Aimi, she would have already died alone. She had come to rely on their generosity, gentleness, and unconditional love so much over the years. Yet, she could not shake a horribly ominous feeling in the back of her mind, warning her that things were about to change. What would she do if anything happened to them?

• • • •

DAYS BEFORE SHE WAS supposed to turn thirteen, Sonika found herself on the shore not long before dawn in the earliest month of summer. The Okami didn't need light to see, but still, she strained her eyes against the darkness, searching, that uneasy sense gnawing at her insides. When daybreak barely touched the blackened waters of the sea, Sonika saw what she feared the most. Her heart dropped into her stomach and terror gripped her coldly as the black sails bearing the Empire's seal appeared on the waves. She folded her arms over her chest, shivering from a chill not caused by the brisk morning. The ship could arrive onshore in as little as an hour.

This isn't happening. She thought as she tried to convince herself that she needed to move, fast.

She bit her lip to keep it from quivering in fear, jumping from her secluded outlook of rocks and onto the wet sand where the tide was beginning to roll out. She mouthed a silent prayer to the elements of the earth and sky for protection, then turned and sprinted toward town, where she easily located Makoto and Aimi's home. Most windows were still empty from the glow of oil lamps and chimneys still free from smoke, but Sonika felt relief when she saw Makoto's silhouette moving across the windows in his home.

"Makoto!" she whispered urgently as she burst through the door. Makoto looked up from his morning tea, appearing as though he had barely slept the previous night.

"What are you doing up so early? Hunting?" he chuckled a little.

"Makoto, I saw—"

"I had the strangest of dreams last night, Sonika. Kept me awake half of the night, too, you know." Makoto mused, speaking quite dreamily for one who was usually so resolute in concepts of logic. "A massive black wolf approached me and dropped a katana at my feet before disappearing again. Perhaps it was one of your ancestors warning me."

Sonika fell silent and felt her jaw drop ever so slightly at Makoto's description of his dream. Finally, she shook herself back to the present. Firmly, she said, "Makoto, I saw black sails."

Makoto jumped out of his chair as if he'd been touched by fire, startling Sonika with his suddenness. Even when he landed and took her face into his hands, she retracted from his movements. His eyes went blank with horror. "No. They couldn't have possibly tracked you all the way here. They should have assumed you dead—there had to be a spy, or-or someone reported..."

"Makoto...?" Sonika was terrified by his change in demeanor.

"You're sure about what you saw?" He asked. She mutely nodded. He looked as if he were on the verge of tears. "We have to get you out of here. Even if they're here for some other reason, you have to hide. You won't be safe here. You have to leave."

"What?" Sonika could not comprehend the idea of leaving the place that had become her home.

Sonika glanced to the window nearest to the door where the morning's light was beginning to cast a warming glow on the houses and shops along the street. The orange rays grew longer, until suddenly her vision filled with the fires that had consumed the Okami village on the night the Giahatio had stolen her homeland. She involuntarily gasped in fear and blinked, noting that everything was back to normal, before turning to Makoto once more.

"You'll die," Sonika said, her voice quavered with terror and guilt. Makoto didn't acknowledge her as he shifted and made his way toward the back of the house where her room was. Sonika followed on his heels, repeating anxiously, "Makoto, you'll die."

"You cannot be found." He looked over his shoulder at her before opening the bedroom door. He gestured for her to go through. "For now, stay in here and pack your belongings. I'll see if I can get any information."

"Makoto," Sonika started to plead again, her voice breaking.

Makoto began to close the door on her. He closed his eyes for a brief moment before he sighed deeply. He said slowly, "If you want to show your gratitude for being here, you will find a way to live and stay out of the Giahatio's hands."

The door slid shut, and she heard his footsteps retreat the few paces across the hall to where Aimi was still sleeping in their room. Sonika listened as he woke Aimi, an action followed by frightened whispers, but she could not make out their words; they had a way of speaking to one another too softly even for Sonika's keen ears to detect. When Makoto left the house, Sonika immediately went to her window but could only watch him until he made a right toward the town square.

Sonika felt sick to her stomach. Her eyes remained on the street for what must have been hours. When midmorning came and Makoto still had not returned, she wrenched herself away to instead pace the length of the room repeatedly, pausing to pack her bag, waiting for some sort of news. Not even Aimi had come to see her. Sonika's anxieties grew tenfold with each passing minute of silence. Finally, she sat on the bed, hoping her breathing exercises would calm her.

As the afternoon warmed the house, a knock came to Sonika's door and pulled her from a sleep she hadn't been aware of falling into. She quickly jumped up from her bed and opened the door for Aimi, whose eyes were on the floor, a look of deep sorrow haunting her features. She held the small blue book Makoto had always kept and a bundle of fabric in her hands.

"This belongs to you, now." She said quietly as she passed it to Sonika's hands. Without giving Sonika time to recover from the shock or ask questions, she wrapped a cloak around Sonika's shoulders. She pulled the hood up before taking Sonika's bag by the door in one hand and Sonika's hands in the other. "You need to go."

Aimi led Sonika to the front of the house once more, tears in her eyes. "Stay strong, little one."

"Aimi," Sonika began, but the woman looked away, trying to hide her emotions. Sonika bit her lip, hugging her tightly for a long moment before letting her go.

"Get away as fast as you can." Was Aimi's final plea before she opened the front door for Sonika and gestured for her to run.

Without any direction of where to go, Sonika decided to slink along behind the row of houses beside Makoto and Aimi's home. Her heart was pounding with adrenaline as she kept to the shadows. The alleys behind the houses were extremely narrow, barely enough to keep homes from touching, but Sonika was thin enough to move through with ease if she could avoid the mud that had not yet dried up from the last time it had rained. Sonika's eyes were constantly scanning her surroundings. Eventually, she came to the town square, where an anxious crowd had gathered, all whispering and looking around furtively. The scent of blood was in the air. Sonika decided to creep closer to the source of the commotion

She had to put her hands over her mouth to keep herself from screaming.

Makoto's head was on a pike, surrounded by tall Giahatian soldiers clad in light gray uniforms. The color drained from Sonika's skin as her knees wobbled. Cautiously, she continued forward, hoping to hear why or how such a tragedy had occurred. She located her answer to her left, where a soldier with a delicately crafted katana stood speaking to a citizen. Sonika backtracked a little in her path so that she could overhear.

"If it weren't for the tip you wrote in, we wouldn't have ever caught on. We thought the wolf was dead." The soldier chuckled; he spoke with a thick Perenin accent, venomously spitting the word "wolf" when he said it. "And to think this one thought he could get away with hiding the creature. Good on you and your son for doing your civic duty."

His son? Sonika's eyes fell on the man, the father of one of the boys she played with. Her stomach churned, burning with the sense of betrayal. The boy knew his father to be a staunch believer in the Giahatio's agenda for advancement and colonization across the known world. His father had once stated that the Giahatio had every right to use the force it did on civilizations standing in the way. The boy hadn't been one of Sonika's favorite playmates, especially since he at one point had tried to kiss her without her permission, but he was intertwined enough within the group of friends that alienating herself from him would have been suspicious. Given their ages, they likely would have sided with him, anyway.

Sonika's eyes roamed over to where the soldiers displayed Makoto's head in open view. Fury took hold of her. She drew a knife from the leather case she kept attached to her right leg for easy access. She stepped away from the crowd, catching the attention of the soldier and the citizens who had been around her.

"What's this, then?" he seemed annoyed. The other soldiers bristled with awareness; they recognized her golden eyes before he did. Sonika made sure he saw her canine fangs.

"You had no right—" She growled over a breaking voice as she threw the knife into his throat. The soldiers rallied from around Makoto and toward her. Sonika ran straight for them, slipping by quickly as they struggled to match her pace. There was no time to cry for either Makoto or the fact that she had just ended another human being's life. Now was the time to survive, and her senses would lead her.

"Damn it all, burn the whole fucking village to the ground and get after that beast!" one man yelled to the others.

She heard a man's voice calling out orders to the others who were behind her as they began to leave the town, where the space between houses was more significant, and a few of the men fanned out behind those buildings. Sonika readily predicted their tactic to divide and conquer, as it was a common one for Okami hunting parties. She prepared an attack once again as she pulled the shuriken from hidden pockets in her clothing. She turned and threw her weapons before landing, unceasingly sprinting toward safety, wherever that may be.

She was beginning to tire, but she drew in a deeper breath and pushed her body further, the open field she had led them to now becoming a blur beneath her feet. An abrupt whistling noise cut through the air as a knife sailed over her head. Sonika looked over her shoulder to see the fastest of the soldiers who were able to keep up with her. Suddenly, an entire onslaught of knives came at her, the soldiers knowing the only way they could slow her down was to keep her dancing around the edges of the blades. One caught her along the cheek, the first of many superficial cuts, but Sonika kept moving no matter how many scraped against her skin.

Sonika was exhausted by the time she came to the edge of a gulley where a river rushed far below. Her muscles and lungs felt as if they were on fire. She paced along a short route as she contemplated what to do. A raven cawed as it circled high above her head. She could still hear the Giahatians behind her. They would kill her if they caught her, and whether that would be on the spot or in Perena, she wasn't willing to find out. She was not ready to die. When Sonika glanced around, she could see the soldiers beginning to climb up the steep hill after her. The guiding spirit of the raven swooped downward at the riverbed and disappeared. Without another thought, she threw the pack containing the blue book and several medicines down to the riverbank where, to her surprise, it landed safely. When she jumped, she only hoped that she could do the same.

• • • •

KULAKO AWOKE WITH A jolt from a strange dream, feeling as if he landed on his stomach after someone threw him from an insurmountable height. The dim light of early morning was sifting through the tiny, dirty window of his now-solitary room in the bunkhouse. Images of a rushing river and the black wolf still lingered before his eyes. He winced as he tried to push himself up, reality finally taking hold. The dried blood from the wounds across his back cracked with his movement. Kulako had slept restlessly on his stomach the night before after being flogged. He had argued with one of the masters about something—he couldn't remember what, now; starting the debate had been a horribly miscalculated risk on his part—and believed it had ended in him calling the master something along the lines of a "fucking idiot." He might have gotten away with only getting hit for the insult if he hadn't provoked the older man's temper in the first place.

Finally, Kulako pressed upward and pulled on his shirt, loosely connecting the ties before he tucked it into the cloth belt at his waist. The light fabric irritated the injuries. He removed his shirt again, pulling on a black undershirt before redressing. It would at least hide any blood that leaked since he couldn't see his own back well enough to try placing bandages effectively. There was one medic on site at Kurushima, but he never touched injuries inflicted by punishments. The man barely did anything yet still held himself in the same high regard as the Healers at the Palace.

Kulako dismissed his thoughts as he realized the time; they would sound off for morning formation soon. He'd just been flogged, and wasn't keen on enduring it again this morning from being late. He tied his hair appropriately and hurried out the door, only barely remembering his katana. The rain from overnight kept the ground slick with mud. When he approached the formation lines in the center of where drills were held, Kulako paused to find where he would be able to slip in unnoticed, as he could already see the masters prowling through the lines of young men who stood firmly in attention with their hands behind their backs.

Kulako caught movement out of his right periphery and noticed a pair of young ones who could be no older than eight, also examining the lines. He knew what would happen to them if they were the last ones to line up. They locked eyes with him, nervous, worried, telling him that they were also aware of the consequences of tardiness.

Kulako hesitated. Him or them?

His eyes went back to the lines for only second before he nodded toward them. They rushed forward toward their designated where they needed to go. Someone else may have said that they would need to learn to be on time eventually, but Kulako didn't want to be the reason they were given that lesson. He exhaled heavily through his nose before loping toward his own area, trying not to think of how much less merciful a second lashing was about to feel.

"Kahn, Kochi..." the master paused, his eyes scanning the area as he saw Kulako finally joining the back of the line. He sighed and said grievously, "Kulako. There he is."

Once formation was dismissed and the trainees went to their designated training assignments, Master Sheng grabbed him by his collar before he could also disappear. When Kulako looked up at him from beneath his bangs, the master grunted and yanked on his clothing before releasing him. Kulako followed behind him to one of the small tents left outside for the masters to rest in.

When they were separated from other ears and eyes, the master ordered Kulako to kneel, and he obeyed without hesitation. He kept his eyes on the muddy ground. His clothing had already begun to soak. Master Sheng sighed again, and Kulako swallowed nervously.

"Late again," Sheng said sternly. "Second time in eight years; usually the consequences of a single tardy mark are enough for one to never do it again. Those other two boys were late, too, but you were the last to fall in line."

"Yes, sir." Kulako's eyes examined the blue veins running beneath the pale skin on his hands.

"And of course you *are* aware of what I meant when I said 'consequences' in regards to this particular infraction." Sheng continued as if Kulako hadn't spoken.

"Yes, sir."

"Given how last night's spat with Master Aramoto ended, especially, I would think you'd be more inclined to avoid it. I suppose I should also take this moment to reiterate that what you said wasn't right."

"With all due respect, sir, it may not have been right, but it was definitely accurate." Kulako cringed, wishing he could have held his tongue.

"Look at me, boy," Sheng snapped. Kulako complied. Sheng's eyes bore into Kulako's for a long moment before he spoke again. "Regardless of what happened to you, you still chose mercy for those young ones. Mercy is not a lesson we as assassins can afford to teach."

Kulako opened his mouth to interject, hoping to prolong the inevitable, but the master ignored whatever he was about to say.

"But it *is* a lesson that needs to be learned." Sheng's eyes softened a little, and Kulako felt as if an entire cartload of iron had been thrown onto his back. "You may stand."

Kulako slowly rose to his feet, not taking his eyes off Sheng, fully aware that his entire expression reflected the surprise and confusion he felt. Northern Nomadic men and women never grew tall, so Kulako had already reached his adult height. He stood six inches shorter than the master. Usually, these differences were a meaningless detail to him, but at the moment, he felt as if it were a three-foot gap between them and he could be crushed.

"Small acts such as that are the things that separate us from the demons we must embody—but we *are* human, Hikari's Creation, not the monsters of Kuro's Hells. Mother Hikari expects that all of us are capable of mercy."

"Even assassins, master?" Kulako kept the disdain he felt toward the subject of religion from inflecting in his voice, as he believed that neither Hikari nor Kuro was in charge of the world and its creation, but such blasphemy was intolerable even here at Kurushima. To deny the Gods was to deny the Empire, or at least that was how Kulako thought the saying went.

Sheng nodded. "Even assassins. Of course, as an assassin, when you dole out that mercy will be at your discretion, so long as your missions are still complete. Now, then, you'll be fifteen at the end of summer, correct?"

"Yes, sir."

"Then get back to your training and train hard—we only have so much of the season, and as you know, you have to complete a preliminary assignment before you can be considered for graduation next year. If we find there's room for you, that could come at any point between autumn and then."

Kulako bowed and dismissed himself.

Six: Paths to Escape

Sonika had been living on the riverbank for several days. The Giahatians who pursued her evidently decided not to track her downstream, as her death should have been more likely than her survival. At first, she suspected that they might be lying in wait on the other side of the river somehow, though she couldn't tell whether or not there was a bridge to connect the width of the gulley. After the days and nights had passed without incident, she stuck to her original conclusion—they assumed she was dead and went home.

Probably the only time anyone would call lazy soldiers a good thing, Sonika wasn't sure if that was quite the right way to look at things, but it helped to keep her concerns at bay.

She found a small cave that was only big enough for her to fit in at night if she slept in a tightly curled ball, and she used her pack as a pillow and cloak as a sheet. She looked for stray sticks during the day and used the twigs for a small fire at night to cook the fish and roots she gathered for food. Fire was a useful tool, necessary for many things, but it terrified her after watching her homeland burn to the ground.

One morning while Sonika was foraging for roots, she saw a young man in the distance. He sat alone on the bank across the way with only a fishing rod and a bucket—Sonika had been using her knives and a load of good luck to fish. For a fraction of a second, she felt jealous of the equipment, then her focus shifted to him. He did not appear to be Giahatian, and it seemed to her from their proximity that he might be a few years older than her. Nervously, she glanced back in the direction of her cave, wondering if she should retreat, but her curiosity told her to duck behind the tall rocks she was near and observe his actions.

He fished for a while without catching anything, and eventually, Sonika determined that she had seen enough. She snuck away without incident, putting plenty of distance between herself and the young man as she returned her attention to her own hunt.

The next day, much later in the afternoon, Sonika saw the young man again, though he still didn't notice her. Her senses alerted her that he could be dangerous, though there was nothing about him that seemed to prove that; he carried no weapons, only the rod and bucket for fish. However, it did not escape Sonika's notice that he'd moved closer to her small encampment from the previous day. She decided to sleep with a kunai at the ready that night.

He did not return for two days. On the third morning, he was near enough to Sonika that when he did glance up at her, Sonika could see the bright green of his irises. She froze in terror, though he remained across the water. He simply waved a greeting before going back to what he was doing, though Sonika did not feel safe enough to do the same. She struggled to think of what she should do.

Finally, after a few hours of silence, he spoke to her. "Fishing isn't much good in this river. I prefer the pond near my house, but so does everyone else lately."

Sonika cautiously looked up from beneath her lashes but did not reply. His eyes locked on her again. He ran a hand through his thick brown hair and sighed before he stood. She watched him uneasily as he moved several paces to his left, where he was now able to sit directly across from her. When he lit a cigarette, Sonika's nose involuntarily wrinkled at the scent of the burning tobacco lifting into the air.

"You look hungry." He called over. "I can't cook very well, but it has to be better than what you've been eating down here."

Sonika shook her head, and he laughed.

"I'm not going to hurt you," he said calmly. "I want to help you. You've been down here for a while, haven't you? You probably need time to decide, so meet me at the pointed rocks at sunset, and if you're interested, I'll help you cross."

Sonika didn't like the situation, but he already knew where to find her, and she hadn't seen many other alternatives for shelter along the riverbank. The river itself would eventually rise enough during the rainy season to submerge her cave—her options were limited. For those reasons, she decided to meet him at the indicated spot. The rocks would be her easiest way across the river from the bank, though not the safest. When evening came, the young man was waiting for her. His teeth flashed in an orange grin against the fading daylight.

Sonika looked over at the setting sun, willing for darkness to wait, and started to crawl across the rocks. It was difficult to navigate, but eventually, with the young man's guidance, she stepped on the last rock, where she then slipped and landed in his arms. He chuckled and helped her steady herself once again.

As he led the way up a steep path onto flat land, he introduced himself as Okubo, saying that he was the son of a merchant who recently perished and so had passed on his business to the sixteen-year-old. Okubo was lively in conversation, not appearing interested in asking many questions, much to Sonika's relief. Still, she could not place precisely why she felt so apprehensive of his presence. When they came upon the small town where he lived, she wondered how much her misgivings mattered.

"Braid your hair," he told her gently.

"What?" Sonika usually allowed her hair to hang free around her shoulders, as was the way of most Okami women.

"Braid your hair." He repeated more firmly, though Sonika didn't notice the edge in his voice. "It's normal. They won't even think they haven't seen you before."

Hesitant, but aware of the importance of blending in, Sonika did as she was instructed and twisted her hair into a braid over her right shoulder. He smiled with satisfaction and gestured for her to follow him through the streets. As they moved through the town, Okubo placed his arm around her shoulders, and Sonika's senses rang with discomfort, though she was equally afraid of appearing out of place.

The town itself seemed trapped in the essence of the color brown—the streets were muddy, the wooden houses were still damp from the most recent rain two days ago, and large, brown oxen strapped to carts roamed along at the demand of their caretakers. Sonika did not like this place. Already, she regretted not staying at the riverbank.

They reached Okubo's home without notice, which was on the corner of one of the wet roads; two houses on each side stuck out from odd angles to accommodate the street. When Okubo brought her inside, Sonika thought the place was surprisingly threadbare. The kitchen was empty except for a table that was falling apart; there was no furniture in the attached living room aside from an exposed pit to serve as a fireplace. At Okubo's explanation, she learned there was a room just down the hall where he—and now she—would sleep.

Sonika felt danger as if it had grabbed her by the throat. It suffocated anything she wanted to say.

"Well, make yourself at home," Okubo said suddenly, interrupting Sonika's attempt to process her surroundings. "I have a few things I need to attend to; I'll probably be back rather late."

Sonika turned to say something, anything, but before the words could leave her mouth, he was already out the door. Despite being confused at his abrupt exit, she decided to explore the house. She found the room where Okubo's bed was, along with some spare sheets in a linen closet. She made a cot for herself beneath the window, on the opposite side of the room for Okubo, ensuring she would have easy access to an escape route.

Sonika paced about the house for a while as the darkness deepened outside. Okubo's sudden disappearance caused her great unease, but the uncertainty of what she had gotten herself into was even worse.

Stupid, stupid. Sonika cursed herself. She found herself staring at the linen closet again, this time up toward the ceiling, where she noticed a loose tile for a crawlspace. She grabbed her pack, which contained her weapons and medicines, and climbed the rickety shelves until she was able to push the tile aside. Dust and cobwebs flew at her face, and she coughed, but soon she blinked the debris from her eyes and was able to see an area where her pack would fit easily and that even she might be able to curl up into.

Sonika paused, unsure of why she had thought of putting herself in such an unpleasant, musty area, but dismissed it as she threw her pack into the crawlspace before launching herself from the shelving. If nothing else, at least Okubo would not know about her skillsets, which seemed more important than ever to keep hidden. Now all she needed was a plan for getting out of this situation, but it would take time.

• • • •

THE FIRST FEW WEEKS with Okubo passed by with complete normalcy. He was as kind as he had been beside the river, seemed willing to help, and praised the cooking that Aimi had taught Sonika. By now, Okubo had explained how he found Sonika purely by chance. He'd been worried for her due to her curious location and gone back to check on her each day until the time she'd agreed to follow him. Whether he did not know or did not care about Sonika's Okami heritage, she could never exactly tell, but she was still young enough to write it off without thinking about it too much.

When Okubo was not around, Sonika would spend her time watching the docks, intent on learning the ships' timing and what each one carried. No one ever interacted with her during these excursions, but she made a point to keep her eyes downcast when someone came too close to her. Most of the ships were cargo ships and kept to regular schedules over the weeks. However, one day, a passenger vessel anchored at one of the piers. Unable to contain her curiosity, Sonika found the bravery to approach.

When she was halfway to the ship, a gentle wind blew from the sea and Sonika saw movement on her left. The white wolf's form appeared only feet away, weaving around the legs of those ambling about. No one saw the wolf, Sonika knew they wouldn't. The wolf calmly swished her tail before motioning with her head toward the boat. Sonika blinked then rubbed her eyes, and the wolf was gone.

Just as Sonika stepped forward, she felt a hand on her shoulder and turned, startled. Okubo's bloodshot eyes were wide with anxiety, and his mouth twisted into an equally fraught expression. He reeked heavily of alcohol, tobacco, and something else Sonika couldn't identify.

He asked with a threatening timbre, "What do you think you're doing over here?"

Before Sonika had time to answer, he grabbed her firmly by the wrist and pulled, forcing her to follow him. When she resisted, frightened by his unexpected change in demeanor, he rounded on her and struck her, hard. Her lip began bleeding as he dragged her to the house. If anyone had noticed, no one had made the motion to defend her—she hadn't even had time to protect herself. Shock and pain still resonated throughout her body when Okubo slammed the front door behind them and hit her again. He was yelling, but Sonika was too terrified to make out the words. She ran from him, locking the bedroom door before frantically climbing into the crawlspace, where she stayed until she heard him leaving the house in a flurry of rage after a solid ten minutes of pounding on the room's door.

The town seemed oddly quiet the next morning as Sonika stepped through the wet streets. It was unseasonably cold and rainy, and she kept the hood of her cloak up around her face to hide the marks Okubo had left on her. She was still in shock from what had happened, having thought that violent natures were more predictable.

She felt stupid. She felt afraid.

Okubo told her to leave for the market, but he failed to name a specific purpose for it other than wanting her out of his sight. His entire disposition was different now, so she did not protest despite the weather, which had begun to intensify. Sonika swore at the sweeping wind that gusted rain into her face as she took shelter beneath the awning covering the several fishmongers' stands. An older merchant grunted unpleasantly at her.

"I'm sorry." Sonika said weakly. Her hood fell around her shoulders as she turned to him. The old man's eyes were cold.

"What're you?" He grunted. Sonika, stunned by the question, shook her head dumbly as she fumbled for an answer. The old man squinted and leaned forward from the chair he had been sitting on. "I see those strange eyes. What're you, ye stupid bitch?"

"Nothing," Sonika replied numbly. After another round of enduring Okubo's harsh words, which had reached the very same conviction continually, she wondered if it were the truth. She sighed deeply and dipped her head. "I'm sorry for disturbing you."

The man bent over before he straightened again and threw a small rock at her. It missed, but his intentions did not. "Then git."

Sonika was not sure how long she had spent aimlessly wandering through the marketplace despite the rain. Eventually, she walked away from the buildings and the vendor stands toward the small patch of woods not far from it, where she settled with her back against a tree. She wanted to cry, but even that emotion felt frozen in her chest.

She debated sleeping outside until another gust of wind knocked her hood down, and hesitantly she decided to make her way back to Okubo's house. It was empty when she returned, and Sonika sighed in relief. She set up a temporary clothesline beside the fire pit to dry out her cloak and what she had been wearing while out. She changed into one of the spare sets of traditional gear Aimi made for her, before she built a small fire for warmth. Her hands shook whenever she lit fires; they still reminded her of death.

She was unsure of Okubo's whereabouts, but did not care to know them. If he was not around, she was safe, and that was all that mattered now. Sonika didn't let herself cry, no matter how many times she wiped away the tears welling in her eyes. She couldn't plan if she cried. She knew her next step would be to begin watching the ships again. The next time she saw the passengers' vessel, she would find one way or another to get on board and get as far away from Okubo as possible.

Sonika carefully began to analyze the patterns of activity surrounding the docks again. She became intensely aware of Okubo's habits, as well, and was always home before him, even if it was only by seconds. He would still yell at her, berate her, and beat her, but Sonika could never predict exactly when those moods would strike him. The most that she could do was survive through each day.

"Get up." He barked at her one night. Sonika blinked her eyes open slowly; it was very late, she could tell by the moonlight cast into the room.

"Okubo, what—"

"Get *up*!" he grabbed her by her hair and pulled, Sonika complied. He pushed her to the other side of the room. Sonika could only stare at him, her heart racing with fear as he advanced on her again. "The hell did you think you were doing talking to that horse-faced idiot earlier today? You're *only* to speak to the merchants and *only* when making a purchase. At *least* four people saw you, so don't bother lying about it."

Sonika barely remembered the young man who had asked her about tobacco prices while leaving the market. "He just wanted to know—"

"I forbid it to ever happen again." Okubo shoved her into the wall.

Sonika caught herself with an outstretched arm and regained her balance. Her brows furrowed at Okubo. She said in disbelief, "Forbid it? You don't own me."

"You don't think so?" Okubo straightened indignantly. She shook her head, her bravery rapidly failing her at the menace in his eyes. He pinned her against the wall and ordered, "Get down."

Before Sonika could decide whether or not to do as he said, he threw her on her back. He was on top of her so that she had no way to escape. A flare of pain from her old wound rolled up her spine, but she still tried to pull up a knee to strike at him. He responded by putting his hands on her throat. Sonika froze at the pressure, worried that he would lose the last bit of his withheld temper if she struggled. His eyes were fierce on hers. Sonika didn't understand the hatred in them.

"Okubo, please," she choked out under the strain of his weight and hands. Involuntary tears stung her eyes. Was he going to kill her? Her nails dug at his wrists in a desperate search for pressure points to push him off again, but he only pressed down harder. Sonika released him.

The expression in Okubo's eyes changed suddenly, and Sonika felt her face reflect her fear. He was gazing at her in a way that she had never seen before. One of his hands released her windpipe and moved down to her inner thigh. Sonika's skin crawled with every agonizing second.

"You don't think I own you? After everything I've done for you?" Okubo's voice was dangerously low as his free hand began to explore her body. Sonika squirmed uncomfortably, but he would not let her go, no matter how much she continued to scratch at him.

"Okubo, stop." Sonika pleaded, unable to control her tears.

"You are *mine*." he snarled as both of his hands went to the waist of her shorts and began pulling them off.

"No!" Sonika's protest was cut off by Okubo's lips pressing against hers in the most horrid way she could have ever imagined. His fingers were in her hair, pulling on her to restrain her further.

Sonika screamed, she begged, she fought as hard as she could, but nothing she did stopped Okubo from doing what he wanted to her body. She trembled violently as he lay beside her when he was finally finished. Her legs covered in her own blood, her fingers stained with his, layers of his skin embedded under her nails. She felt raw, exposed, empty, disgusting, helpless. However, when he began snoring, Sonika pushed down the sobs that threatened her willpower. She thought that if she were to cry now, she would never be able to get up again and would instead risk being at Okubo's expense for the rest of her life. She found her scattered clothes quickly in the nearing daylight. He had not torn them as badly as she had suspected. She decided she could still wear them until she was in a better place to change out of them. Her body ached all over, but despite her soreness, she pulled herself up the shelves of the linen closet in agony and carefully grabbed her pack from the crawlspace, silently extracting herself before landing on her feet once more.

The noise she made when dismounting seemed to be the loudest sound she had ever heard or felt, but the sensation did not resonate. Okubo made no motion to get up. Sonika released the breath she did not realize she had been holding before drawing it in again and making her way out of the house.

She thought she began to breathe easily when she made it down the street. Dawn was starting to break over the horizon, but she still had just enough cover from the long shadows of night that normal eyes would not be able to trace her movements. It hurt to run, and she swore every few seconds under her breath, knowing that she could not stop, knowing that she needed to leave. She would run back to the riverbed, to the decimated town on the other side of it, anywhere else, even directly into Giahatian territory. Anywhere that was away from Okubo.

She stopped as the looming masts of ships caught her eye at the docks, and she changed her course. The passengers' vessel was nowhere to in sight, but she could still choose her destination between the several cargo ships. Sonika pulled herself closer, keeping to the shadows as much as possible. A light in the shape of the white wolf danced before her and ran to the ship on Sonika's far left before evaporating into thin air. Immediately and unquestioningly, Sonika followed the spirit's advice.

She still had no plan for boarding the cargo ship, but that did not prevent her from creeping along the loading ramp left down the night before. She knocked out two crewmembers who tried to grab her before she disappeared below decks. When Sonika found the cargo area, she crammed herself into an empty crate before pulling a heavy canvas tarp over it, leaving only a slight amount of space so that she still had air to breathe.

Sonika shuddered as hot tears slid down her cheeks. She hated herself for how much she had trusted Okubo, for how much she had ignored her instincts, and swore that it would never happen again.

• • • •

KULAKO WAS NOT AFRAID to kill. Ever since it had been brought to his attention that graduation was within his grasp, his requirements to commit murder even in the sparring rings were more frequent than not—he had taken down so many opponents over the summer that he felt nothing toward it. Hikari's mercy had no place at Kurushima, but perhaps Kulako's version of it did. He killed quickly and efficiently, to the point where his target spent little time in pain before they died; they didn't lie on the ground and vomit blood and spasm wildly for minutes as he noticed most of his comrades' kills did. One clean, deep cut through bone and sinew and Kulako's targets were down in an instant.

Tonight, however, Kulako's ability to remain unseen and still finish his assignment was all that mattered in order to complete the last step toward graduation. He felt no hesitation—the masters were in the habit of beating hesitation out of the trainees until they acted first and thought later. Kulako was still able to think before acting, but his calculations all happened within a matter of seconds, even when those seconds felt like agonizing minutes.

Preliminary assignments were not particularly difficult by design, but rather for observing whether the prospective assassin could kill without the immediate threat of verbal or physical repercussions from the masters. To see if they had grown cold enough to kill of their own volition. Kulako had known for quite some time that he could. The selected brother of a noble would be an easy task.

He also knew something few others did. Despite what they said, the masters would be watching either from secret perches or through the eyes of a trusted spy. It wasn't common knowledge, but years of watching the ritual had brought him to this conclusion. Master Sheng, now Master Hoji's replacement, confirmed this suspicion without saying too much more on the matter.

Kulako traveled the entirety of the day to reach the Wen Valley. It was the furthest he had been from Kurushima since he had arrived there. Trips to the Capital city, which lay roughly five miles from Kurushima's gates, were reserved once weekly for those who were fifteen and older. Kulako knew from the stories those boys told that their intervals were mainly spent in taverns. He usually turned away from the conversation when they began going into details about the brothels and gambling halls. Perhaps at his age, he should have had more interest, but Kulako thought it seemed like a waste of their temporary freedom, although he didn't know what else would be done with such time now that it was the end of summer and he'd aged into the same opportunities. Maybe he would track down his brother.

It did not matter; nothing else really did at this point. The world began to fade away as coldness struck Kulako's heart. Movement on his left. He crouched, watching his target from the shelter of the quiet, cooling bellows of a forge at rest for the night. The nobleman's brother was said to be a useless drunk who had been caught selling iron from the family's mines to warrior clans on Oshosha. The Wen Valley provided nearly all iron and steel for the Empire—not only were his actions cutting into the family's profits, but the Giahatio's supply as well. It seemed as though the government and the family forged the contract on his life from a mutual agreement. Kulako's target swayed from the emptied wine flask at his hip. Kulako crept forward.

Master Hoji observed silently from a covered ox cart not too far away from where he thought Kulako might be. The flash of Kulako's katana caught in the moonlight before it was swiftly covered in blood and Kulako retreated. Master Hoji closed his eyes solemnly. He hesitated, resentful to admit that he was pleased with Kulako's efficiency—drunk or not, the man hadn't even had a chance to notice that his death was near. Sheng had respected his wishes when Hoji asked to bear witness to this moment; he'd wanted to see if all the effort in training the slaveborn had been worth it. Hoji looked at the stars above, wondering how he could have ever doubted Kulako's coldness. This same young man had begged the recruiters not to return him to his father once they learned that he was six rather than seven, the age children were supposed to be when taken into the institutions of intelligence and assassination.

He scribbled a note down on the parchment he had been clutching. Kulako would graduate at the age of sixteen. He was cold and merciless as any of the other killers roaming through the streets of the Empire's settlements.

The only challenge to face now was the ceremony.

Seven: Only the Strong

Kulako looked at the clothes laid out on the bed he had not slept in the night before. The formal uniform had a thick red line of embroidery along the lapels and at the cuffs of the sleeves to signify rank, along with a red cloth belt. The standard all-black uniform that assassins wore daily didn't have the embroidery, but the color of the belt never changed unless rank did. Kulako chose to wear the gray shirt of a soldier's uniform. It fit better and allowed him to blend in a bit more. One of the older assassins he'd gotten to know liked to say it took the honor out of earning his place in the ranks. Kulako's stomach twisted in disgust when he thought of how a ceremony once intended to represent valor and honor had been changed into a drama, then again at the connection of words like "valor" and "honor" to a harbinger of death such as the graduation ceremony from Kurushima.

Although, he thought, perhaps he'd never actually known what they meant, anyway. Most days, Kulako felt more like a dog with a broken will than a bloodthirsty assassin. Where was the valor or honor in that? Did people actually believe the ceremony granted them those things?

The graduation ceremony traditionally took place in the spring, when the cherry tree blossoms were in bloom, and the days warm with cool and comfortable evenings. It was held on the last day of the weeklong Spring Festival. Later at night, street performers would act out the fights for those who had not seen such horror for themselves—typically women, children, and low-class citizens who had not wriggled in between the nobles and wealthy merchants for a place to view it. The acrobats turned their performances into a comedic feat. Kulako wanted to hate them all for the entertainment they found in the ritual, but had long exhausted his reserves of the feeling. They were just as powerless as he was to stop it.

Besides, he thought he knew his place well enough by now, and it didn't involve questioning the new Emperor or his motives.

The recent death of Emperor Akuwara and the rise of his son Akuko to the throne had inspired the unusual circumstance of a second ceremony being held during the week of the Winter Festival. Emperor Akuko already had a reputation for cruelty, whispers carried through the streets told that he was fond of torture and dismemberment to criminals and innocents alike, just as his father had been. However, the official coronation was still going to be attended by as much of the city as could fit inside the temple on the Palace grounds; those whispers were already garnering fear among the new Emperor's constituents. Kulako wondered if there was any truth to the other theory he'd heard: combining the events of the coronation and the graduation was a way of guaranteeing Emperor Akuko unwavering loyalty from a group of assassins who had never served under Emperor Akuwara.

Kulako shivered from a chill running down his spine unrelated to the snowfall outside. Emperor Akuko hadn't put a stop to any of these speculations yet for a reason.

Due to his status as a trainee attending the ceremony, Kulako had been living within the Capital's assassin quarter for the last two weeks. If he survived fighting to the death, the flat he had been assigned to stay in would become his. If not, it would likely remain empty until spring. He and the others in the same situation were granted the freedom to roam the city as they pleased during the day. Despite his best efforts to remain solitary during those days, worried that his emotions might finally surface in the face of such an awful trial, the young men with whom he had spent the majority of his life with insisted on several final gatherings. They spent their fledgling wages on booze, the rich foods offered by vendors, and women. Kulako wasn't exactly proud of that last part, but he was human, too, wasn't he?

Kulako laughed, pushing the hair away from his eyes. In what could be his final two days, he surprised himself at the things he chose to dwell on, though he wasn't convinced they were wasted thoughts. He wondered if this was closer to how normal men his age thought rather than about surviving and how to effectively kill in order to do so.

"Enough of that, I guess." He murmured to himself.

He folded his formals into a neat pile and placed them in a pack. He had to report to the Palace later in the evening, where he and the others would stay in an isolated barracks until the ceremony commenced. He dismissed his thoughts and set out into the city, knowing it was for the sake of doing something to distract him from the upcoming event rather than needing to accomplish a task—it was uncharacteristic for him, as he preferred to stick to the shadows where he belonged unless necessary. Kulako felt the distraction to be as essential as anything else he would have to do that day.

Kulako always felt as if he observed Giahatian and Perenin cultures more than he would ever actually participate in them. He watched from his unnoticed perch on a rooftop as people passed by in the street below. Women wore silk kimonos with equally long jackets and, depending upon rank, wore their hair in the simplest or most complex of braided styles. Noblewomen painted their faces, whereas commoners did not. Common men could wear their hair long, but it had to be tied low, and it was never allowed to be as long as Kulako's now was, which fell to just above the middle of his back when not restrained.

In comparison, noblemen could wear their hair cropped close to their scalps if they chose. Noblemen had delicately embroidered tunics and shirts, whereas a commoner's clothing more resembled what Kulako normally wore and mimicked that of a military man's. Men's beards were expected to be trimmed neatly along their jawline. Kulako subconsciously scratched at his cheek, knowing that it was unlikely he would ever grow one to have to worry about. From what he could remember, the Nomadic men never seemed to grow one.

Kulako turned on silent feet, abandoning his perch on the rooftop, knowing that if he ever wanted to see the real state of the Empire, all he had to do was duck into the rows of carts and booths just two streets over from where the successful merchants placed their shops. Despite Emperor Akuko's insistence that everyone in the Empire had benefited in some way over the last year, Kulako could tell by the disrepair of the buildings how untrue that was—at least for anyone not within an elite circle.

A hand suddenly touched Kulako's shoulder, and he grabbed it instinctively, pulling at it and the sleeve attached to it as he dropped his weight to throw the other person to the ground in front of him. Kulako pinned the arm he had initially grabbed and was on top of the other man with a knife drawn, his knee in the person's chest, only now taking the time to register who it had been.

Teiji glowered at Kulako and put the palm of his free hand on Kulako's face, pushing Kulako off. "What in Kuro's Hells is your problem?"

Kulako rubbed his face to soothe away the red marks Teiji's fingers had left, blinking. "You expected differently?"

Teiji paused, then laughed, much to Kulako's irritation, and deftly sprang back up to his feet. Kulako slowly rose from his crouched position. Teiji's face was alight with amusement. "I really didn't expect you to be so lost in thought that you wouldn't have heard me."

"I know, thinking. You should try it sometime." Kulako rolled his eyes.

"Next time I catch you that off-guard, I should just kill you," Teiji smirked again, and Kulako tried to ignore how possible that could be with Teiji's skills. "I wanted to see you get bloodied to death in the ring, but I guess I'm being sent out long term tomorrow."

Kulako's expression changed to one of disbelief. "Long term? You only just graduated in spring."

Teiji shrugged and twirled one of his kunai by the pommel on a finger. "When you're skilled, they recognize you for it—quit rolling your eyes at me—and when they do that, you'd be surprised what sort of assignments they hand out to you."

Kulako dropped his gaze to the disturbed patterns in the snow indicating their brief scuffle. Teiji sighed heavily and half-heartedly shoved him.

"Look, just don't get yourself killed in the ring. I want us to be able to work together one day."

Kulako winced as Teiji turned and melted back into the shadows of the snowy alley. Though the ceremony sat weightily upon his mind for the last two weeks, it was the first time he had considered the possibility of his own mortality in stride with it. There were several opponents Kulako might face whose skills intimidated him, but the masters rushed to present before the Emperor. Kulako thought it to be worse to be paired with someone who was not ready for the bloodletting; in this group, there were even more who were unprepared than who were prepared.

Heavy bells began ringing in the distance. Kulako jumped from surprise and looked toward the Palace all in the same motion. The coronation had begun, which meant he was expected. The masters told them to anticipate instructions about how to properly enter the Palace grounds and find the barracks where they would wait in holding until the day of the ceremony. Finding the instructions and following them were both part of the final test, which began the moment Kulako unfolded the formals. Kulako probably wouldn't have noticed them if he hadn't laid the uniform out on his bed, where the parchment they were written on had fallen from. Kulako wondered if anyone else found them; the uniform wasn't meant to be worn until the day of the fights.

The Palace itself was a marvel of architecture, built from black volcanic rock with looming towers standing sharply against the sky during the day and grounds that seemed to span for miles. There was a single path of cobblestone, which wound toward the main gate. Kulako hesitated when he came to the head of it and then walked to a small, barely noticeable trail to his left. From there, he was able to navigate around the outer wall until he came to a crumbling, mossy pile of bricks. He climbed over them and then went under the iron bars on the other side. In the distance, Kulako could see the temple's silhouette, where throngs of citizens dressed in furs for warmth waited outside in the snow to catch a glimpse of the coronation. He stepped toward them with a pit in his stomach, hoping to remain unnoticed as he approached the barracks where he and the others were to stay.

Kulako crept along in the shadows of a wall, intently watching a guard. His foot dragged over a rock, scraping it against the wall with an impossibly loud noise when it moved, or at least he felt as if it had. Kulako froze, cursing his carelessness. The guard turned his head slightly, but faced away once more after a brief scan of his surroundings. Kulako quickened his pace until he was able to slip around the temple and into a courtyard. Across the yard, Kulako could see the barracks. There was nothing else to hide behind, but the night was falling rapidly, so he darted for the building on the other side.

All was quiet in the barracks. The outer walls were made of stone and reinforced within by plates of iron. Even for Kulako, the silence was unsettling. He found the bunk assigned to him for the remaining days of the Winter Festival and set his pack with his formal uniform inside down beside it. He listened restlessly to the worsening weather outside. Surely, someone else would be joining him soon, though he hoped it wouldn't be too long before a military officer came to retrieve weapons until the ceremony. Kulako had heard enough stories about others being eliminated to diminish the number of competitors before the fighting officially began.

The wind howled miserably outside, and Kulako shuddered as he sat down on the bunk. Finally, after what felt like an eternity, the iron door swung open again. Twenty-three young men clamored in over one another to escape the cold, though they brought plenty of it and a gust of snow in with them. They looked as surprised to see him as he was to meet them all disheveled as they were. Their ages ranged from sixteen to twenty, but they were all the size of fully grown Perenin men, who were generally taller than Giahatian men. Kulako couldn't imagine how they could have possibly arrived in such terrible shape.

"Akahana?" Haru stepped forward, obviously vexed. "How in Kuro's Hells did you get here? We've been getting shoved around and harassed by guards for the last hour."

Kulako blinked and unfolded the note that he had found earlier that day. He extended his arm forward to show them. "They told us how to get in."

Haru ripped it out of his hand and tore it to pieces. Kulako rolled his eyes as Haru stepped up to him and tried to use his full height as a way of intimidation. "How the fuck did you get that?"

"It was in the belt on the formals. Look at yours."

Haru eyed Kulako suspiciously but still set his pack down on the ground and rummaged around. He swore when he crinkles paper between his fingers. The others began to copy his movements. Kulako grinned as twenty-three annoyed expressions grimaced at him.

"You'd better hope you aren't against me in two days, Akahana. I'll remember this." Haru seethed as he threw his pack onto one of the bunks.

Kulako laughed.

Not long after everyone settled in, the military officer came by to gather weapons to put into storage until the day of the ceremony. Along with him came a surprisingly generous meal, which everyone ate in utter silence. Contrary to the companionship they experienced up until that morning, Kulako could tell the reality of what was about to come hit them as suddenly as it had done to him. In the next two days, if they were not dead, they would have to kill someone they grew up with.

The next morning, everyone was brought into the arena, which had been cleared from the previous night's snowfall, to practice for the ceremony with a military general. The man's shoulder-length hair hung loosely, and his perfectly trimmed beard had flecks of gray and white. Kulako wondered if it was better to notice that rather than to stare openly at the general's eyepatch as Haru and Eiji were doing. Plenty of the masters at Kurushima had old wounds to display, which they did often and proudly, especially when someone complained about an injury of their own, but none of them were missing an entire eye.

The general spoke with little room for questions and even less patience. "The posts are where the ring is indicated. If you go outside of the ring, you risk getting blood on the nobles. Do *not* get blood on the nobles, or—will you two *stop gawking at me*?"

"Hardly a ring," Kulako muttered as the man stomped over to the two who had been staring at him, all the while threatening to show them the hole where his eye used to be. "More of a rectangle."

The general cuffed Kulako on the back of his head immediately after doing the same to Haru and Eiji. "The three of you are going to be shoveling out horse stalls tonight if you don't give it a rest. I highly doubt that sort of work is what you want before the ceremony tomorrow."

Kulako rubbed the sore spot on his head before straightening back to attention. The general massaged his temples in annoyance, trying to remember where he had been in his instruction before the interruptions. He inhaled deeply, trying to contain his vexation.

"Tomorrow morning, you will be divided evenly into two teams of twelve. The matches will be decided randomly by a tactics master. Your weapons will be returned to you at dawn. Now, then. Let's go over the formation one more time. It *must* be perfect."

"This is the fifth time," Sota complained. The general rounded and smacked him on the back of his head.

"It *must* be perfect," he repeated firmly. "Now let's move. You're all wasting precious daylight with your stupidity. If you were in my troop, you would've already lost your weekly rations."

Kulako looked around at the others as he fell in line at the back of the formation, suddenly feeling as though pushing his emotions aside would not be as easy as he had first expected. He breathed deeply as the general stood at the front of the group and began explaining when they would be called into the ring and when the Emperor would arrive. His voice became distant in Kulako's ears. He swore he saw the black wolf sitting behind the general, staring at him pensively.

Get it together. Kulako told himself firmly while they all stood straight with their hands behind their backs, desperately trying to recall the patterns he had let his emotions continually cycle through over the years in order to appear numb to it all. *Only the strong survive here.*

Eight: Fangroot

A gong sounded above the fighting ring. Kulako didn't dare glance up and see which of the looming outer ledges the reverberation was coming from. His heart was pounding, he was sweating despite the swirling snow, and all he could do was keep his eyes forward on the general who was directing the ceremony. The general's right hand remained held out in a fist, signaling to Kulako and the other young men to stay perfectly still.

The Emperor was approaching. Kulako didn't shift in the slightest to try stealing a glance when the crowd of gambling noblemen and merchants fell deafeningly silent. He wondered if he was still the only one who could hear his throbbing heartbeat.

The general spread his hand and delicately lowered it. As one, the graduates went to their right knee, their right arms over their chests and heads bowed. Kulako's breath was shaking. The cloth over his mouth was the only thing preventing the escaping puffs of air he exhaled from showing as much.

Kulako could sense Emperor Akuko's eyes on him, on all of the gathered trainees, from where the Emperor stood on the high balcony far above any of the others who had come to witness such horror. Kulako slowly raised his eyes to the base of the stone tower; it was as far as he dared to look.

The tension in the air slipped out just as suddenly as it had appeared. The new Emperor had taken his seat on the throne. Kulako took a deep breath and closed his eyes. The general began his speech about honor and tradition, which was mostly the same as the one given during the spring, but he added passages to include the rare occasion of the coronation along with the Winter Festival. It faded to a hum in Kulako's ears. He chose to concentrate on the cold ground numbing his knee instead.

Finally, when the general turned to the graduates with an upturned palm, they stood fluidly at attention. He extended both arms out to his sides. The graduates fanned out to their respective edges of the ring. As the general stepped off to the area where the tacticians sat, Kulako thought he looked relieved to have his part in this game of death over with. Another uniformed soldier stepped forward from a tunnel likely connected to the Palace itself and took the general's place where the front of the formation had been. He announced the first match, and two young men took their positions before him. They bowed first toward the Emperor, to the proctor, and then to each other before they each drew back by four long steps. They unsheathed their weapons, and Kulako noticed that the tips of their katana were shaking.

That isn't a good sign. He winced as their match began.

Kulako watched as ten matches passed, as young men who had known one another most of their lives now vied to slaughter. The lifeless bodies were carelessly drug away from the frostbitten, packed dirt of the ring by fully masked undertakers, trails of blood in the snow all that was left behind. Kulako shivered and glanced across the ring at Eiji and Sota, who were the last ones along with him and Haru waiting for their turn. He could only see their eyes because of the masks covering their faces, but Eiji seemed petrified. Sota appeared as if he had accepted his fate. Kulako was somewhere in between; he wasn't ready to die, but he was far from eager to enter a match with either of them.

As Kulako heard his name called, his heart plummeted into his stomach. He swallowed nervously as he entered the ring with Eiji, who was still barely holding himself together as they pivoted and bowed to the Emperor. Kulako panicked, trying to remember Eiji's exact skills when they bowed to the proctor. Eiji whimpered a little when they bowed to each other.

Kulako drew his sword and aimed at Eiji's throat. If nothing else, live or die, Kulako was determined to have this over with as soon as possible. He lunged at Eiji, who barely ducked out of the way. Kulako felt the shallow scrape of a knife against his arm as Eiji passed. They both spun around immediately and charged each other again. This time, Kulako went low to sweep his opponent's feet. Eiji went down, but as he did, Kulako also lost his balance.

Kulako's blood rushed in his ears as he struggled to rise. Eiji kicked the katana from Kulako's hand before coming back with another knife aimed at Kulako's head. Kulako rolled out of the way and managed to stand up, dizzy. He stumbled but remained on his feet realizing, as the onlookers must have, what was going on. Kulako could hear their rather loud speculations:

"Poison!"

"Cheat!"

"Show us some blood!"

He drowned them out again.

Coward. No one uses poisons in this ceremony. Kulako reached shakily into his belt for a knife. He looked at it dumbly for a second before, by only a paper's width, he was able to dodge another swipe from Eiji's blades. From the effects, Kulako thought he recognized the fast-acting poison as fangroot, which meant that it wouldn't be lethal or last long, but that he *did* have to survive through Eiji's attacks as it worked through his bloodstream.

Kulako looked up at Eiji hazily as the fangroot made his vision sway. He blinked. No change. He blinked again. Eiji's fist hit him in the jaw. Kulako hastily grabbed at the outstretched wrist as he turned from the force, pulling the arm forward and bracing his shoulder against the outer elbow to throw Eiji into the packed dirt. Kulako was breathing too heavily for the battle at hand. His lungs were on fire. This was the last phase of the poison before it would leave his body. He knew he hadn't locked Eiji's elbow enough for a break. He took a knee as Eiji rose again.

There was still a knife in his hand; his adrenaline shot up when he remembered it. He slowly stood. The fog was beginning to clear from his mind, but he wondered if Eiji had been able to keep track of time as he would have in a setting where he had more control. Kulako knew he would be pushing how much his body could handle immediately after the fangroot, but it was his only chance. Eiji could kill him if he wasted any more time. He took a second knife into his left hand and put them both up to guard, eyeing his katana briefly before Eiji began to circle him.

Eiji lashed out with a strike, Kulako blocked it with his first knife and followed up with a retaliating slash with his second, giving Eiji no time to recover from the unexpected outburst as he kicked him in the stomach. Eiji shook the shock from his features and put space in between himself and Kulako. Kulako glanced at his katana again as he put away one of his kunai, and this time Eiji noticed. He ran at Kulako with a black-dipped blade in his hands.

Now he uses a lethal one. Fucking idiot. The one thing he shouldn't have listened to Master Aramoto about. Kulako pivoted out of Eiji's reach as the other man stabbed at him and was able to roll away to pick up his katana in one fluid motion. He rounded on Eiji, and could focus normally enough to see he was still petrified with fear.

Eiji took a step back as soon as he realized that Kulako had successfully retrieved the sword. Kulako threw his remaining kunai at Eiji's hand, effectively disarming him of the poisoned blade. Kulako moved forward, and Eiji pulled a foot back to retreat, the kunai still dug into his hand.

"Draw your sword," Kulako said quietly, barely able to control his anger. Eiji complied, his eyes wide with terror as he noticed the expression in Kulako's.

"Kulako, the poison, it was the only way—" Eiji tried to plead as he pulled his mask down, barely able to put his sword up in time to block as Kulako came at him with a strike.

Kulako disengaged and turned his blade downward for a low cut, which he stopped just short of Eiji's leg where he had inflicted a long scar only a few years prior. "Then you should have had another plan."

Using his opponent's confusion, he took his sword's hilt and drove it into Eiji's windpipe. The other man fell, gasping for air while spitting blood. Kulako remembered his initial drive to end the fight quickly through the burn of his anger. Rather than letting him suffer for too long, he stood over Eiji and drove his katana straight down into the solar plexus, closing his eyes as he delivered the killing blow. Kulako sheathed his sword and retrieved his knife from Eiji's limp hand. He turned to the proctor, who hesitated before nodding curtly. Kulako bowed and left the ring, refraining from glancing back when he heard the undertakers moving Eiji's body.

Exhaustion ripped through his body as the after-effects of the fangroot began to take hold. He sank to one knee again as Haru's match against Sota started, using his katana for support. Kulako's hands were shaking. He could have collapsed, but refused to appear weak before the Emperor. He rested his forehead against his sheathed katana as he heard blades scrape over and over until finally, there was a sudden thud and then absolute stillness. Haru, for all of his confidence, looked shaken to have won.

The twelve remaining trainees exchanged glances of shock, confusion, elation, and relief. They were finished. Years of brutal training were over and they survived the last of the gauntlet toward becoming assassins. Kulako dug his sword into the ground to pull himself up, a helpless smile crossing his features as Haru dragged him over to where the other eleven men gathered in the center of the ring, awaiting the Emperor's announcement of their official graduation.

However, the Emperor did not rise. Stunned silence rose into the air.

Kulako glanced up from the corner of his eye. Emperor Akuko was shrouded in shadows on the dais, leaning to his left to speak with the man standing there, who nodded curtly and then stepped forward to the railing of the balcony. Kulako couldn't make out his face very well, but he heard the name "Master Ewah" breathlessly whispered by one of the few surviving. Kulako tried to slow his breathing.

The man cleared his throat loudly and spoke in a broad, projected voice. "His Highness has decided that there are still too many of you."

Kulako's shock was drowned out by the uproar of excitement from the crowd. He looked around in panic at the other exhausted young men, whose expressions mirrored his own. They were searching each other's faces for answers none of them possessed. This had never happened before. Kulako thought it was a flex of power, but quickly banished the idea from his mind. Now was not the time, and it was not his place to question Emperor Akuko.

Ewah continued, "The last five who remain shall be considered graduates of Kurushima."

Kulako's survival instincts seemed to take over just then as he counted out the twelve of them who still stood. Five of them needed to remain? Kulako blinked the malice from his eyes as a clear thought finally came to him. It was an uneven number of matches.

"Melee." Master Ewah said. "Hitokiri, fan out."

It was an order, and they all complied instantly. There was nowhere to hide in the ring, which Kulako realized would make this much more difficult as he sized up his opponents, all with weapons at the ready. He knew he would need to rely on his speed and accuracy the most. He sheathed his katana.

"Begin," Ewah growled.

There was a moment of hesitation, but soon after, everyone went toward the center for one another. Kulako held back to circle the battle, waiting for an opportunity. Madness or not, if this was the game he needed to play in order to have some semblance of freedom, he would participate until his death.

Kulako threw a kunai into the midst of the chaos, landing it in the eye of the only other young man the same age as himself, who was then quickly finished off with a slit throat from someone else. The first of seven to die left the others locked in stalemates. His body was not removed as had been done with the other fallen before him. Kulako remained on the outside of the main fight and waited for another window in which to strike.

Haru pinned and killed a second boy, but an arm wrapped around his throat from a third. He stood and used his height to try shaking his attacker with no luck. They began to struggle. Kulako ran in and tackled the pair, grabbing the one who had attacked Haru by the hair before dragging the point of his knife across the opponent's jugular. Haru exchanged a wary glance with Kulako once the young man had dropped, resentful gratuity in his eyes before he flipped away to avoid a slash at his head. Kulako also took that moment to retreat, giving him enough time to draw his katana before he charged back into battle. He locked blades with a trainee a year his senior. They pushed against one another without any give when they both heard the thud of a body beside them. Kulako counted the fallen bodies.

Seven.

The remaining five looked at one another fearfully; all too afraid of what could happen if they let their guard down too soon. Kulako thought he was breathing more rapidly than when the fangroot was coursing through his blood and his heart was pounding worse than it had been at the beginning of the ceremony.

Master Ewah came to the railing again, this time with Emperor Akuko at his side. A blowing of snow obscured them from view. The five young men all knelt as they had before. The general reappeared from the tent of stunned tacticians and stood at the forefront of the formation facing the balcony, but not the young assassins. The gong sounded again.

The general turned to them, a haunted look in his eyes. "Congratulations, hitokiri."

Kulako couldn't believe the words even as they fell on his ears. Finally, it was real.

They were escorted back to the barracks to gather their things. They all refused to acknowledge the emptiness that seemed to exist in the absence of the nineteen others who had not survived the ceremony's ritual, and none of them spoke about what had happened in the ring. Kulako stripped the sheets from his bunk and listened as the others did the same in utter silence.

Killing then returning to life as if nothing had happened was precisely the sort of thing that an assassin was supposed to be able to do. Kulako had accomplished it several times during training, but he still couldn't shake the fact that he had killed two people whom he had lived with for the last thirteen years—though the cycle was always the same, there was a false sense of hope that the ones who had survived for so long would always be around. A hand was suddenly on Kulako's shoulder, he jumped, though he did not have the energy to retaliate. He blinked in surprise when he saw Haru, whose eyes were also troubled.

"Look," Haru began hesitantly. "You saved my ass in the ring earlier. How about we go out for a drink tonight? The usual spot?"

Kulako, taken aback, could only nod.

"We'll all go." Haru continued, raising his voice and catching the attention of the other three. "Then we can remember the fuckers who left us."

• • • •

LATER THAT NIGHT, ONCE everyone scrubbed blood and dirt from their skin, and they were able to rest in safety in their flats for a few hours, the five new graduates arrived at the tavern. Kulako was convinced that at least two of them were about to be kicked out by the owner; they sounded determined to test the poor man's limits. Though he tried to relax and enjoy himself, he couldn't stop thinking about how they had dragged Eiji's body away and of the others who the Giahatio tossed aside after premature deaths. He felt Haru sit heavily beside him.

"Fine, give it over. What's on your mind?" Haru asked, sounding bored already.

"Where do the bodies go?" Kulako asked somberly.

Haru took a long drink from his mug. "They bury them in a mass grave just off of the Palace grounds."

Kulako glanced over at Haru, his brows furrowed at the image. "They don't even burn them?"

Haru shrugged, trying to seem nonchalant, though there was obvious disgust in his eyes. "They're failures in the Empire's mind, and failures don't receive a proper funeral. Guess it's just a good thing that we aren't. At least not for now. I'll bet you two silvers that you fuck up before I do."

Kulako rolled his eyes and finished his drink in silence.

Kulako hadn't lingered at the celebration and was more than happy to leave just as a brawl started. The streets of the assassins' quarter were usually empty at night, and he was grateful for the peace the silence provided him. He tried to both ignore and process what had happened that day.

He sighed. No matter what, he would see them in his nightmares all the same when he finally did sleep that night. When he came to his flat, a paper pinned to the door rustled in the cold breeze. Kulako cautiously took it down and brought it inside where he could read it by the light of an oil lamp.

In his hands was a black envelope, his first official assignment as an assassin.

• • • •

SONIKA THOUGHT THAT Itake's village gave a home to a beautiful little community. It possessed many of the same qualities that she remembered from Okami life: people worked together, helped one another, and the elderly were not without assistance as she had seen in her most recent venture. However, Sonika still felt like an outsider. Though they had welcomed her, many still seemed wary.

After days of sneaking around for supplies in the hull, Sonika arrived on Itake. When they unloaded the cargo ship, Sonika waited until she could no longer hear the voices of the crew before she slipped out from beneath the protection of the canvas tarp. They left the crate she hid in unattended in a loading area near the docks, among the rest of the cargo, where she then managed to get away without notice. After unwittingly wandering into the market area, a pair of sisters swooped in to help her after her eyes accidentally locked on them. It had taken them only seconds to realize that Sonika was Okami, but the sisters were unbothered by that. Instead, they began battering her with many racing questions about how she had gotten to Itake. Over a year passed since then. Sonika still found it hard to believe.

With her cloak wrapped around her tightly to fend off the chill of the damp weather, Sonika leaned further against the tree she rested on. She had taken a seat in the smallest of dry patches where constant rain of Itake's winters wouldn't reach. The spirit of the white wolf was lying next to her with her soft head on her knee. Sonika closed her eyes and breathed deeply as she stroked the fur along the wolf's neck. Itake was home for now; she thought she might be able to find peace with that.

She felt the earth shift beneath her, and familiar footfalls belonging to Lady Kiki began to approach. The warmth of the wolf spirit left her, and when she opened her eyes once more, she turned her head to see Lady Kiki walking toward her. Unable to contain it, Sonika smiled, proud of herself for recognizing who was coming and happy to see the older woman. Lady Kiki was the elder of the two sisters who had found her.

They had a strange agreement, at least in Sonika's opinion, but Lady Kiki wouldn't hear anything of it: Sonika could live with Lady Kiki and be formally trained as a medic, so long as Sonika gave over her list of Okami medicines. Sonika thought it was an uneven trade, but Lady Kiki would hear nothing of it. She told Sonika with acid in her voice that the Emperor was wrong for what he had done to her people.

"Another lazy afternoon in the woods?" Lady Kiki raised an eyebrow at her critically. "Where are the herbs I asked you to pick?"

"I've already washed them and set them to dry on the table, Lady Kiki."

Lady Kiki's expression softened after just a moment. "It's the rainy season. Are you going to be coming into my house soaking wet again? Shouldn't you be doing something else right now?"

Sonika stood and brushed herself off, grinning wolfishly at her mentor. "I suppose I can make more time between weapons training and your training to get underfoot."

"Your peoples' spirits have mercy on me, girl." Lady Kiki grumbled before pressing her lips together in consternation. She folded her hands delicately in front of her. "Listen, Sonika...Magistrate Tomio wishes to speak with you."

"W-with me?" Sonika felt her heart drop into her stomach like a rock.

The village's magistrate was an official appointed by the Emperor himself to preside over Itake. Was he going to take her to Perena and end her evasion of the Giahatians? Sonika could only hope she was wrong; Tomio seemed like a kind man, but Sonika had learned not to trust appearances.

Feeling somewhat like a small child, Sonika sheepishly asked, "Will you come with me?"

Lady Kiki's eyes and demeanor were nearly always stern, but she was not unforgiving or heartless in nature. She nodded solemnly, turning without so much as a gesture for Sonika to follow along. The magistrate's house was near the inn, where on most days he would wait to greet passengers from the ships. He spent more of his time being out among his people, which Sonika liked. Lady Kiki often stated that the Empire held disdain for how he ran his village, as he had never held an execution or sent anyone off to Perena for such an event. Sonika was thankful it remained true after Magistrate Tomio learned the truth about her heritage.

Lady Kiki let herself into Magistrate Tomio's home, where his son, Teiichi, let out an exclamation. Teiichi was four years older than Sonika, but Lady Kiki always spoke to him as if he were a small child. He resented her for it and had no issue making it known to anyone who would listen.

"Lady, you aren't supposed to be here without permission." He said scornfully.

Lady Kiki only acknowledged him long enough to respond, "Then talk to your father about it and leave me be, boy."

Sonika hid a grin behind her hands as she followed Lady Kiki's swift pace to the magistrate's office, leaving Teiichi stammering for a retort.

"I'm glad you two came so quickly." Magistrate Tomio greeted them as soon as they crossed the threshold. He ushered them into the room. "There's some dire news that I just received: Higia Akuko has been crowned as Emperor this week."

Sonika looked between Lady Kiki and Magistrate Tomio; "Higia" was the name of the dynasty currently holding power over the Giahatio, but she still wasn't accustomed to the fact that the surnames of richer Perenin and Giahatian families came first when stated. It always took her a moment to make the mental adjustment. Thankfully, her pause to consider it hadn't taken any time away from the rest of the conversation at hand.

Lady Kiki looked at him sharply. She dared to allow a tenuous hint of hope to touch at her inflection. "But isn't that a good thing? Without Akuwara, doesn't that mean there's no longer a contract on Sonika's life?"

Tomio gravely shook his head, shooting a furtive glance at his son, who stalked near the doorway, though he had not been invited in to listen. Sonika followed Tomio's eyes, accidentally locking her gaze on Teiichi, who grimaced hatefully at her before storming away. She looked back to Lady Kiki; she'd witnessed the exchange, but chose to say nothing.

Sonika turned her attention to Magistrate Tomio, her heart in her throat. "Does this mean I have to leave?"

The magistrate paused, looking at Lady Kiki for a moment before his eyes fixed on Sonika. "No. It means that if any military men do come to town, you'll be protected from immediate apprehension. Itake is a neutralized province. You'll still have to be careful, but unless an assassin is specifically dispatched, you cannot be touched by soldiers."

"This *is* a good thing, Sonika," Lady Kiki urged. "Hardly enough, but it's a start."

Sonika glanced out the window to her left, wondering, *How much longer until those treaties get broken, too?*

Nine: Nightshade

The sun rose red over the Capital city. Kulako watched with weary eyes from the small yard of his flat as it ascended from the horizon. He had barely slept the previous night, or most of the nights before. Unless he smoked white leaf, which got him high and prevented him from dreaming altogether, nightmares still haunted him. Lately his nightmares were filled with endless rivers of blood and the dying gasps of men barely aware it was their last second to breathe. He was nineteen, now, and already his heart was heavy from the weight of life. Kulako shuddered as a cool, early autumn breeze touched his skin, and wondered how he could survive another day as the monster this blood-lusting government had turned him into.

A stray leaf from the tree above him gently floated to the ground, and Kulako caught the motion out of the corner of his eye. He sighed reluctantly as he placed his sword in his belt, recognizing the time, and the need to go to his commanding officer for yet another assignment. Kulako had only been home for perhaps five days since his last mission, and most of that time had been spent giving accurate reports to his commanding officer and reorganizing after his absence. He was tired of being sent away; it felt like it happened to him more often than the others.

Kulako still did not enjoy killing and avoided it as often as possible, but few could stop him if his mind was set to it. The masters who once taught him and beat him without mercy at Kurushima now refused to acknowledge him when they passed through the assassins' quarter during their rare trips into the city, afraid of what they had created.

Kulako's skills in combat were nearly unmatched by the other hitokiri—the formal name given to assassins—who occupied the quarters alongside him. Because of his age, however, his rank among them was low. He didn't mind. He had always been different, from his actions to his appearance—he still demonstrated an uncommon sense of calmness and preferred to stay far away from the usual skirmishes and other violent nonsense, which even older assassins frequently engaged in. The others often teased him for his isolated nature, but it had saved his life on more than one occasion. His silent footing, sense of when to disengage, and the katana at his hip were the only things he'd found to be reliable over his years of training. Kulako was well aware how dark that line of thinking made existence, but he had little else to draw from.

Despite early graduation, he still felt ill with the thought of the things witnessed and the scars he had received over the years. The soldiers who formed the Giahatio's main army were trained less brutally, and it showed in the way assassins and soldiers behaved and in how they regarded one another. Soldiers were boisterous and frequented popular areas of the city, whereas assassins kept to their home in the shadows and were generally only welcome in more low-end taverns and brothels; even the market Kulako shopped in was considered undesirable. However, a hitokiri of Kulako's rank was paid well, certainly better than the average foot soldier, and more often than not, they could afford wages for maids or company of their choosing.

Kulako skirted around the main gates of the Palace, the path now memorized from many trips since attending the ceremony. The others saw him as odd for not engaging in either of those things, as well. The very thought of having anyone else in his flat filled him with dread, so he cooked and cleaned for himself, and he often donated wages to a couple of the city's poorhouses in secret. The Giahatio paid assassins more than what they needed to survive, and Kulako had spent almost his entire life in survival mode.

When he arrived at the old, unused part of the Palace that had become the workplace of the assassins' commanding officers, someone grabbed him by the shoulders and pulled him into a room. The door locked behind him. Before his vision could adjust to his surroundings, his shoulders were pinned against a wall and the cool metal of a knife touched his throat.

"Stop that." he told Obito irritably, who laughed when Kulako shoved him off in an equally annoyed manner.

"You were really just going to let me kill you?" Obito was still snickering as he allowed Kulako to regain his bearings.

Kulako rolled his eyes, although he was unable to prevent an amused smile from forming on his face. "Do you think you could? You are the least of my worries as far as people who would want me dead—besides, I heard you coming."

Obito laughed again. "You know my stealth is nowhere near yours. Why do you think I've been holed up in an office the last several years?"

After he shook the shaggy bangs from his eyes, Kulako found what he thought was the only comfortable spot inside the dusty room, on a windowsill that framed a view of the Palace gardens. Obito has been introduced as his commanding officer the same night as he'd received his first assignment. They rarely saw one another outside of professional reasons, but enjoyed one another's company. It was the closest thing Kulako found to friendship over the years.

"Are you ready for your next assignment, Hitokiri Nightshade?" Obito chuckled at his own joking inflection.

"No, but do I really have many other choices?" Kulako replied with a roll of his eyes. Both peers and military officials typically held hitokiri with a nickname in high esteem. "Nightshade" was given to Kulako as a sort of snide acknowledgment of how his skills and rank were extremely disproportionate and as an equally snarky reminder of how much he stood out during the day. However, once night fell and assassins stalked the darkness, Kulako was the last anyone could find.

"Not if you want to live a few years more, but with you, I guess that always is a matter of question."

"I haven't let myself die yet."

Obito went to a desk nestled in the far corner of the room and flipped through a short stack of black envelopes, each containing missions. He turned to Kulako when he at last found the one he was looking for. He eyed the other young man thoughtfully and then spoke with the same seriousness in his voice. "I want you to know that this assignment is far above your rank, but we had few others to give it to."

Obito handed Kulako the envelope, visibly anxious. Kulako watched him with undisguised curiosity as he removed the parchment from its inky folds. He glanced at the paper, which only contained the date he was to depart and where he was being sent. Usually, there would also be a day written down to indicate when they expected him to return and report in, and supplemental information about the target, but this particular order fulfilled none of those expectations.

"Is this a joke?" Kulako looked at Obito with tightly controlled annoyance. "You had me wake up before dawn for this?"

"Forgive the early hour, but this is a big responsibility, Kulako. I wanted to cut down on eavesdroppers." Obito noticeably retracted defensively. He took the paper back and wrote something down on it, then handed it to Kulako again. "What was the last that you heard of the Okami?"

The name of the tribe of wolf-people slaughtered by Giahatian forces nine years prior rang in Kulako's mind, reminding him of the roaring fires he had dreamed about on the night of that attack. It made him think of the black wolf again, who had not visited his dreams in at least three years. There was an old Northern Nomadic superstition stating that they only dreamed when necessary, but Kulako didn't believe it, especially not with how nightmares plagued his sleep.

However, looking at where Obito had written the word "Okami" on the parchment, he was questioning how much he could cling to any of his disbeliefs.

He cleared his throat to shake himself from these thoughts to not allow Obito to notice the reverie he had been caught in—he always saw too much too quickly. "Not much beyond what anyone else knows: they were destroyed almost ten years ago, most Giahatians hated them due to their supposedly savage nature, and the Emperor at the time viewed them as a large political threat. Was there something I missed?"

"It's a fairly large detail that we've been trying to fix for years, practically ever since the wolf-people were taken off their isle. You see, as it turns out, not *all* the Okami are dead."

Kulako's expression turned to one of skepticism, and Obito shifted with discomfort at bringing the military's incompetence to light. "The assassins who helped attack Othakra likely would've used chained scythes for range. Is this why they took the kama out of training?"

Obito nodded. As his story continued, he told of a drunken soldier's confession about failing to kill a child attempting to flee Othakra, which was when Emperor Akuwara placed a price on the wolf's head. Intelligence then uncovered a young Okami child kept in hiding for four years after the massacre. He said that even though the Giahatio sent men after her, she escaped apprehension again. It was vital for someone who did not at all resemble a Giahatian to take this assignment.

"I suppose all of that makes sense, but they really should send Haru; he's never looked right." Kulako and Obito grinned at one another. "But even all of that doesn't explain why there isn't a date for a report on here. How long am I expected to be gone?"

Obito fixed Kulako with a serious gaze. "You won't be able to get close to her unless she trusts you fully. Our reports show that she is well-trained and exhibits powerful traits even among her people. She has also been given instruction from the local medic over the last few years. As a female Okami, medicines would have been part of her arsenal all along, which means that she may also be skilled in poisons and their antidotes. You have a lot to contend with, and as I've said, she has escaped our army twice, now."

"I'm not sure if I'm right for this one," Kulako said hesitantly. "Besides...a woman?"

"You've killed women before, Kulako." Obito reminded him indifferently before he looked Kulako over once and then smiled at his friend. "I have faith in you to do what needs to be done with this. I do have to warn you, though: this has been a highly coveted mission for quite some time. Do not be surprised to meet opposition from some of your more experienced comrades."

Kulako mumbled something foul under his breath at the thought of having to fend off other assassins. "You really need to think about keeping your 'open secrets' less open."

"If I did that, then I wouldn't be able to trade information with the spies. Really, it's their fault how much of it leaks out."

"A kunai to the throat could fix that quickly enough."

Obito laughed, "Don't kill my personal economy. Now, then, you'd better get moving. You're supposed to leave today, remember?"

"I remember." Kulako absently looked at the paper in his hands again. He watched Obito for a long moment before adding, "Speaking of that, I've been trying to find Daisuke all week. Could you tell him that he's an idiot the next time you see him?"

Obito smiled. "Will do."

He and Obito bid one another a brief farewell, and he made his way back through the winding, crowded streets of the city to his flat, where he began to prepare for his departure. This part of his career was routine by now, but the very nature of this assignment was something he never experienced before. He'd never been sent beyond the shores of Perena, as those assignments were reserved for higher ranks; he still only had the red embroidery on his uniform, and the average level that should've been selected would have had at least a silver strip. Given the details, Kulako already knew he would be beyond the reach of his skillset—he was horrible with people and even worse when it came to women.

Since Kulako had been given written instruction to leave as soon as possible, he decided to head for the wharves before anyone could suspect that he was not following orders. As he walked along, he lowered his hair from the high tie that signified his position as an assassin and gathered it at the nape of his neck where most foot soldiers wore theirs.

He felt better traveling this way no matter where he went if it were outside of the city limits, as most of Perena's civilians were quite aware of what each hairstyle meant. This way, he was welcomed a little more openly when he entered a new town. His required uniform was a long sleeve, lightweight black shirt that tapered at his wrists, a cloth belt at his waist, and pants made of the same materials met at his knees by hard-soled boots. Soldiers wore gray for their shirts, which was what color Kulako often decided on when not expected to present a more formal appearance. He figured that, if nothing else, it was better for the assignment if people viewed him as a soldier rather than recognized him as an assassin.

By the time mid-afternoon rolled around and the warmth of the day finally began to touch the breezes, Kulako found the ship that would be taking him and several other travelers to his new destination. He paid his fare and settled in the tiny cabin provided for him below decks. For such a critical undertaking, someone else with more experience really should have been going. Even a spy would have been a better option.

Despite his best efforts to prevent the memory from creeping toward him, the unforgettably deep, rumbling voice of the black wolf who had once visited his dreams resonated in his mind, *"This is your destiny."*

Ten: Wolf

Sonika watched the lifting darkness with tense eyes as the sun began to peer over the horizon. Itake's cliffs allowed her an open view of the ocean from where she sat, and she inhaled deeply as a warm breeze rolled up from the waves to run along her skin. She had come here every day since Lady Kiki left two months prior, hoping and waiting for her mentor to return, but somewhere in Sonika's heart, she knew that was unlikely.

Lady Kiki had departed for Perena upon receiving a letter supposedly from her sister, who was currently residing there to further her own medical knowledge. The sisters hadn't seen one other since Sonika's first winter in the village, so at first, it seemed believable. However, one day while Sonika organized the medical kits in the linen closet of their home, the letter had fallen from its hiding place on a shelf. After reading it, Sonika ran to Magistrate Tomio with it.

The sender's scent was still faintly lingering on the paper, enough so that Sonika could tell it was not from Lady Kirimi, whose scent was similar to Lady Kiki's. It had been signed with nothing more than an Imperial Seal. Though he was the village's magistrate and his first loyalty technically belonged to the Giahatio, Lady Kiki trusted Tomio, which was the only reason why Sonika decided to show him the letter—Lady Kiki trusted very few people. Sonika had come to be much of the same way. Tomio reacted the way Sonika worried he might; he formally named her as the village's medic and gathered the town to announce Lady Kiki's death.

The villagers were angry, shocked, and afraid. Many had refused to believe it initially, just as Sonika tried to now, though she couldn't convince herself that Lady Kiki had survived past landing on Perena. Magistrate Tomio only stated that someone framed Lady Kiki for committing a heinous crime. He did not reveal the contents of the letter, but two months later, Sonika had the words memorized: *for the crime of harboring a dangerous fugitive, you will pay for your sins against the Empire.*

Sonika still couldn't say why Lady Kiki had obeyed the order, other than to protect the village. Very few people on Itake knew about Sonika's heritage—Lady Kiki, Magistrate Tomio, and a friend—and because Itake was considered neutral, those accused of such felonious things were summoned to the Capital rather than the Emperor wasting time and money on dispatching an assassin. If Lady Kiki chose to ignore the letter, she would have risked forcing Itake to suffer the same fate as Othakra and Makoto's village.

Sonika clutched at the kunai case at her side on the ground; her heart stopped briefly when she remembered there was another on Itake who knew of her Okami blood. Teiichi was also now living on Perena, shadowing a magistrate who was not his father, a tradition to help prevent biases in practice when he eventually took Tomio's position. Sonika wondered if Teiichi had truly hated Lady Kiki so much that he would send her to death. It meant death would soon come for her, too.

The sun was bright red when it finally broke completely over the horizon, and another warm breeze swept through her hair. She thought it possible that she was only paranoid, but with the ways that her life had already been threatened in the last nine years since the massacre, Sonika had become vigilant in listening to her senses when they warned her of trouble. Her ancestors' strength ran boldly through her blood. Through the valor and courage of many previous generations of Okami, Sonika had been able to find her own power to continue existing in a world that wished to see her dead. In every inch of her being, she could never be anything besides who she was.

Sonika pulled the kunai case onto her lap, knowing that she would not train today like she planned to, as she did most days. In addition to the overwhelming stress of her senses, the gnarled scar from the chained scythe was agitating the nerves along her spine, as it sometimes still did, so instead, she stood to leave.

She desperately wanted her thoughts away from where they had been all morning thus far, but they were already beginning to crawl toward a less favorable place. If the Giahatio decided to send more soldiers after her this time, she could not back down if she were to keep her own life, but she also would not risk the lives of the villagers who so selflessly offered her solace these last few years. The people of Itake had come to be incredibly accepting of her, and she felt there was no proper way to compensate them for their generosity and open hearts. Itake was a place of cultural convergence, and the locals had learned to treat her no differently than they treated those who arrived from any other part of the world. With Lady Kiki's house now belonging to her, she offered free medical visits as often as possible and worked long hours without complaint when her skills were required. It was a small offering to compensate for safety, but it was all she really had.

Sonika began to feel a familiar stir building within her chest that wanted to be free. Feeling emboldened by it, Sonika cupped her hands around her mouth and let out a long, loud howl, sending an echo across the waters. The Okami used the wolf's call as signals and for music, but to her, it was as if she had called out her defiance to the very Emperor of Perena and the Giahatio himself, and she wanted to find out whether or not her challenge would be answered.

As she made her way back to the village, the morning birds songs began, and she felt content once more as she always did in this setting. Itake's rustic appearance with a thick layer of woods and fields and plenty of hiking trails made her feel at home in a sense. Surrounded by the docile creatures that lived in the trees, she, too, could find peace. Not wanting to disturb anyone, she quietly moved through the village to her small home. She glanced toward the smithy, where she could see the fires and smell the metal of her friend Maru's work even in this early hour. Sonika was able to catch the sound of his wife's laughter floating on the breeze.

Never forget who you are as Okami, she repeated to herself off-handedly, and a voice Sonika buried into the folds of her childhood came to her.

"I will always be with you." Takeo's last words filled Sonika's ears.

She shivered at a chill in the air and retreated into her home before her emotions became more than she could control.

• • • •

EWAH WATCHED ROKU FROM a high balcony of the Palace as the assassin faded from sight. He felt anxious; it was abnormal for Ewah. Roku was not easily able to abide by missions that ordered him to take the sideline, but it was necessary to have a secondary hitokiri available should a failure occur.

The Emperor had taken a personal interest in assigning the first hitokiri because of the circumstances surrounding the contract. Although Ewah had to abide by His Highness's choice, Emperor Akuko allowed it to ultimately be Ewah's decision to send a shadow ahead. It was vital that the dispatched hitokiri finally put the matter to rest, and there was no room for chance. He could only hope Roku would not try handling things himself.

Ewah finally shrugged and turned away from the window, knowing there was little else he could do but leave it in Hikari's hands. No matter what, the man who succeeded would receive a generous award—at least, that was what he'd made Roku believe.

• • • •

KULAKO HAD BEEN AT sea for a week and feeling awful for second of it. He hadn't been on a ship since the recruiters took him from Okara as a child, and couldn't remember much of the experience, though he was sure it couldn't have been like this. In between the churns and flips his gut seemed intent on performing, he managed to do a bit of extra research from notes he had copied from Obito in his illegible handwriting. It did little to clear the heavy cloud of doubt that overthinking the situation left him with, but it did give him a distraction from it for at least a few seconds at a time.

He learned that since the disappearance and the declared death of their last medic over two months ago, the people who resided on Itake had become very protective of their current one—the Okami. Very few people were aware of her tribal origins; in fact, the report of her existence on Itake was from someone who did not live there, but the spies had confirmed it eagerly, hungry for new information to trade with one another.

Itake was considered more of a wayside rest for travelers. Due to the lack of resources and skilled men, it had been left out of any significant conflicts throughout Imperial history; children weren't even recruited for Kurushima from Itake. All of these circumstances put together were why the late Emperor Akuwara had declared Itake neutralized and made the rules considering apprehensions by soldiers and kills made by the hitokiri. That was all the information Kulako had, so that was when he stopped reading, which was usually when his stomach started acting ridiculous again. He was sure he'd survived poisons training with less inconvenience.

The ship was drawn to port on Itake Island in the early afternoon. As passengers milled about and began to leave the boat, Kulako decided he could only follow those who were also moving to locate the inn. However, as he lifted the bag he had brought with him to his shoulder, he felt another presence before seeing it. He watched the underbrush of the nearby line of trees for a moment as he slowed his pace as to not draw attention to his suspicious actions and again saw the subtle movements in them that did not belong to any creatures.

Kulako hesitated, then padded toward the forested area where a man's figure dissolved once again after successfully catching Kulako's notice. For reasons Kulako could not explain, he thought of when the black wolf had warned him of Teiji and Haru approaching with the intent to harm, wishing the wolf were there now to warn him of what he was walking into.

Once Kulako merged far enough back within the trees, the other man who lured him in this far dropped down in front of him. The man lowered his hood and loosened his scarf before he quickly drew a knife,

Fucking hell. Kulako's expression betrayed his thoughts, no matter how he tried to conceal it. He cleared his throat and spoke aloud, hoping that perhaps there had been a misunderstanding, though he knew better. "Name and stripes?"

"Roku Himewa, red-and-silver." The man returned with a confident grin on his face. "I already know you, Kulako Akahana, Hitokiri Nightshade."

Kulako tensed further as Obito's warnings came back to him. "Why are you here?"

"Word from Obito's purse said that a foreigner got sent after the Okami. I just couldn't believe it." Roku sneered. "The title and reward promised with that mongrel's death are too great to be given to you, foreigner. This is a matter of Giahatian pride."

"There's no title or reward. Where the hell did you get that idea?"

"Master Ewah," Roku smirked. "Perhaps it wasn't offered to you for a reason. He isn't shy about which groups of people he dislikes."

Kulako rolled his eyes, but was forced to quickly put his forearms up to block his face. Roku had attacked without warning and didn't hold back. He used his entire weight to push against Kulako, who slid backward. The tip of the kunai Roku had first drawn threatened the space between his eyes. Kulako separated the cross his arms made to catch the down strike and used one to launch himself off Roku. He rolled away and stood in a flash.

Roku turned toward Kulako and flexed his fingers, the glitter of expensive, jewel-encrusted rings catching in the sunlight filtering through the treetops. Kulako had no desire to fight the other hitokiri; if civilians caught either of them, they would likely have to kill the unsuspecting villager, something Kulako was desperate to avoid.

"You didn't really answer my question," Kulako said, hoping to buy some time. "Why are you here? Do you really think you could just walk right up to the wolf and stick her with a knife? With the way you look, I don't even like you being near me."

Roku angrily bore his yellowed teeth and threw the kunai at Kulako, who sidestepped out of the trajectory path. It had been stupid to provoke Roku, but Kulako knew well how exhausting anger was, and he hoped Roku's fury would cause him to expend too much energy, make too many mistakes, and decide to fall back. Roku lunged at Kulako, using their difference in reach to grab Kulako at the lapels, pulling him closer and then launching a successful strike at the left side of Kulako's face. Kulako fought through the shock of the hit and grabbed Roku's hand that was gripping his lapel with his left. He twisted Roku's wrist, which made the man's arm snake in response, before he drove his elbow down into Roku's, digging into the pressure point at the joint. Roku swore and released Kulako as he began to sink to one knee, but not before another punch connected with Kulako's cheekbone. Kulako noticed the taste of iron as he clambered away. He put the back of his hand to his bleeding lip.

Fuck, His only clear thought, realizing he'd turned this into even more of a confrontation. Black dots began to litter his vision from the hits he had taken. He tried to shake them away, but no assassin's skull was that thick.

Roku quickly recovered and was running at Kulako again, this time with his scarf at the ready. Kulako only had time to duck, which was an even worse mistake than provoking Roku. Roku easily hooked Kulako's head into the loop he created with the scarf and now stood behind him. Holding the fabric taut, Roku pulled it tightly against Kulako's throat.

Roku threw a couple of strikes at the back of Kulako's head, and he could feel the stinging of broken skin from the stones on the rings. His heels left the ground as his opponent further restricted his airway. Desperate, Kulako drew a knife of his own and blindly thrust it back into his opponent's side.

The other man howled in pain, and after a quick jerk backward, he released the scarf. Kulako fell to his knees and gasped for air, relieved that his plan had worked, until he heard the grass rustle from beneath his opponent's feet.

"Won't you draw your sword on me, *Nightshade*?" Roku hissed, his black eyes flaring with ire. Kulako was about to try getting up, but Roku grabbed him by the leg. Roku's arm locked dangerously around Kulako's knee, forcing the younger man down by placing his weight over Kulako's abdomen with his knee. He eyed Kulako again. "Am I not worth your time?"

"No." Kulako braced himself as Roku brutally twisted his arm around Kulako's knee and then sent an elbow directly into the joint multiple times until they both felt it weaken. Kulako's opponent released him and then stomped on his shin multiple times. The entire world became unbearably bright and then dark all in the flash of a few seconds as Kulako reeled from the pain. Kulako did the only thing he could think of. He reached up and, with every bit of strength he had left, shoved the heel of his palm into Roku's nose, able to feel the cartilage crumble as Roku pulled away. Kulako turned on his side as if to try and get away from his attacker.

Roku held his profusely bleeding and broken nose as he reeled backwards and onto his feet. Roku kicked Kulako in the back of his head out of a reflex of anger and self-defense, sending him into unconsciousness. He turned Kulako onto his back, swearing as he began to retreat. Ewah meant for him to be a shadow, not an opponent. He knew that if Master Ewah found out about this, he would likely die for defying orders. This had not gone to his plan at all; rather than intimidating the lower-ranked assassin into tucking his tail and running from the assignment, he'd driven him right into the medic's care. He had to hurry away to tend to his wound. He had to devise some sort of lie and file a report.

Besides, he only had a small window of time to cover up his scent from the wolf.

Eleven: The Wreckage

Okami medicine was strong. Sonika always made her medicines to be potent as most Okami remedies first. Then she diluted half of the solutions, kept in the forms of topical balms or easily swallowed liquids—she never had learned to make Lady Kiki's pills. That way, she could ensure a steady supply for those not conditioned to handle intense treatments. She used as many local items as she could grow in her garden. If she had to send away to Perena or Othakra for ingredients to more complex emulsions, she asked the islander next leaving for such a trip to find what she needed, drawings and diagrams included.

While going about her nightly routine of stirring together the mixture she liked to use on sore muscles, burns, and bruising, she sensed as the earth shifted beneath her, like a flex of the ground as someone moved across it. Simultaneously, the sound of hurried footsteps rushed to the short set of stairs before reaching her porch. She quelled the fire beneath her medicine pot and turned to her door, opening it after a single knock.

"Lady Sonika!" One of the villagers said breathlessly, trying to compose himself. "We-we found, there was a—!"

Sonika raised a hand in the air between them, trying to keep the man calm enough so that he could adequately explain what was going on. She reminded him, the words more automatic than expected, "'Lady' was a very suitable title for Kiki and is for most medics, but it does not belong with me. Now, please, tell me what's going on."

Embarrassed at the scolding for the use of a designation with her, he glanced away for a moment before gaining enough control to relay the message he needed to give. "Please, excuse me. Lady Kiki has not been gone for very long, and I forgot that you dislike the title."

Sonika, ignoring the shameful pit in her stomach for the way she had spoken, waited for the man to go on.

"A few of us were out for a walk in the woods, you know, looking for a good patch of trees to clear for the cattle we're about to get when we stumbled across someone. We think he's a Giahatian soldier, but he looks like he's been beaten pretty badly. And recently. We were worried that an assassin was after him."

Sonika slipped on her cloak to protect herself from the evening's chill, pausing briefly out of worry when the idea that an assassin may be encircling the village crept into her mind, but she banished this concern. She needed to focus. "How bad does he look?"

The man stepped aside, allowing her to exit. After shutting the door behind her, he retraced his steps to where the other men were waiting to help carry the injured man to safety.

When they arrived at the designated location, each of the four other men stood from where they were seated beside the body of the individual in question. Sonika greeted them quietly and knelt next to the young man on the earth, taking note of his Giahatian clothing.

She noticed the katana at his side and slid it out of his reach, urgently telling the man who brought her there, "Bring this to Maru and have him store it, please."

She turned back to the injured man. Examining his face, she saw dried blood in the corner of his mouth from where his lip had been split open, and then she looked up at his bruised eye and cheek; a few small cuts were scratched into the skin around them, though Sonika couldn't be sure what those were from. It was hard for her to say if his vision would suffer any permanent damage, but Sonika doubted it, as such results seemed to be rare. She cocked her head to one side curiously, a wolfish manner that no amount of trying to conceal herself could ever take away, noting the pallor of his skin. She peeled back the hood from his head, flinching as the dried blood caused it to stick to his fiery red hair. Sonika stared in complete surprise for a moment. Unable to help herself, she touched the ends of it, but recoiled as if she expected him to wake and lash out at her. She looked away.

"He doesn't look at all Giahatian," she teased the remaining villagers who stood around her. They all mumbled some form of embarrassment for acting paranoid, and she grinned at them. Sonika didn't want to admit that they were right about the soldier's clothing. She touched the scarf at his neck where a second scent mingled with his, most likely belonging to his attacker. His assailant had attempted to strangle him with it. She pulled it down just enough to see the deep red line at his throat she suspected would be there.

"What about his leg, L—Sonika?" Another one of the men piped up. She turned to him, broken from her entrancement with the damage done to his top half.

Sonika's stomach churned as she shifted for a proper look at his leg, where there was noticeable swelling on his shin and knee. She could not yet say how severe the injury was or where it was.

A medic's job isn't done until the patient is healed. She recalled one of Lady Kiki's first pieces of advice for patient care. With a sigh, Sonika realized that she would be taking this one in for a bit; he needed a place to heal and rehabilitate where she could track his progress—considering his condition, she also assumed he had few other places to go. She wiped her hands, red with his blood, on the grass beside him and stood.

"I need some help carrying him back to my house. He needs to be cleaned up and fitted with a cast."

"Are you sure that's a good idea? What if he wakes up?" One of the men protested.

"With that injury to his leg, he won't be much of a threat to anyone. And don't forget, I'm good with knives. Please?"

Another man nodded firmly, which seemed to rally the others around him. "Of course."

Sonika instructed them on the best way to carry him and prevent further agitation to his injuries. Shortly after they were all in a position to lift him off the ground, they marched back to her home in the dim light of early autumn's dusk. He was lightweight even for his height, and they managed the journey in a short amount of time. They placed him in the small, unused room, which had been hers when Kiki still inhabited the house, and gently lowered him onto the bed. Sonika thanked each man who helped her and bid them all a good night, wanting to begin treating him immediately.

Though already exhausted from a long day of work, Sonika braided her hair back and lit a couple of oil lamps before gathering a few medicines and rags along with a bucket filled with water, and then she began to clean the young man's wounds. She washed out his hair and inspected the injury at the back of his skull, which was easy to stitch. She placed a touch of ointment over his bruising before opening his eyelids to shine a light in each eye. Each pupil constricted normally, however, the color of his irises startled her. She had never seen violet eyes before and was highly intrigued, though she knew better than to allow herself to look longer, as they was still plenty of work to do.

She looked over his torso to ensure that nothing else suffered damage. The source of his shallow breathing revealed a patch of bruising on his ribcage where something struck. There were old defensive scars scattered along his skin, some had gone light enough to blend in with his skin—typical enough for soldiers, she thought. She pressed against his abdomen, and his body involuntarily contracted a little. Other than medication for pain and the balm for bruising, there wasn't much she could do for those areas. Okami medicine was strong, but Sonika didn't have the magic of a Healer; if his organs were bleeding, she might lose him.

Last, she rolled up his pants to look at his leg. She examined and then correctly set it. Even in his unaware state, his body twisted, and she had to force him to stay steady by placing her full weight on him. She braced and wrapped it properly, and with a shaky breath, sank against the wall opposite of the bed, relieved that her work was complete except for a treatment for pain.

She stared at him for a long while with scrutiny, finally asking his unresponsive form, "What are you doing here?"

At the sound of her voice, his mouth twitched subconsciously, and Sonika had to stifle a laugh. It was rare that she struck up a conversation with unconscious individuals, and even more uncommon that they seemed willing to respond. She decided it was time to give him a dose of medicine for the night and cleaned up the scattered debris left in her wake of tending to him as quickly as possible. She gathered the knives removed from his clothing prior to treatment, as well as the scarf found around his neck, unsure of what she should do with any of it. She finally decided to lock the knives in her dresser, and thought that she should keep the scarf for the sake of remaining familiar with the scent of the assassin should he return.

••••

KULAKO AWOKE WITH A start in the early hours of the morning, mouth dry, head throbbing, and pain radiating from his right foot all the way to the base of his skull. Every inch of his body ached. He attempted to sit upright, but settled for propping himself on his elbows and glanced out the window at the wan light of dawn. He remembered very little of the day before other than arriving on Itake Island in the early afternoon. There was something else; a man who called him aside from the rest of the crowd while leaving the small port. He remembered the nature of his attack through a thick screen of exhaustion.

Thunder rumbled. He ran his hands through his hair, pausing when he felt a ridge in his skin, freezing when he realized that the length of his hair was unrestrained. Kulako vaguely reached out to fumble for the tie he could barely muster the energy to find when he realized that he had been disarmed. He grabbed for one of the knives usually stored in his open shirt, hoping to prove himself wrong, but his fingers brushed fabric. He scanned the room. Where was his katana?

His attempt to leave the bed was met with excruciating pain throughout his right leg, and his head swirled with a final memory of all that had taken place before he'd blacked out. He looked down at where he could feel the brace around his leg from knee to ankle, grateful that someone had taken care of him.

He could see a bit of the village from his window, although the rain soon blurred most things from view within moments of looking outside. He half-heartedly tried to force himself to get up again despite the agony in his joints, but was unable to move from the comfort of the blankets placed over him for the duration of the night.

Trying to remain calm, he ran two things over in his mind continuously: one, the assassin who assaulted him faced consequences for defying orders upon returning to Perena, or they would send someone to deal with him before then. Two, the person who had taken such care of his unconscious form was not highly likely to attack him in this state. He decided he would instead work to rehabilitate himself as quickly as possible; the longer Kulako stayed, the more likely he would be to catch the village's general attention. Though these thoughts did little to truly cure his worries, the drowsiness from the medications he had previously been given sank into his mind, and his body called for rest once more. Unwillingly, he gave in to sleep, lulled by the thunder and rain.

• • • •

"MARU SAYS THAT EVEN for an assassin, that katana would be pretty high quality," Mitake told Sonika as she poured tea. "Well, a low-ranking assassin. It's definitely impossible for a foot soldier to get something like this—unless it was inherited from a disgraced member of the military."

"I'm not so sure that helps me much. All that really tells me is that I have a beaten soldier with a dead soldier's sword." Sonika answered, a dubious expression marking her features. She had decided to visit her friends at the smithy to gain a little more intelligence on her patient. Taking a long sip from her cup, she mulled over what she had been given thus far to work with, which was very little.

Maru chuckled from the other side of the room at his friend's frustration. "You know, Mitake thinks of herself as something of a spy these days, Sonika. Give her some credit."

Mitake's dark brown eyes alighted, and her expression made Sonika nervous. Though she knew that Mitake's heart was generally in the right place, her suggestions were usually ludicrous. "You said his leg is really bad, right? Maybe if you just—you know—threaten to punch it or something..."

"And give myself more to do?" Sonika couldn't help but laugh. "This one's going to be enough work as it is, especially since I'll have to learn how to share my house until he's ready to leave again. I stopped by to see Magistrate Tomio before I got here; he said he didn't recognize anyone with his description."

"It's been years since he's seen any soldiers, Sonika," Maru said critically.

Mitake quickly added, "I doubt Tomio would know anyone from the Capital right now. Think about it, though. You've definitely got leverage here, and if he's going to be living with you and you think he could be dangerous, I suggest you learn how to use it."

Somewhat unwillingly, Sonika considered her options. "Well, no matter what, he isn't going to be up for answering too many questions today. I gave him quite a bit of medication to keep him tame until I found some crutches for him."

Mitake smiled, gesturing to where her husband was working over on the other side of the smithy. "Maru *claims* that he isn't much good with those sorts of things, but he should have them ready soon. For now, why not go home and rest? It sounds like you had a long night, and Maru can bring them when they're done—probably sometime later today."

After some idle chatter not involving the stranger, Sonika finished her tea and bid Mitake a farewell, pulling up the hood of her cloak and clutching it tightly against her to protect her from the rain. She passed by familiar faces on her way home, and each had questions about her new boarder. She answered vaguely, wanting to keep what little she knew confidential until he could provide her with more answers.

Sonika did rest for a little while when she returned home but soon grew restless as she usually did on rainy days. She felt that being indoors rather than out in the garden or training in the woods always made the day feel twice as long. In the house's small sitting room, she lit a fire to fight off the dampness seeping into the indoor air. She went into the stranger's room and decided to bring in one of her medicine kits to work on a new dosage to alleviate any pain he would feel upon waking. She set out several jars in a neat row beside her mortar and began to work with her back turned to him. Sonika knew she wouldn't be able to focus if she felt as though he could somehow see her, though he was still sleeping heavily.

• • • •

HIS MIND WAS STILL in a fog when Kulako regained consciousness, this time in the late morning. He felt rested, which was odd. Kulako couldn't remember the last time he slept well enough to claim that—there were many nights when he hadn't slept at all. A few strange yet wonderful herbal aromas drifted through the air to him, along with the unseasonal scent of cherry blossoms, which encouraged his eyes to open. He forced himself to sit up, though his body wildly protested the action, and he slowly realized that another presence was in the room with him. She stood from where she had been sitting on the floor, her length of dark hair falling over her back.

"You shouldn't be up yet." A firm yet soothing voice came from her as she wiped her hands on a towel slung over her shoulder. She didn't turn around. The sound of her voice caught Kulako off guard. He hesitated for only a second, reminded of his need for information.

Feeling a little embarrassed over his injuries, Kulako asked, “Where am I?”

When she rounded on him, her golden eyes immobilized him. Kulako was frozen, taken aback by the fierceness in her gaze and the strength of her stance, though she was small even compared to him—he would have never dared to assume that she was fragile.

The Okami, his mind whispered as if even his subconscious was afraid to draw attention to itself in her presence.

Twelve: Rain and Roses

"You were a soldier in the Giahatian army, but decided to leave?" The Okami woman asked Kulako as she reached out to hand him a cup of hot liquid. After determining him cognitive enough for conversation, she produced what she claimed to be a mixture of medicines with tea for him to drink and began to interview him. Her stern eyes never left his as she sat on the edge of the bed.

Kulako looked warily at the cup containing the strange-smelling fluid. She set it on the bedside table when he didn't take it. The deserter story was the first thing that had come to his mind when she asked him about how he had come to Itake, and, surprisingly, she seemed to believe it. At least for now. Kulako wasn't sure he would be able to keep up the premise for long. Lying never had been one of his strong suits.

Kulako reminded himself that he wasn't likely to be in much danger considering the care he had already received. He nodded in response to her question, and finally, she glanced away. Kulako silently exhaled in relief. The intensity of her gaze made it feel as if she could see right into his soul.

"I suppose that *would* explain why the assassin came after you, then, wouldn't it?" She spoke as if to herself, then directly to him again, anger now bright in her eyes and the annoyance on her face revealing one of her prominent canine teeth; Kulako almost didn't believe he saw it. "Innocent people live here—why would you choose to endanger them like that? What if he comes back?"

"I doubt he will. The hitokiri are usually confident about their kills." Kulako said offhandedly. Despite his injuries, he felt it was safe to assume that Roku wouldn't come around again for some time. "And even if he does, he can really only try to kill me again."

The medic rolled her eyes and paused for a long moment. "Well, either way, that means you're stuck with me for a while until you heal."

"Don't you think it's the other way around?"

"With a mouth like yours, no wonder you had to leave the army."

Kulako started to laugh, but a sharp pain from his side flared, and he leaned forward to try and ease it. The medic tapped the table at the bedside and held out the cup of her medicated mixture for him again. Begrudgingly, Kulako reached for it, but his perception was off, and the extension of his arm stopped too abruptly; he'd nearly knocked the cup from her hand.

"You're pretty lively, but I'm not surprised," she said before he could apologize. "The medication I gave you last night is still working through, so your movements will be off for a bit."

"What, did you give me poison instead?" Kulako rolled his eyes.

"You're tempting me. Now, drink." She took his hand firmly and wrapped his fingers around the cup so he could take it from her. "I haven't even introduced myself yet, have I? My name is Sonika."

"Kulako," Perhaps she had been right about the previous medicines making him feel off; Kulako's face felt hot, and not just from the warm liquid he'd taken in at her command. Despite the strange smell of the concoction, it didn't taste terrible, but Kulako had a feeling that whatever was in it would hit him hard once it started cycling through his system. "Sorry, I guess I should be nicer. You *are* healing me, after all."

Sonika paused, and then gave him a troublesome grin, which fully revealed her fangs as she took the empty cup back. "You'll have some time to learn. Severe leg injuries can take up to six months to heal, and that's if you behave. More bed rest for today, and then tomorrow, we'll get you up and about. I know some medics will say to rest the whole time, but I'm meaner than they are; I worry about one's blood sitting still for too long."

Kulako rolled his eyes, this time out of amusement, and the rest of the room swirled with the action. He leaned forward again and put his head down.

It was no secret among those in the Giahatian ranks that still remembered the Okami—one shouldn't waste time considering them as more than the animals they named themselves after. Those only a few years younger than Kulako were usually clueless that the tribe had ever existed. Though Kulako had never agreed with the sentiment to begin with, likely because of how the slave trade viewed his own race as subhuman, he was now confused as to how those thoughts were once applied to the Okami. Sonika acted more human than most hitokiri he knew. He wasn't sure what else he had been expecting.

What? Did you think she'd be an actual— the last word came out of his mouth accidentally as the medicines made his mind fog again, "Wolf."

Sonika's posture visibly tensed and her fingers tightened around the cup, but she only stared at him in disbelief. "What?"

Kulako shook his head. "Wolf."

"Are you insulting me?" It was a quick reaction, Sonika was aware, but she had only ever heard the word used as such since she had been forced to flee Othakra.

Kulako's eyes were glassed over from the treatments she had given him and he started to sink into the bedding again. "You're Okami, aren't you?"

"You can't prove that." An involuntary growl rumbled in the back of Sonika's throat.

He was already asleep again before he could reply. Sonika glanced over at the small utility knife near the bandages she kept in the medicine box she brought in with her. She shook her head in frustration; it would be an insult to her honor as a medicine woman to slaughter a defenseless patient and cause a larger crisis to her beliefs. However, it was undeniable that Kulako had known what he was talking about, at least on some level.

Wolf, Sonika repeated to herself with a scowl as she packed up her things. She thought the word again when she was nearly out of the room, but this time how it sounded when he had spoken it. It hadn't been harsh. It hadn't been contemptuous. It had just been a word.

A name.

Sonika's face turned warm.

• • • •

THAT NIGHT WHEN SONIKA fell into dreams, the white wolf greeted her in the familiar safety of a forest. She happily knelt to scratch her companion's ears, and the wolf licked her face before she turned to lead Sonika up a trail.

"What do you think?" the white wolf asked her calmly. *"This one feels different than others, doesn't he?"*

It was true; Sonika had noted Kulako's aura lacking in aggressive traits during their earlier encounter. Really, he emitted little presence at all. As soft and quiet as a shadow, as calm as a midnight snowfall. She supposed most men would take those comparisons as an insult to their masculinity, but she had a feeling she was dealing with a different type for now.

"He knows I'm Okami—that isn't a good thing. The Giahatio have only ever taught their soldiers that we're subhuman savages. What if he finds a way to make contact with someone in the Capital?"

The wolf swished her tail in amusement. *"He won't be going anywhere for a while. Perhaps you can convince this one differently."*

"How am I supposed to do that?" Sonika knew she sounded as desperate as she felt. *"Would it even be fair of me to expect anyone in his position to listen? I know I don't know much about the Giahatian military, but they don't exactly have a reputation for making soft soldiers."*

"If you can learn his heart, he can learn yours."

The white wolf stopped, motioning with her head for Sonika to lead them up the steep path. Sonika pushed back the thin tree branches and stepped over bushes as carefully as she could. The trail ended at a cliff, where a terrible storm raged around the edge. In the center of the storm, Sonika thought she could see a figure similar to Kulako's standing amid the black clouds and raging winds, looking down at the sea below.

• • • •

KULAKO'S DREAMS WERE troubled by strange images that night. He at first stood on a tall rock overlooking an enraged sea. Surrounded by flashes of lightning and bellowing thunder, the wind and high waves threatened the safety of his perch, until he blinked. Then he was deep in a forest, the canopy of trees protecting him from the same storm that continued overhead. He tried to walk forward, surprised to find that even in his subconscious, his leg injury persisted. Suddenly, there was a large mass of black fur beside him, and he found himself looking down into the hypnotic golden eyes of the wolf from his childhood.

"*Hello, Takeo.*" He heard himself say. It surprised him, as he had never asked the wolf's name, nor had it been given. His voice echoed despite the roar of the ongoing storm.

The wolf inclined his head ever so slightly in a greeting. His voice rumbled more deeply than the thunder above when he said, "*Come, Kulako.*"

It was a childhood habit to place his hand in the thick fur at the black wolf's shoulder, but it was no less comforting now that he was an adult. His ebony companion leaned into him, providing Kulako's injured leg with stability as he guided them down the forested path.

It was barely past midnight when Kulako awoke from his visions. He was upright before he fully pulled himself from sleep, and in the silence filling the house, he was able to find calmness again. A gentle breeze made its way in from his open window, alerting him to the rustling of parchment on his lap. Curiosity overcoming panic, he warily picked up the folded note from the sheets.

Akahana,

> *We'll both lick our wounds for now. Master Ewah originally ordered me here as a shadow, and so a shadow I will stay until you can admit that you are incompetent. When you inevitably realize your worthlessness and need an out, you may find me at the inn. One of us will kill the wolf, no matter what. His Highness will not allow failure this time.*
>
> *Roku*

Kulako looked the letter over twice and again regretted not disposing of Roku when he should have. Had it not been for the allegation that Roku was acting on Master Ewah's orders, he may have been more compelled to do so. Master Ewah was a man cloaked in mystery, but his methods when dealing with those who disobeyed his command were not. Kulako didn't know who he feared worse between the intelligence master and the Emperor when the idea of facing punishment for failure crept into his mind. Kulako glanced out the open window again and watched the moonlight as it danced between the trees swaying on a light breeze.

When taken from home as a child and nearly every day since, the Giahatio told him that he belonged to them for the entirety of his life and that he was only a tool to be used at the Emperor's expense. When the wolves came to him, they made him believe that he could change such a fate. He wanted to fight against the direction his thoughts tugged him toward, but nonetheless, he wondered if he could still accomplish such a thing.

On Itake, he was mostly free from the Giahatio, save for Roku. Roku wouldn't be of much concern for a little while, either. Kulako had never been able to place much faith in gods, goddesses, spirits, or superstitions. Perhaps while separated from the Giahatio and allowed to think freely, he would be able to figure out what the apparitions really meant.

Anxiety curled into a ball in his chest. He worried that he may not like the answer he found, but was more afraid of what it meant if he agreed with that conclusion.

The black wolf's eyes flashed intensely before his once more.

Thirteen: A Home for the Restless

Kulako was convinced that he was losing his grip. In the two weeks since he had be taken under Sonika's care, it felt as though the darkness in his heart was beginning to lift. It had been there for years, and only in its absence was he able to acknowledge its existence. There was no need for the constant vigilance with which he normally watched his surroundings, his nightmares dwindled, and he found that he could sleep dreamlessly most nights. He enjoyed the change of pace thoroughly, even if most of his time was spent repaying Sonika for her care by managing little chores around the house. She argued at first, but after some—gentle, slightly terrified—insistence on his part, she begrudgingly accepted it.

Thirteen years of training and carefully building up his emotional defenses, and Kulako felt it all slipping away at the first real instance of human kindness in his life. Something was definitely wrong with him. Perhaps the faith he had in the image of the black wolf wasn't so misplaced, after all. Kulako shuddered the thought. The wolf had not returned since the dream, but the appearance still unsettled him. What did the sightings of the wolf mean, and why did he continue appearing?

He was trapped in these thoughts when Sonika sat down at the kitchen table with him one day. She noticed his distraction and descended upon him with that captivating gaze of hers.

"At ease, soldier." She teased.

Kulako rolled his eyes. "Don't pick a fight you can't win, wolf."

"I might be able to right now." She glanced down at his injured leg briefly and grinned before her voice became teasing again. "Besides, you wouldn't fight a woman, would you?"

Kulako watched as she set a few shuriken on the table. Sonika had been upfront with him about her own experience in training. "That depends. Are you using those?"

"Do you want me to?"

"Nobody has that much time to ask that many questions during a fight."

"Or be this selective." Sonika shook her head in exasperation.

Kulako touched the edge of one of the blades on a throwing star. "You know, these aren't seen very often, and I've heard they aren't exactly easy to master; you must be a skilled distance fighter."

Sonika looked at the shuriken fondly, remembering Takeo's deep voice and warm eyes during their practices together. The present called to her once more, and she glanced at Kulako. Avoiding her memories, she answered, "I've been using them for a long time. Enough about that, though. Something's bothering you. What is it?"

Kulako felt a pang of guilt; whatever he said must have triggered something painful, and it played into his hesitation to respond. He looked at Sonika uneasily and, as she set down a sharpening stone for her weapons, her expression changed when their eyes met again. Who was better to ask about wolves than a wolf?

"What is it?" She asked him again, this time softly. *That* tone; Kulako wasn't used to it, and he still wasn't sure whether or not he should trust it. The sound alone was too kind to be real, but Sonika never spoke with malice or heartlessness as nearly everyone Kulako had known to this point did, even when he purposely exasperated her. The wit and sarcasm she usually gave him, as she had been doing only moments ago, had been less difficult to adapt to.

"This might surprise you, but not much is known about the Okami anymore." Kulako said cautiously. He was sure he was going to offend her and earn a strike to his leg—he would consider it fair at that point.

"That's shocking." Sonika laughed when Kulako rolled his eyes.

"Giahatians don't really believe in this, but...did dreams mean anything?"

"I guess it would depend on the dream," she answered slowly, not expecting what he asked.

"A recurring one?" he said vaguely, not wanting to risk sounding more ridiculous than what he was sure he already did. Sonika rolled her eyes at his response, unimpressed by his lack of detail.

Sonika thought on it for a moment. "Since the Okami believed more so in spirits—that Earth, Water, Wind, and Fire all had different lives and different tasks of their own—than an actual deity, the idea of spirit guides was generally accepted, either a wolf or a raven. There used to be a saying among tribal Elders: 'if a dream keeps coming back to you, you have received a message from the spirits.'"

Kulako considered that for a bit, drumming his fingers against the table lightly. Finally, he picked up one of the other throwing stars on the table and asked for instruction on how to care for it properly, which she demonstrated for him before he took over the process. Sonika leaned back in her chair, smiling to herself a little as she watched him work. While it was true that their situation was what likely made him so amiable, he always found ways to place just a small amount of peace within each day, and she truly enjoyed his presence.

Not wanting to linger over how that idea made her feel, she decided that it was her turn to have a few questions answered. "You know, there are a few things you haven't told me yet."

He looked up at her hesitantly from beneath his bangs. "Like what?"

"Why did you leave the Giahatio?"

"Don't push it, wolf."

Sonika blushed a little at being called "wolf" so casually for a second time and hoped he didn't notice.

Kulako put down the tools in his hands and sighed. "Look, even among soldiers, few are given a choice in joining—most families send their sons to have them avoid poverty. After a while, it just left a bad taste in my mouth."

"Is that all?" She teased.

"Well, that, and I made a terrible soldier." Kulako laughed at the annoyed expression crossing her face.

"One more thing," she challenged, and Kulako waited. Sonika's countenance was set bravely as if she knew she was stepping into dangerous territory. "You say you were a soldier, but you don't seem entirely dangerous. Have...have you ever killed anyone?"

A heavy silence filled the room after her inquiry, and Sonika's eyes widened a little as she dropped her gaze from his. She hadn't expected the question to freeze the both of them.

"Soldiers kill," Kulako nodded and inhaled deeply.

Sonika felt a chill at his confession. "So can wolves."

"Does that worry you?" Kulako asked her.

Sonika tilted her head to one side as she examined him, her relentless eyes seeming to stare into his very soul. At last, she said as she pushed back from the table, "No. Now, come on. You haven't walked yet today."

• • • •

THE APPROACH OF WINTER rains set a damp chill in the air, and each day fewer villagers walked the streets. The cold on Itake was different from the brutal and freezing winter on Perena, and Kulako thought he could adapt well to the climatic differences. He usually enjoyed winter, but he found he was looking forward to not seeing snow this year. He hadn't asked Sonika to return his katana or kunai. In truth, he felt relieved at being separated from the weapons. Though Sonika didn't talk much about her past, he suspected the things she had faced to escape the Giahatio taught her to be wary. If he pushed too much for their return, he risked frightening her.

Now and then, he could sense Roku stalking in the shadows around Sonika while they talked if they were outside or moving through the village, but eye contact scared the other hitokiri off again. Sonika would tense in those moments, and Kulako knew that she could also sense the other presence, but he told her nothing. He didn't know how, but since she couldn't seem to detect Roku by scent, he saw no reason to cause undue panic. Roku had promised to stay out of the way, and Kulako would make sure that he stuck to that promise even if it meant taking a rock to his skull. The will to keep his cover was eroding, but he didn't want to risk it by revealing Roku.

When he had the rare moment alone, Kulako stared up at the leaden sky, wondering what he was supposed to do. The only reason Sonika hadn't already unveiled his lie was that they, with little choice, surrendered some trust to one another. Had she remained suspicious, he likely would have had to either fight her off or try to escape already, whether he was still injured or not.

Sonika had been spending more time at home lately, the number of times her medic skills were required faded with the warmth of the rest of the year. They talked frequently and laughed together often. He learned how to help her portion out ingredients for her medications. She had already begun to amass a stockpile in preparation for the inevitable sicknesses that would plague the villagers during the winter. Slowly, she would communicate small things about herself as they worked, or as they sat together in the evenings beside the fire, sweeping him up entirely in her presence with everything she did.

Sonika had gone to the forge to drop off some ointment for Maru's burns and to check on Mitake, who had been complaining about not feeling well for quite some time. Kulako listened to the heavy rain falling against the roof of the house. His leg was strong enough to have walked with Sonika, and he'd offered to do so, but she insisted that she wouldn't be long and all but commanded him to stay. Kulako stared into the low embers of the hearth; it was as high as Sonika would willingly build a fire. She always looked nervous when he made bigger ones.

The front door opened and Sonika swept into the sitting room not long after, drenched from head-to-toe and looking positively miserable about it.

"Out for a swim?" Kulako raised both of his eyebrows, surprised at how soaked she was just from a short walk to the forge and back.

"Hell, no. The closest I get to swimming is a nice, long bath." Sonika laughed as she wrung out her hair before braiding it over her left shoulder.

Kulako looked at her curiously as she disappeared toward her room and contemplated her answer. She reappeared in dry clothing not long after. His expression hadn't changed by the time she returned, and she teased him for it by making the same face before tilting her head to the side.

"It's not that weird to not like swimming." She said defensively, wrapping herself in a black robe and folding her arms in front of her chest for protection.

"No, but, that along with the fact that you only ever build small fires—what happened?" Kulako flushed, embarrassed at his question and how direct it was.

However, Sonika's eyes softened a little as she made her way over before sitting down beside him, Kulako watching her the entire time. She was silent for a moment, looking at her feet. She sighed deeply, and her eyes held him when she looked up once more. "The Giahatio happened. They ruined...*everything* I used to love, that I still love. My family, my homeland, our way of life, they destroyed all of it. The Okami used to celebrate everything with bonfires and gatherings. Now I can barely stand some embers in the hearth or the little fire that I make for the medicine pot."

Kulako opened his mouth, but the intensity in Sonika's eyes stopped whatever he could have thought about saying. Sonika breathed deeply and began to speak. She told Kulako of the genocide of her people how she remembered it, not the way the Giahatio told it, and about the loving care she'd received from Makoto and Aimi. Kulako learned of the wound on her back they'd helped heal into a scar, which rarely caused trouble anymore, but put her in severe pain when it did. With evident emotional strain, she said how she wished she could thank Makoto and Aimi for everything one last time. The image of Makoto's head on a pike still featured in her nightmares.

Sonika talked about her narrow escape from Giahatian forces that involved throwing herself into a gulley, where she wandered until she met a man who promised to protect her from whatever it had been that she was running from. Sonika's words were halting and scared when she confessed that this man instead beat her and eventually raped her, abusing any little bit of trust she had been able to build up since the Okami had been slaughtered.

She explained her careful watch over the ships and how she, by complete chance, had boarded a vessel to Itake, where the local medic trained her to enhance some of her skills. She told him about the note that summoned Lady Kiki to Perena. She knew Lady Kiki had been executed for harboring her for years, and that it had been meant as a warning to her.

She told Kulako all of this with what details she thought *she* could stomach, and Kulako found that even those were hard for him to swallow. He could only watch her while she spoke, completely wrapped up in her expressions and stories, and utterly baffled she had convinced herself to survive through it all.

Had he only slightly less control over his emotions, he thought that he would have found himself in tears. When Sonika had finished speaking, she, too, seemed to be unsure of the grip she had over herself. Aware of the desire for her head after the Okami massacre, the ways Sonika guarded herself were expected. Knowing everything else she had been through, Kulako felt as if he were looking at a completely different woman than the one who had been in the room with him when she first started speaking.

"Sonika," Kulako said quietly, gaining her focus, though he still struggled with what he wanted to say as he began to say it. "I...I'm so sorry; I wish there was a way to change any—all—of what you've been through."

Sonika sighed deeply before faintly smiling. She looked at Kulako with warmth in her eyes and gently touched his arm. "You know, Kulako, you're pretty compassionate for a dejected foot soldier."

"I told you I wasn't good at my job." Kulako grinned half-heartedly, and Sonika laughed genuinely.

An expression filled with curiosity crossed Sonika's features as she looked into Kulako's eyes. Though he was steadily growing more accustomed to it, something about how she understood him with that simple glance made him feel uneasy. Uneasy, yet comforted. He didn't understand it.

"That does make me wonder, Kulako, what about you? You were a Giahatian soldier who decided to *desert* the military. There has to be a story behind that."

"It's my favorite. That's why you've heard me tell it so many times." Kulako told her dryly.

Sonika was quiet for a moment, clearly thinking. Finally, she asked him sympathetically, "What were you before you were a soldier?"

"A slave. Most of the Northern Nomads are slaves on Okara, now. I was six when recruiters stopped by. My father sold me for a few pieces of silver. He probably would've done the same to my brother, Daisuke, but he joined the military on his own the year before. The moment he turned eleven, he was gone."

Sonika was horrified at the thought of anyone selling their child. She pushed it out of her mind by asking, "Why did your brother leave?"

"Half to get away from our father, the other half was to avoid a life of slavery. Soldiers get some recognition, at least." Kulako shifted uncomfortably, and Sonika looked away from the pained expression in his eyes, feeling guilty for her insistence. Kulako paused, remembering the glassy look that had been in his mother's violet eyes as his father dragged him away by the hair to where the recruiters waited. He swallowed dryness at the back of his throat. Visiting those days did little else but make his chest tighten and his muscles feel weak, even after all these years—Kulako had buried himself in surviving Kurushima for the very purpose of avoiding his memories.

Kulako hesitated further at Sonika's genuine concern; it did little good to discuss these things with people who found them normal, and he'd never spoken with anyone who saw otherwise. However, he was willing to open up to her just as she had done for him. Kulako had been born to house slaves on Okara, and he and his brother had learned to hide and protect each other from their violent father, a man with no sense of decency and certainly no paternal instincts. When Daisuke left him behind to pursue a military career, all Kulako felt was gnawing sense of abandonment, which eventually grew into bitterness; Daisuke switched to a career in intelligence, anyway, so he knew better than to expect much out of a relationship with him. He told her what he cared to remember about life at Kurushima.

When he first arrived at Kurushima—he simply called it "the barracks" to keep up with his weak deception—the masters had cut everyone's hair to make them all the same. They had placed a wooden sword in his hand and told him to block. The masters' wooden swords struck him continually for months on end, always covering him in welts and bruises, before he was finally able to deflect a single strike. The boys who were not as light on their feet as Kulako would have the bottoms of their feet whipped. Kulako had that happen only once when another trainee fell on him and pushed them both onto a creaky board, but he could not avoid floggings at the post for various other infractions, like the one time he was seconds late for morning formation. If Kulako remembered right, that wasn't long before the dream with the wolf began, but he didn't tell Sonika about that.

He told Sonika about how the masters branded trainees with the symbols of a military oath to remind them of where their focus should be. The absolute law of kill or be killed to survive most nights, bloodshed, and training brutality. Finally, he admitted he felt as though he had forgotten, until now, what it meant not to be viewed as a tool for killing and enforcing terrible laws. He only barely remembered to embellish bits where it would have been required to continue with the front that he had ever been a soldier instead of an assassin. Even as he spoke, he wondered if there was a purpose in keeping the façade, though he was well aware of the treasonous undertones in such thinking. Treasonous thinking often leads to treasonous actions, and Kulako knew well the path he was headed down.

They sat in silence for a long while, Sonika searching for words to say, and Kulako waiting for what those would be, his entire body stiff with tension. He had never spoken at length about these things, as he usually tried to rid himself of these thoughts as soon as they occurred. He stole a glance in her direction—she looked disgusted by what he had told her.

"Look, my story isn't all that different from ones the others could tell," Kulako added quietly after he felt the silence had persisted for too long. "Why else would they all be such bastards?"

Sonika then reached out, placing a hand over Kulako's heart. The motion startled him, and he was sure his expression reflected as much. She smiled at him, not teasing him as he had expected her to for the way he had reacted, and he felt peace take over his consciousness again.

She said, "It *is* unique, though, because this still works, and from what I've seen, quite well as a matter of fact. No matter what you've been through or what you were made to be, you're still very human underneath it all. There's no shame in it. I...I think you should even be proud of that. I've met soldiers before—they forget their humanity because of how they've been raised and the things they've done. You haven't."

Fourteen: Lady Okami

Sonika's fingers worked nimbly on the quilting pattern that she had agreed to assist Mitake with. It was always an excellent way to find time for good conversation between friends, though this was one of her least favorite activities alongside making flower arrangements. She hoped that if a man ever did want to marry her, he would know better than to expect a traditional wife in the widely accepted sense. She would make a perfectly good life companion by Okami standards.

Mitake had plenty of early pregnancy woes to share with Sonika. Lady Kiki taught Sonika how to midwife, but the advice she offered was more clinical than helpful, so they agreed with laughter that Mitake would do better speaking to other women in the village.

They talked about their excitement about the upcoming annual midwinter festival. The celebration was a way to break the monotony of the season for villagers. Because of the large gathering, couples often chose that time to celebrate weddings or anniversaries, no matter what time of year their unions had taken place. The festival involved music, dancing, and a good portion of the harvest saved just for the occasion. It coincided with the formal Winter Festival that took place in the Capital. Sonika also knew from experience that it was a time for accidents involving ale or wine, and had learned to bring bandages and other supplies with her.

Mitake gave Sonika an uncommonly serious look, and Sonika placed her end of the blanket in her lap, waiting for whatever her friend had to say. Rather bluntly, Mitake asked, "So, you and Kulako are getting pretty close, aren't you?"

"I'm not sure if that's the right way to put it—"

"If you two dance together at the festival, Maru and I will have to think that you're engaged." Mitake suddenly clapped her hands together delightedly. "Now, wouldn't *that* be something? Would you make him marry you under Okami law?"

Sonika gave a miserable roll of her eyes, hiding her face in one of her hands to shield her furious blushing from her companion. Muffling her voice with her palm, she groaned, "Why do I come over here? And since when does dancing lead to marriage?"

Mitake paused, a devious grin spreading across her face. "You aren't *denying* that you have feelings for him. And I *do* remember being told that the Okami only marry once—I think *you* were even the one to explain that to me—so they're pretty choosy about the person they fall for; let's not even get into the fact that the Okami married for love. Aren't they, you know, *drawn* together?"

"They were called a 'bonded pair' for a reason," Sonika said, desperately wanting out of the conversation and suddenly regretting everything she had told her friend about Okami traditions.

"That sounds even more permanent than marriage."

"*Even* if I gave what you said any thought, Kulako isn't Okami." Sonika replied, her face blocked by both palms now. "There's no guarantee that he would feel the same way. Plus, once he's healed, he'll likely just be on his way again, anyway. He's a deserter, remember? We can't keep him here more than he can stay here."

"But you *do* have feelings, yes? I mean, you're already seventeen. Noshians would be appalled that you aren't married by now, let alone not even betrothed—and let's not mention what my own Perenin mother would have to say about it if she were alive. The one thing all cultures seem to agree on is that we come of age at seventeen." Mitake arched her eyebrows. "As mother would have put it, you're behind."

Sonika growled, giving Mitake a withering glare from between her fingers.

• • • •

KULAKO CAREFULLY PLACED what weight he could bear on his right leg as he stood from a bench in the inn's main room. He sighed with relief; every few days showed improvement. Due to the treatments he received, his recovery had gone more smoothly than anticipated; broken bones at Kurushima and in the assassins' quarters were reset, wrapped, and then the injured man was on his own again. Kulako wasn't sure if Sonika's method was uncommon or not, but it definitely seemed to be the better practice.

The original cast was now a tight wrap, still extending from ankle to knee. Though he couldn't stand or walk on it for terribly long, he was lucky that Obito had been right in assuming the effectiveness of Sonika's medical skills.

Kulako had hardly even thought about Obito or the Giahatio in recent weeks.

Four full moons had passed since Kulako came to Itake, which meant that he'd been living with Sonika for the same amount of time. Gradually, she'd become more open about her heritage and Okami culture with him. He liked to ask her questions; her face always brightened as she answered them. Now more than ever, the idea that the Giahatio considered Sonika or any of the Okami as savages was an impossible thing for Kulako to grasp.

Try as he might to ignore it, Sonika had a peculiar hold over him, even though he was sure that she didn't realize it. Between her passions, compassion, the way she spoke and laughed, and her physical and emotional strength, he could see everything in her that made her a resilient force against the Giahatio and shook them at their core merely by surviving. He had never known someone who could possess such amounts of inward and physical beauty. If the Okami had endured the Giahatio's advances to this point, he thought that with Sonika leading her people, the Giahatio might not have survived the Okami.

She made him feel alive. She commanded him in a way that required no consciousness of doing so; he would do anything for her.

"Kulako, are you daydreaming again?" Maru called to him, breaking through his thoughts and causing him to jump. A devilish smirk crossed the blacksmith's face then, and Kulako already knew he wouldn't enjoy where the conversation was going to go. "I bet I know exactly what's going through your head right now."

Kulako shook his head in exasperation and made his way over to Maru to help throw some wood into the main room's fireplace in preparation for the festival occurring later that evening. "Fine, then. What are you betting?"

"No, Kulako, it's just a thing that people say...surely they use it the military." Maru seemed to have been brought up short until Kulako grinned at him. His shoulders slumped in annoyance before he perked back up. "So, what's your next move going to be once that wrap comes off of your leg, deserter?"

"Does that have something to do with our bet?" Kulako tried to avoid Maru's eyes as he continued placing wood in the fireplace.

"Only everything," Maru's brows knitted sternly. "You don't think you can take our medic with you, do you?"

"I know I can't." Even though Kulako laughed, a small hint of sadness at that truth touched his heart. He forced it away, not wanting to think about how his options and likely time for the assignment he'd been given initially were running low. "Besides, we both know she's too good for me."

"You're damn right about that one."

Later on that night, the festival was fully underway. Kulako enjoyed the ones in the Capital city, though he hadn't directly attended one since the Winter Festival he graduated during three years ago. Itake might not have fireworks to display, but the sense of community felt all the same as people danced, sang, and drank with palpable joy lingering in the air. Kulako breathed easily, wondering if there really could be a place for him outside of the shadows.

Sonika was on top of one of the inn's tables—Kulako wished she would stand still; he couldn't move fast enough to catch her if she fell from her broad movements—telling a wild tale about a mountain troll and sword made of bones. He was sure that she had the complete attention of all in her vicinity; she certainly had his. Sonika paused in her story for effect, and her eyes found his from across the room. She smiled at him and continued with her story. Kulako's heart fluttered.

Sonika had told him at one point that there was a method of communication used among the Okami known as Mindspeak, describing it as a gentle push on one's mind to connect thoughts. Their leader used it to communicate to everyone during battles and hunts, and individuals could use it for private conversations. As she kept telling her fable to the small crowd gathered in her corner of the room, Kulako felt something he couldn't control interrupting his thoughts. It was careful, curious, and when he closed his eyes to relax, he could hear Sonika's voice speaking in whispers.

Sonika turned to him slowly as she, too, sensed what had just occurred. There were occasional instances of Mindspeak being compatible with those who were not of the tribe, although it was rare. The individuals had to forge an undeniable bond. Mindspeak was a form of pack communication, and in acknowledging they could speak in such a manner, Sonika had no other choice but to accept that somehow, they were part of each other's pack. She didn't know what to expect out of this newfound connection, and even though she was afraid, the leap to figure it out didn't seem so far.

She had come to realize some very complicated feelings. She still believed that it was not in her destiny to pursue romance or anything like it—with the way the Giahatio continuously sought after her, how could she reasonably justify allowing anyone else to be involved in her life in such a manner?

Her story concluded, and as people applauded, Kulako moved through the crowd to help her down from the table. She graciously accepted his extended hands as she stepped down.

"You are the strangest wolf I have ever met." Her voice joked inside his mind. *"Or maybe just the strangest person."*

"You've known that." Kulako audibly laughed when she playfully nudged him with her shoulder.

"Come dance with me," she spoke aloud after watching the festivities for a moment. She felt her face turn hot even as she made the suggestion, trying to ignore the conversation she'd had with Mitake earlier that week.

Kulako's face turned a light shade of pink; he averted his eyes from her. "Do soldiers dance? I don't think they do."

"You mean you've never tried." Sonika snickered before taking his hands into hers and pulling him from the shelter of where they were standing. Kulako's face was now on fire. "Don't worry, it won't be too hard on your leg, and I'll lead."

• • • •

SONIKA GUIDED KULAKO through the village's streets; his knee was aching from the day's activities, and she had decided that they needed to return to the house.

The first time they'd tried to leave, Maru found them on their way out and dragged them back into the party, begging them to play along with the drinking game he created just moments earlier. They were finally free two hours later, both slightly intoxicated. Kulako had tapered off from drinking in the last few years and now rarely imbibed, and Sonika was generally even less inclined to do so. The blindfolded leading the blindfolded, finding their way home was an adventure.

Kulako stopped against a building to rest his leg, the unexpected force of his weight pulling Sonika with him. He caught her in his arms, a quick reaction of his trained reflexes, her glowing eyes widening as she processed what had happened. He looked at her with uncertainty, but when she laughed, he did the same before she set herself upright once more. He shifted a little and felt her hands on his shoulders, as if for balance, and then Sonika moved her fingers, lightly gripping his shirt. Whether from the ale or his own human impulses, Kulako felt suddenly compelled by something far outside the control of his better senses. He leaned toward her while she did the same to him. For a moment, the rest of the world seemed to fade out.

A young man's shout from across the street to a group of his peers broke them free of the realm they had become ensnared in. Kulako looked away from Sonika, able to feel how red his cheeks were and how embarrassed he was at himself—a second's worth of a lapse in self-control, and he had honestly considered kissing her. He didn't inherently consider it wrong, but he was sure it wasn't right.

Sonika glanced up at him from beneath her thick eyelashes and offered him a small smile. Kulako swallowed nervously, his head reeling from something besides the ale. When he looked up, in the distance beyond Sonika's shoulder, Kulako met Roku's disapproving gaze, soon followed by the flash of something in the light of hanging lanterns. He jerked them both out of the way as a kunai sailed past Sonika, the action agitating the ligaments in his knee.

"What was that?" Sonika asked urgently as she helped him stand straight again, her eyes wide with concern.

Kulako looked up again to find that Roku was no longer nearby. He steadied himself against the building they were near so that Sonika could let go and glanced over his shoulder to see if he could trace the kunai.

He fumbled for a lie when he spotted it. "That drunk, I guess."

"Let's get you home."

Later, long after Kulako was sure that Sonika would remain in her bed despite any quiet disturbances he may cause, he made his way toward the inn once more. When he arrived, the main room had fallen into near silence compared to the boisterous activity from the celebration; a few conversations still drunkenly buzzed about the room. Kulako looked around for only a moment before he saw Roku near the fireplace with his back to the rest of the room, something he was never comfortable enough to do. He limped over and sat down on a nearby stool. They did not speak for a long time, but Kulako knew that Roku was well aware of his presence.

Finally, Roku chuckled. "She's making you weak, Kulako."

"You should leave." He bluntly replied as he tossed the kunai recovered from the earlier incident to Roku's feet. His entire leg was throbbing, and his patience with the man who caused the injury had worn thin enough to resemble nonexistence. "If you do now, they might not behead you. We both know you shouldn't have stayed here."

"Fuck off." Roku smirked when Kulako rolled his eyes. "No, I think I'll wait and see how this plays out, first."

"Then you've built your own funeral pyre—if they'll give you that much." Kulako tried and failed to mask an involuntary grunt of discomfort from his throat as he rose to his feet again. "Use some sense."

"Bold words coming from a man who let a woman—if you can call her that—take all of his sense. This is not the cold hitokiri that I expected to meet. It's rather a disappointment, really. You don't hear about yourself the way the others get to do. I'll make sure you regret this encounter when the time comes."

Kulako glared at Roku, but said nothing more as he left.

Fifteen: Assassin

Magistrate Tomio had been feeling under the weather for months, occupying a majority of Sonika's medical attention. Sonika hadn't been able to cure his illness yet, but she had been able to manage his symptoms and keep him well enough to perform his government duties, though with each day that passed, he acted less and less of himself. She supposed anyone would if they continuously coughed blood and ran a fever. Sonika sighed as she set out on the village's main road that would take her home, wondering what exactly it was that she kept missing. She had already tried several different methods and combinations of medications.

If only he hadn't sent his Healer with Teiichi. She thought as she watched the gray skies above; the rains were beginning to slow, though it would still be a week or two until they finally ceased altogether. Healers could use magic and cure just about anything they faced. The Empire provided each of its government officials with one. They came either from the Temple of Hikari in the Capital or from varied other locations around Perena, where they were trained by priests. When Teiichi left for academic training in the Capital two years ago, Tomio had insisted that his son take the Healer along with him, confident in the care anyone could receive with a medic.

Sonika sighed again. *That was when Lady Kiki was still here.*

The teahouse was the halfway point in the village between where Tomio and Sonika lived. Sonika had asked Kulako to meet her there. If he could make it there and back to the house, then she would be able to clear him to take the wrap off his leg. By the time the rains ended, he could be a free man again. Sonika smiled at that, even though the idea that he might have to leave saddened her greatly. He made a good companion, but not all friends could stay forever. At least she could get one patient healed.

Kulako's bright red hair made him easy to pick out, especially with his back turned to her. Forgetting her concerns, Sonika's thoughts turned more mischievous, and she wondered if she could surprise him. She slowed her movements as she got closer, knowing it was lucky he was facing the other way. When she was close enough, she jumped for his back, though he caught her off guard when he pinned her arms down first with his left forearm and then his right. Kulako shifted his weight, and when Sonika started to move over his shoulder, he froze.

"Good thing you wear perfume. I almost threw you." He told her as he released her so that she could slide down before he looked around at her.

Sonika felt a little embarrassed by both her impulsiveness and her carelessness. She put her hands behind her and began to back toward the street. "So I *did* surprise you?"

Kulako rolled his eyes and smiled helplessly at her as he started to follow her. A man wearing a long black cloak with his hood up went directly behind Sonika as she turned. She bumped into him, and he shoved her back with barely a pause in his stride. Kulako caught her when she stumbled. The man kept walking.

"What's your problem?" If Kulako had a knife on him, he might have drawn it.

The man stopped without looking back. Roku disguised his voice with a craggy, dry intonation as he said, "You'd do well to keep that savage out of public."

Kulako heard a sharp gasp from Sonika as his own eyes expanded in disbelief. Perhaps he had been away from Perena for too long. No one spoke that way on Itake, least of all about Sonika. Kulako looked down at her, but it was an eternity before she returned his gaze. With all previous light sapped from her face, she silently started for her home again with her head down. Kulako was only able to follow.

They returned just as the rain began again. Still saying nothing, Sonika went to the linen closet in the short hallway between the bedrooms, where she stored her meticulously organized boxes of medicines. While she was busy putting away the things she had brought with her to the magistrate's house, Kulako remained in the front room. He found her jar of dried tealeaves, thankfully labeled, as was the neighboring pot of ground water hemlock. As he prepared the tea, he thought it was far easier for somebody to accidentally die in a medic's house than in an assassin's flat. At least, if the chances were between Sonika's house and the apartment he lived in, it would have been. He'd heard once that some hitokiri set traps around their residences to ward off intruders, but assumed it was a myth. Even he wasn't *that* paranoid—he chose the practical route and walked in with a knife leading the way.

When Sonika emerged again, she wordlessly directed Kulako to come to the table with her. Her eyes briefly fell on the steaming cup of tea he brought over for her, and a small hint of their normal warmth returned. She pulled out her chair as he had done with his and sat down, putting his foot on her knees. She had a small knife on the table to her right; she was the only person Kulako trusted enough to be this close with a knife of any kind. She pulled up the edge of the wrap at his ankle and began to cut.

"Do *you* think that I'm a savage, Kulako?" Sonika asked him quietly, pausing when she was halfway through cutting the bandages.

"No." He answered immediately. He took the knife from her carefully and continued cutting the wrap himself, smiling a little as he spoke again, "Maybe a little strange, but definitely not a savage."

After a moment, Sonika finally returned his slight smile and laughed a bit. "You're one to talk about being strange."

She pulled the bandages away before carefully touching the sections of his leg where it had been fractured or otherwise hurt, then she pressed down more firmly. When he didn't react to either, her smile reappeared. The gloom in her features receded as Sonika reached over and took a sip of the tea he made for her. Kulako was relieved.

"I suppose the next step is getting your weapons back to you. It's been years since I've had a sparring partner. It'll be fun." Sonika said after a moment. Kulako hadn't expected that, and the way he looked at her must have demonstrated as much. She held his gaze evenly. "I trust you. You haven't tried to kill me yet."

• • • •

A WARM WIND SEEPED into the air from the south, and finally, the rains ceased. The ground dried and allowed wildlife to begin flourishing anew. In the early hours of one of these spring mornings, Kulako was in a clearing facing Sonika, who from the very first day of pleasant weather held to her promise to help him regain some of his other strengths now that his leg had fully recovered.

Kulako discovered one of Sonika's greatest gifts was her speed. She was difficult to keep up with even when she slowed as not to lose him on her usual running trail; Kulako knew he would have a hard time catching her if she ever decided to outrun him. Though he knew several of her shuriken and kunai patterns well, when she dropped her weapons and turned to her hands and feet, he often had to resort to a few dirty tricks to overpower her. She was strong and swift in her movements, and though he had been granted the return of his katana, he refused to draw it on her, which forced him to try other techniques.

"One more time," she insisted as she brought a kunai to her hand. Kulako nodded in agreement, a weapon already in his left hand. Being left-handed, Kulako usually had an advantage when it came to throwing opponents off. After a few exchanges on their first day of working together, Sonika had already developed ways to counter.

They moved rapidly around one another; the control they exuded over their trained muscles barely allowed blades to scrape; no contact made with skin, hands and feet made no connection. Kulako felt his years of conditioning return to him all at once. Suddenly, in a surprising shift, Sonika grabbed him by the lapels and flipped him over her back. He landed on his feet, and she swept his ankles out from beneath him, laughing when he was unable to recover his balance.

A hitokiri is nothing compared to someone who grapples for fun. Kulako thought as he dusted himself off, also able to find humor in the situation.

"You got lucky, wolf." He told her with a grin.

Sonika snickered, a glint of the sunlight catching her canines. Picking up the scattered weapons they left in their wake from their hours outside, they decided to take a walk up to the cliffs to enjoy the expansive view over the ocean. The breeze from the water cooled their skin nicely as they sat on the edge of the hulking rock formation. Kulako caught himself admiring how Sonika's aura relaxed in this peaceful setting as they talked frivolously of things that had recently taken place around the village. Even after several months of living alongside her, he couldn't escape how her presence occasionally entranced him completely.

In Kulako's dreams that night, the large black wolf sat before him, his golden eyes holding a sweeping melancholy in them as they kept their usual, penetrating gaze on him. Finally, the wolf looked away and stood, beckoning Kulako to follow him through the forest he had seen many times in these visions.

"The winds are changing, Kulako. You will be expected to return to Perena very shortly." His voice rumbled.

"How can I leave?" Kulako asked. He'd been dreading the thought of being in the Capital again. Itake had provided him with such peace, as had living with Sonika, that he could barely imagine returning to his normal life.

Takeo laid his ears back sadly and shook his massive head, silently encouraging Kulako with a nudge to place his hand in the soft fur at his shoulder as he had always done. *"You know what to expect if you do not. Your leaders aren't known for their ability to be forgiving or understanding. You know what you must do."*

When dawn broke the next morning, Kulako's heart felt heavy as he looked out his window and into the pastel-painted sky above. There would be a few ships leaving during the evenings for Perena that week, and he thought that perhaps he would have at least a day or two to think of something while he figured out how to leave behind a life he had finally come to love.

Though it was accurate he had only known Sonika for a short amount of time, they had not been apart for more than a few hours at most each day in almost six months now. Their spirits were connected. She understood him in a way that no other human had ever bothered to do before. She knew how to soothe his temper on its rare occasions of appearance by only saying his name; she completed him in a way that he could not even begin to explain. Perhaps most importantly, she reminded him of the fact that, despite his past and the horrible crimes he committed at the Giahatio's order, he was still very human. Provided with the space to accept such a thing, the scars in his heart were healing, something he never expected could happen.

Kulako loved Sonika in a way that he didn't think was possible. Having that vulnerability with another was a frightening thing to acknowledge, but he wasn't afraid to feel it toward her.

As the wolf in his dreams indicated would happen soon, he received a notice beneath the front door the next morning while Sonika was out. They wanted him to report in the Capital, and Kulako knew that it was time to reveal everything to Sonika. He couldn't stand the thought of her fate at the hands of the Giahatian government and had, quite knowingly, written off his orders to kill her months ago. As this thought occurred to him, he felt Roku's very near presence, and he knew that he had another thing to do before he left Itake.

"I guess it's time." Kulako muttered to himself, looking over at the katana in the corner of his room that hadn't been unsheathed for fighting since autumn. "Are you ready?"

When evening began to fall, the beautiful spring day's rush drew Itake's inhabitants to early retirement for the night. Sonika and Kulako remained outside to enjoy the air and watch as oil lamps began to dot the village. Though Kulako knew he would soon have to leave her, he couldn't tear himself away from her companionship. He was determined to enjoy every single moment of it while he was still allowed to be with her. However, Sonika could feel the heaviness from Kulako's heart, almost as if it resided in her own.

"Something's wrong," Sonika gently probed. She looked at Kulako and delicately touched his cheek, turning his face ever so slightly as if to better analyze his expression.

Kulako sighed, bracing himself. No matter how often it happened, he frequently forgot how quickly and easily Sonika could read him. He nodded in assent to her suspicion, and the curiosity in her features grew.

He could barely meet eyes with her. "There's...there's something you deserve to know the truth about."

Roku's feet softly crushed the grass beneath his steps, instantly grabbing Sonika's attention. She turned and drew a shuriken in one fluid motion, a low growl in her throat; she recognized the scent from the scarf she had kept all this time. He glanced at her only briefly, his blazing eyes then flicked to Kulako. Kulako slowly looked over from where he had been standing beside Sonika on the house's small porch, anticipating what his next move should be as tension began to amass in the air.

"*You* finally came back." Sonika growled at Roku again.

Roku chuckled. "'Came back?' Wolf, I never left."

Sonika drew back, her eyes wide with surprise. She subconsciously touched her nose. "How is that—?"

"A dab of brewed iceweed behind the ears like some frilly perfume is really all it took, is it, wolf?" Roku said the last word malevolently, then turned his attention to Kulako. "You are pathetic, Nightshade."

"Not here," Kulako warned, an unexpected tone of harshness creeping into his voice as his hand touched the hilt of his katana. "We're too close to civilians."

"Have it your way—the wolf will still watch you die before *I* kill *her*." Roku's lips twitched in an attempted smile, but he quickly turned on his heel and disappeared into the forest with the rapidly fading daylight.

Anger burned at Kulako's lungs, and he darted after the other assassin, forgetting Sonika's presence altogether.

Sonika blinked the confusion from her head as she attempted to comprehend the exchange that had just taken place. Her mind raced with unanswered questions. Though she dreaded what she might find, she decided to follow Kulako. Sonika swallowed her anxieties and pursued them.

They all met in a clearing. Kulako, realizing that Sonika had followed him, glanced over his shoulder to warn her to stay back. Shocked by the expression in his eyes, she unquestioningly shrank behind a tree as he and Roku approached one another. Roku drew a knife, adding a bit of a flourish as he spun the pommel between his fingers. Kulako remained unchanged. Roku's dexterity wouldn't be enough.

"Would you really betray your duty to the Empire? For her?" Roku glared at Kulako hatefully. "Would you really consider risking *death* for that *savage*?"

"You chose the wrong assassin to make your enemy." Kulako said lowly, threateningly, beginning to draw the katana from its sheath.

Sonika froze at the way he spoke. It wasn't the voice of the man she knew; this was the voice of a killer. Kulako raised his arms and drew one foot back. He held the katana with the blade facing the sky and the back parallel to the ground. Sonika shook as the present faded, and in his place, she briefly saw one of the Giahatian hitokiri who had attacked her village.

"Last chance, Roku. I'm faster. I won't hold back this time."

Roku smirked. "Fuck off, Kulako. We'll see who's faster."

Roku yelled as he charged at Kulako, but Kulako did not move. Roku's knife was raised and he was about to make a final leap toward the space between Kulako's eyes, when in a swift lunge, the tip of Kulako's sword pierced through Roku's throat, and the other man sank against his blade until slumping forward on his shoulder, blood bubbling and foaming at his lips.

"I still wish I would've done that in the first place," Kulako muttered as he gave a simple turn of his wrist and Roku's lifeless body fell to the ground just as the point of the katana directed it to. "See you in Hell, Roku."

"Kulako...?" He heard Sonika's voice, and his eyes widened as he turned to her, his cheeks flecked with another man's blood.

Sonika approached him cautiously, a shuriken and a kunai at the ready and her golden eyes glowing fiercely in the encompassing darkness. He cleaned and sheathed his sword quickly, putting his hands in front of him, but she remained prepared to attack. When she was an arm's length away, she dropped her weapons and flew at him. She pinned him against a tree with her arm across his throat, and he narrowly avoided a strike she sent for his skull. He didn't try to fight her. She wasn't pressing on him in a way that threatened his ability to breathe, but Kulako didn't want to push her into feeling as if she needed to.

"An assassin?" She choked out the words despite the growl they were carried over—her arm was shaking, her whole body was. "How long until you were finally going to kill me? As long as *he* didn't get around to it first?"

Guilt kicked at Kulako's stomach, and he pushed her off. "I wasn't going to—I wouldn't. Ever."

She swallowed a lump in her throat. Tears stung at her eyes as she withdrew her fighting stance. She forced herself to look him in the eye just as he did with her. Kulako wasn't sure how long they held one another's gaze, but each passing second was agonizing. Finally, Sonika broke the silence.

"I can't believe I was so stupid. I *trusted* you. I thought we—" She shook her head firmly, dismissing her emotions. She showed him her canines, and Kulako understood the depth of how he'd hurt her. "It all makes sense, now. Get the hell out of my sight before *I* kill you; you've made an absolute fool out of me."

Kulako fought the thoughts and feelings flitting through his mind. He didn't have time to sort through them all; with Roku dead, he needed to return to the Capital as soon as he could manage. He knelt and bowed his head.

The weight of a thousand words was on his tongue, but he could only think of one thing that seemed appropriate to say. "Forgive me, Lady Okami."

Sonika placed a hand over her mouth, attempting to repress a wave of misery. Kulako made a farewell gesture before she could retort and disappeared into the deepening twilight. Devastated, she sank to the ground, sobbing despite her efforts to resist the reaction as the familiar feeling of heartbreak ripped through her entire being. The warmth of the white wolf's figure was beside her, the spirit's head resting on her shoulder. The spirit whined as Sonika buried her face in the wolf's fur, willing the rest of the world away.

Kulako boarded the ship that would return him to his life as a Giahatian assassin, looking up to the first stars for answers, searching for anything to calm his ringing senses.

What a fucking mess I've made. Kulako thought while he rubbed his face, frustrated. As Itake's shoreline began to fade from sight, he asked the night sky on an octave barely above a whisper, "Is that what you meant by doing the right thing, Lord Takeo?"

"Be safe, my son."

Sixteen: On the Edge

Kulako hadn't dreamt or slept much since returning to Perena. He was unsure how long he'd been on the mainland again, but had lost count of the number of contracts he'd been given in that time. He refused to think of Sonika, and instead turned his heart cold to the world around him; it was the most familiar feeling he knew. He didn't dwell on the loneliness he knew would consume him should he allow otherwise. The other hitokiri who lived around him did not engage with him in conversation or antics as they once had. Instead, they now eyed him warily, sensing the numbness that had settled back into his heart.

He ignored the emptiness around him after sunset. He did not acknowledge the whispers of longing floating through his flat as he minded trivial tasks around his residence. Yet try as he might, Kulako could not disregard the presence of the Okami Lord. His howls echoed through Kulako's open windows in the dead of night.

His sleeping consciousness carried him through the familiar forest until he came to the edge of a clearing. When he stepped forward, he was transported to Takeo's side, where they stood among the smoldering rubble of a decimated village. The sun was bright in Kulako's eyes. When he glanced again at Takeo, he noticed how the black wolf's eyes regarded their surroundings sadly, though he remained silent. Finally, Takeo gave a heaving sigh and looked up at Kulako.

The wolf spoke calmly but sternly, *"Keep your head low and your eyes down, lad."*

Though confused, Kulako did as instructed, and soon after, three other wolves materialized, each from a separate rush of wind, all equally massive in size to his ebony companion. Each wore a golden pendant around their necks and sat on their haunches, watching Kulako with piercing amber eyes.

"Kulako, these are three of the previous Okami Lords. The first to enter was my predecessor, Lord Minoru." The wolf was dark brown with a white patch on his throat just above the pendant.

"After him was Third Lord Ayumu." His fur was brown and white.

"And finally, Second Lord Daichi." The wolf bore a stunning black coat with a white spot almost covered by his pendant.

"Is this the lad your instincts told you to so foolishly trust, Lord Takeo?" Lord Ayumu snarled, baring his teeth at Kulako and raising his hackles. *"You should be ashamed of yourself. Our fate is no safer now than it was beforehand. In fact, we're probably worse off."*

Kulako shrank back timidly from the wolf and lowered his body, disappointed at what he, too, considered his failure, but Takeo stood defensively. Lord Minoru put himself in between the two other wolves.

"You were always too quick with your anger and too harsh with your judgment, Lord Ayumu," Lord Minoru said.

Ayumu snarled back, *"And you have always been far too liberal with your forgiveness. I had once hoped leadership would harden your heart."*

"Are you truly so blind that you can't tell how the lad feels?" Takeo interjected. *"Why else would we all be here?"*

"Those Giahatian scum *are all the same on the inside, no matter how well you think you know them. Why else would we have ended like this?"* Lord Ayumu glared at Kulako. *"Even* he *is no different from the worst of them, always running from failure. There is nobody left who can help us."*

"You fools!" The voice of Lord Daichi boomed, eliciting startled yelps from the three Okami and causing Kulako to jump. *"Have you become so lost in your bitterness that you forget the odds this lad was against? We aren't the only ones the Giahatio has been cruel to. Our daughter is safe thanks to him."*

"Enough of your bickering, all of you." A calm yet authoritative voice came from the rubble. A silver wolf, larger than the others, strode over the destruction on soundless paws. He carried himself with pride, with serenity, and with power. All eyes turned to this wolf, but he ignored them until he came to Kulako.

"Lord Kohaku." The other Okami Lords solemnly greeted him in perfect unison as they bowed their heads.

He examined the human, then commanded him to sit. Kulako obeyed the spirit's order without hesitation. This majestic wolf stared into his soul the same way only Takeo and Sonika were capable of doing. Kulako's heart thudded wildly against his ribs.

"Kulako," he began peacefully. *"You are not well, lad. You feel as though you have failed us—and yourself. You have not. Should you continue as you are and not complete your task, then you and Lady Sonika will surely suffer untimely deaths."*

Kulako averted his eyes from the intense watch of Lord Kohaku, unable to handle the pressure of the wolf's presence. He looked toward the Okami Lords for assurance, and a massive silvery paw landed on his shoulder. A cold shudder ran down Kulako's spine.

"I have trusted Lord Takeo for a very good reason, lad. Allow your instincts to lead you just as a wolf's would. Your destiny is still to protect our fallen. As an assassin, you will never be strong enough for this fate; as a human, *however, this will prove simple. Do not forget who* you *are beneath all of the hatred they have tried to instill in you."*

A persistent knocking on his front door pulled Kulako from sleep. At some point, he'd rolled out of bed and onto the floor. Trembling from the weight of what he had experienced, he weakly pushed himself off the ground and toward the door.

Obito stood on the other side of the threshold. Still bewildered by mental fog, Kulako stared at his friend with an uncharacteristically shaken expression. He blinked, hoping to blame his awkwardness on drowsiness.

"Perhaps it *is* a good thing I decided to pay you a visit this morning," Obito mumbled as Kulako motioned him inside.

Finding some semblance of his sanity, Kulako managed to respond, "You can't be telling me that the others enjoy being woken up this early to find you at their door."

Obito chuckled. "Even less than you do, I'm sure."

"Why would you even be over this way, anyway?" Kulako asked after a moment, his cognitive thought finally following along with the rest of his awareness. "You haven't been in the assassins' quarter for a few years, now."

Obito pulled paperwork from the folds of his uniform. Kulako's stomach lurched with dread at the thought of taking another contract. Obito placed the few papers on a small kitchen table and took a seat. As he prepared a pen, he gestured for Kulako to accompany him across the table.

"I don't suppose you have tea," Obito wrung his hands, a sign that something was upsetting him, though Kulako would never be privy to the details. "Sorry, I know it's early."

"I might; I haven't been to the market yet this week. But what does that have to do with you being here?"

"Well, truthfully, you were due for an evaluation when you came back from Itake since you'd been remote for so long," Obito explained urbanely as Kulako dug around to fulfill the request for a drink. "You've been so busy that this is the first chance I've had to get it done. We're going to talk, and I'm going to write a few things down. This will just prove you're still fit to serve."

Kulako paused while making the tea he found, glancing over his shoulder. "What happens if I'm not?"

Obito looked pointedly at him, and Kulako's hand subconsciously went to his throat. He could only nod his compliance. For about an hour, Obito wrapped a strange, often contradictory strand of questions around him, each designed to pluck out disloyalties or learn where such treasonous thoughts had been obtained.

"Do you know how to prepare wolfsbane tea?" Obito asked.

"Yes." Kulako decided he would keep his responses short lest he incriminated himself.

"Where did you learn how to make it?"

"We learn it at Kurushima. You should know that already." He had also learned an improved version of the recipe from Sonika, but that was a detail Obito didn't need.

Obito chuckled and wrote a note on the side. "I need *your* answers. I can't rely on my flawed memory."

Kulako scowled. "You wouldn't have your job if your memory were flawed."

The spy met his gaze with cunning eyes. "A hitokiri wouldn't have his job if his willingness to kill was flawed. Now, next question. Have you heard His Highness is immune to wolfsbane?"

"No."

"Has anyone ever suggested poisoning the Emperor's tea?"

"No, that's ridiculous."

"You're right. He only drinks the blood of the slain, and from a wine glass made of their skulls."

Kulako rolled his eyes. No matter what Obito asked, he calmly diverted any topic away from Sonika. The thought of keeping her survival a secret drove him to concentrate where others would have failed.

When finished, Obito collected his papers and congratulated Kulako on surviving the interrogation. Kulako relaxed, though he tried not to let his expression reveal how tense he'd been.

"I'll be seeing you in my office at the end of the week," Obito told his friend. "Try to get some sleep. Your missions will suffer if you keep that vacant look on your face."

"Maybe I could get some sleep if I didn't get visitors in the middle of the night."

Obito shook his head then looked down to the stack of papers in his arms. There were more notes than he'd needed. Kulako wondered if they included information from other informants. Perhaps Roku had sent messages over the last several months. Kulako hadn't given it much thought before; he'd been too incapacitated to take care of the matter when it would have been an issue.

"You assassins are too much work," Obito groaned as he took his leave.

• • • •

SONIKA USED TO THINK that being alone meant she was safe from the evils humans could conjure. She once found solace in the idea of returning to an unoccupied house in the evenings. Now alone felt empty; she hated herself for being so vulnerable that she would feel such things from another person's absence. She was hardly even able to find enjoyment in training. Like many days before this one, she decided to end her training session early and head home through the village.

There was a strange amount of tension in the air, she thought as she came to the market, but everyone she looked at seemed as if they were pressed to reach their destinations quickly. It was odd, but Itake had irregular rhythms now and then, especially during the spring after everyone holed away in their homes all winter.

I'm sure it's nothing...I shouldn't be so paranoid, Her attempt to calm herself was futile.

Sonika froze at the sound of rough voices attached to Giahatian accents and glanced over her shoulder. Though she could not see the men they belonged to, she knew they were very near. She swallowed a nervous lump at the back of her throat and quickened her pace through the market, trying to disappear into the crowd, desperate to lock her front door and stay hidden until the Giahatians left. She heard heavy boots in the dirt behind her. She didn't look back but instead increased her pace again. The boots were coming faster, and Sonika's wildly pounding heart leapt into her throat. A strong hand gripped her shoulder.

"Let me go," she said, trying to make her voice firm despite the fear rushing through her blood.

"Your time's run out, wolf." The man said into her ear, running his nails across her throat before pulling them through her hair. Sonika shivered.

"Itake is neutral," Sonika said frantically, hoping to cause the soldier to hesitate long enough so that she could get away again. When he did not back down, she reached over for her kunai case, but his fingers wrapped around her wrist tightly before he twisted it around and pinned her arm behind her back. Sonika gritted her teeth to suppress the pain.

"Your assassin failed. Do you want this to turn into a fight? Are you going to put all of these innocent people in that much danger?"

Sonika's eyes widened. "...No."

"Then you'll come with me. The Emperor wishes to speak with you."

• • • •

KULAKO TRUDGED THROUGH the streets of the Capital on the way toward Obito's office. The haze he'd been living in since returning from Itake was beginning to lift, and he wasn't sure if he carried himself properly. Hitokiri were publicly respected and privately dreaded, but he caught a few furtive glances from citizens uncertain of which they should show.

His instincts alerted him when he set foot on the threshold of Obito's room. He hesitated before advancing into the room, trying to ignore the pit in his stomach. No one attended Obito's desk.

"Traitor!" Obito spat as he sprung from the shadows and backed Kulako into a corner. He put a knife to Kulako's throat, this time pressing with sincerity against his skin. "I knew something was off about you when you came back from Itake. You should be killed for this. *I* should be the one to kill you for it!"

The passion Kulako suppressed reignited as he pushed back against the attack. He scowled and spoke with mercilessness in his voice as he disarmed Obito. "You don't have the courage to try."

Obito retracted from his offensive posture, alarmed by Kulako's tone. "Why would you do this?"

Obito heaved a sigh and folded his arms across his chest when Kulako's expression gave nothing away. A voice from Kulako's past spoke out, "Did you think you were doing the right thing?"

His eyes expanded with dread and shock as they shifted toward the scrawny form of his brother. Daisuke's shoulder-length raven hair was tied back in a messy ponytail. His pale skin adopted the ruddy hue of the oil lamp as he entered the room, his violet eyes hardening on his younger sibling as soon as they fell on him.

"We don't get to decide that. Did you really think no one would find out?" Daisuke's voice was flat as he scolded his brother.

Daisuke more than happily revealed his lack of fighting skills to anyone who asked, but his profession was information, something that could be a deadlier weapon than any Kulako ever held. Daisuke was rumored to have an entire network of connections the Empire didn't know about despite his struggle to rise through the ranks. Though Kulako wasn't sure about the credibility of those claims, as many things about Daisuke were shrouded in mystery, he knew he should have expected that his brother would be aware of the rapidly unfolding situation.

Not long after Kulako's graduation from Kurushima, he'd set out to find his brother within the city. Establishing contact had been difficult, as Daisuke made a point of being difficult for anyone to unearth. Nonetheless, when Daisuke realized that Kulako was again seeking out some sort of relationship with his older sibling, he tried putting some effort in on his end as well. Daisuke had much more practice with placing emotional distance between himself and others than Kulako, and contact was frequently broken off because of that or their assignments. Often, Obito served as their only source of reliable communication.

"Why the hell did you bother showing your face here, Daisuke?" Kulako seethed. "I haven't seen you in *months,* even before I left for Itake." Uncertainty flickered in Daisuke's countenance for the briefest of moments. As subtle as it was, Kulako's time with Sonika had taught him a trick or two about reading faces. He regretted his harsh words.

"You'll have plenty of time to hate me in prison," Daisuke snapped. He pulled himself together before Obito noticed the nuance, twisting one of the two studs in his left earlobe thoughtfully. "For now, though, it looks like I'm going to have to save your ass. You're *welcome.* Here are the simple facts: if I know, Master Ewah knows, which means that His Highness has already made arrangements to have the woman brought here. You don't have any more time to fuck around."

"The woman?" Kulako shook his head with disbelief. He backpedaled, hoping to pass off his worries as confusion; the Giahatio never referred to Sonika as human. "You mean the wolf?"

"You failed to report immediately when you returned," Obito explained while glancing at Daisuke a little irritably; he'd wanted to approach the situation more delicately rather than play moderator between the brothers. "I wanted to question you myself, but I had to send you out again before I had the chance."

Kulako suspected Obito would bring this up and had prepared his argument. A lie layered on top of another lie; Kulako wondered if he would ever be able to keep them all straight. Or if it would matter for much longer whether or not he did.

"She was protected by some hitokiri named Roku. When I got to Itake, Roku tried to kill me. He knew I was coming to kill the wolf. He injured me, and I couldn't strike back until healed. I used the time to learn his schedule, and the wolf's..." Kulako's eyes opened wide with mock surprise. "Did he send messages trying to frame me for his crime?"

Obito and Daisuke shared conspiratorial smirks.

"Indeed he did," Kulako's brother replied. "We got all sorts of reports from him."

"We wanted to hear your side of the story before making any rash judgments," Obito added. "We are also wondering why you didn't offer to tell us any of this. Or why you kept Roku's murder a secret."

Kulako gritted his teeth and clenched a fist. "Roku outranked me and was sent personally by Master Ewah. I feared I would be punished for killing him. I apologize for not coming forward with this information. As for the wolf, she was long gone when I confronted Roku the second time."

"A lousy assassin like Roku can be written off, but that's the least of your concerns." A satisfied grin pulled at the corners of Daisuke's lips. He asked his younger brother with dangerous quiet, "How will you save her now?"

"Save her? Daisuke, you're making even less sense than usual."

"Bad idea play dumb," Obito said blandly. "We know the true story. Nicely done swapping the role you and Roku played in that story. You might have fooled stupider people. Look, you don't need to get defensive. We're not here to sentence your execution. Our goals align more closely than you think."

Kulako released a tense breath. "Explain."

Daisuke twisted the two studs in his other ear this time. "I think we can all agree that what happened to the Okami was revolting, but His Highness isn't interested in humanitarian issues, so we had to think of a different route."

"Breeding Okami traits could prove useful to the Empire." Obito grinned upon seeing the look of mortification on Kulako's face.

"Breeding with what, my love? There are no other full-blooded Okami left, and even though there are rumors of half-breeds around the world, there is no proof." Daisuke playfully leaned into Obito.

The two spies stared Kulako down with such intensity that he could not avert his gaze without looking weak or—worse—suspicious. Kulako retreated to the corner that he had originally occupied. Obito answered quietly and with utmost seriousness, "With his most valued assassin."

"Hold on, both of you," Kulako growled, albeit out of some desperation, as he looked between the two other men. "Sonika isn't an animal, despite what the Giahatio says."

"Sonika? Is that her name?" Daisuke teased. "Sounds pretty. Don't try to convince me that you still plan to kill her."

"Shut up, Daisuke," Kulako grimaced. "So what's your cunning plan?"

"Do you want me to shut up or explain?" Daisuke snickered at his annoyance and straightened a little. "Think about it, stupid. The Okami scares the Empire so badly that they've wanted this *one* girl dead for nearly ten years. His Highness carried it over from his father's reign, who carried it down from *his* grandfather's reign. Imagine if you convinced His Highness that he could have that power under his control. Even if it's a lie."

"Another lie?" Kulako grumbled.

"You two wouldn't even need to see each other again after the deed is done...rather, after you *said* the deed was done," Obito pressed. "Although I am beginning to think you don't want it that way, but that doesn't matter. His Highness would not resist the idea of your talents combined with Okami assets. Once Sonika is no longer 'needed,' you could always hide her further down South."

"Why do either of you care?" Kulako pleaded with them as he, too, realized that he had begun to consider the weight of the conversation. "You shouldn't even be discussing this with me—you should have already turned me in."

"So eager to die," Obito laughed. "I like puzzles. You know this."

Daisuke's eyes and bearing relaxed, as if coming to peace with some mental anguish. He even offered a genuine smile to his sibling, which soon shifted into one of his more common, sly expressions. Kulako understood, and years of bitterness left.

"Call it a favor," Daisuke said. "You can owe me later."

Kulako looked over at Obito. "So, that whole 'traitor' thing earlier? Pulling a knife on me?"

"I told him to make it dramatic." Daisuke shrugged and Kulako rolled his eyes. "What? Be pissed all you like. You fell for it."

Seventeen: The Pledge

The Palace issued an order later that day summoning all available assassins. Kulako felt unease coldly grip his insides as he prepared to leave under the cover of early dusk. They had been instructed to ensure their identities remained concealed, and so he and the roughly twenty others that slipped into one of the great halls wore cloth over their faces. Only their eyes remaining visible, ranks were indicated by the embroidery on their their formals. As for his red hair, Kulako stayed against the wall where the torchlight barely touched him. No one noticed his presence as they all filled in by rank—red embroidery at the back and up to gold-and-purple at the front. Kulako should've been lined up with the others toward the back of the room. However, he stayed in the shadows where his smooth stealth reminded the others of what the name "Nightshade" represented in the first place.

Murmurs of confusion drifted through the room on tense air as moments passed and still no one entered the room to greet the assassins. If Daisuke was right, Kulako thought he knew what was about to happen, and dreaded it. He looked to the grand double doors on his far right, heart racing as they creaked open.

In strode two large foot soldiers with what looked to be like several long claw and canine teeth marks littering the skin beneath their tattered sleeves. The men held a length of rope tightly around Sonika's neck, forcing her to stay close as she walked unsteadily between them. Her hands were bound behind her back by chains, and from Kulako's standpoint, he could see bruising all along her arms and legs. Most of all, it was the terrified expression that haunted her eyes and face that triggered an explosion of anger, guilt, and ignited a blaze in Kulako's chest—the first real bout of emotion that had slipped past his defenses in weeks. He barely held his position.

The soldiers reached the front of the room, turning and facing the gathering of manslayers. One pulled a bit of metal from a chain around his neck. When he put it to his mouth and Sonika winced with a muffled cry of pain, Kulako recognized the piece as a dog whistle similar to the ones used to train the royal hounds. They were using it to demonstrate her sensitive hearing, managing to dehumanize her before all present by likening her to the "savage" wolf in her blood.

"She's Okami!" Haru's familiar voice spat with undisguised revulsion. Kulako thought bitterly about how Haru hadn't changed in the last three years. "Wasn't that Akahana's objective? Where the fuck is *he*?"

Amid the following rumble of assertive agreement and a few calls for various actions to be taken, Sonika's eyes met his despite his otherwise unnoticed placement. It didn't surprise him that she sensed him so easily. Still, he held his ground, no matter how badly he wanted to go to her.

"I'm sorry, Sonika." His thought connected with hers as he felt a gentle push from her on his mind. *"I'll make this right somehow."*

Tears shone in Sonika's eyes. She looked to the ground so no one else would notice her emotions. *"I let my anger get the best of me. You tried to save my life and I'm grateful for it."*

"I'm not done yet."

"Do we have orders?" An older assassin asked, breaking them both from their inner realm. His hand was already on a knife in his clothing as an eager grin played about his lips. Kulako swallowed nervously.

As if on cue, both soldiers removed the ropes from Sonika's throat. Kulako could see flaring red lines in her skin. She glanced at him quickly, her eyes clearly warning him against taking immediate action. He planted his feet firmly on the stone flooring, though he was unable to ignore how completely petrified she was. When his temper bubbled, he struggled to repress it and the taste of iron it left in his mouth.

"Draw Akahana out," one soldier sneered as the men grumbled in disgust. He pushed Sonika forward. "We know he's here somewhere, and Master Ewah seems to think this *thing* will stir something protective in him."

Haru wasted no time in descending on her with a curled fist. Sonika ducked out of the way and sent a kick for his knee while another man's gleaming knife slashed at her. The weapon caught her on the arm and drew a small amount of blood. Kulako watched the first soldier blow his whistle, forcing Haru to stop, allowing a third to land a hit to Sonika's face when she froze in agony from the whistle's pitch. Faster than Kulako could think, he was in front of her with his katana drawn and eyes blazing fiercely. The other assassins stopped, as unsure as he was about attacking a comrade. He pulled the cover from his face, Haru and several others copying his action.

"Disgusting." A voice snarled from the back of the room, causing all to turn and face in that direction. "You would sooner threaten your own rather than allow this thing—this *wretch* unworthy of a human name—to be killed?"

From the shadows emerged the form of a man standing at about six feet, with his shortened hair tied high and a few small scars riddling his stony, pockmarked face. He nodded curtly at the surrounding men.

"At ease, all of you."

Kulako straightened and sheathed his sword at the command, feeling Sonika press against his back for protection. The man's dark green eyes locked on the pair with pure hatred, his nostrils flaring as he tried to remain in control of his authoritative demeanor. Kulako hadn't been able to get a clear view of Master Ewah during his graduation ceremony. However, as the man currently stood directly before him, he was twice as intimidating now as he had been in the past.

"Akahana," he said stiffly. "Now that you're both here, the Emperor will see you. The rest of you, dismissed."

The soldiers grabbed Sonika, replaced the ropes about her neck, and then demanded Kulako's weapons from him before allowing him to walk freely at her side; it was obvious enough that he would not leave her. They glanced at each other once, both desperate for something to say, though no words came forth. The rage and hate in the air from Master Ewah was palpable, suffocating all energy surrounding them as they made their way through many long corridors.

At last, they came to a small room located on the other side of ornate double doors where elaborate tapestries and gorgeous paintings hung from the walls. Ewah signaled with a raised hand for the troupe to halt and glared at Kulako before knocking on the door.

"*I* will be meeting with His Highness to brief him, and then I will send for the two of you." He barked before he entered, and the door slammed behind him.

A sharp whistle through one of the soldier's teeth caused Kulako to turn and give him a withering look. The soldier smirked. "He sure is pissed. I'd absolutely hate to be either of you right now."

"They always told us in training that disobedience for an easy lay isn't worth it." The other soldier chortled.

Kulako rolled his eyes and turned to face the doors again, though his eventually shifted to Sonika, who was examining one of the paintings with horrified eyes. He recognized it as one that depicted Emperor Akuwara hunting wolves on horseback through snowy woodlands.

Unexpectedly through the Mindspeak of the Okami, she said, *"I sure hope you have a plan, Kulako. I'm out of ideas."*

"Just one, but I'm sure you're going to hate it." He paused. *"I know I shouldn't, but can I ask you to trust me again?"*

Sonika sighed, her breath shaking as she did so, but nodded, giving her assent. Kulako's eyes caught hers, and she bit her lip nervously. Finally, she relented and offered a small smile, putting Kulako slightly more at ease. The soldiers tightened their grip on her ropes a little, as if they knew when the doors would open again before seeing it happen. Kulako watched his feet as they entered the throne room, remembering the danger he felt whenever the Emperor was near.

Throwing them to their knees after a few strides, one of the guards pulled Kulako's hair at the roots to force his eyes forward.

Absolute power rippled unquestioningly throughout the room, and as his eyes adjusted once again, Kulako could feel his arms begin to tremble ever so slightly as his vision settled on the ominous figure that sat upon the throne. He was paler than most Giahatians, though he still carried the traits of ebony hair and obsidian eyes—he could even pass for Perenin. His delicate, almost feline features were cold, frozen to the slightest flicker of emotion. Kulako could sense Sonika's fear of Emperor Akuko, but he couldn't tear his gaze away to look at her and attempt keeping her calm.

The Emperor scrutinized the assassin for a moment, then his eyes flicked to Sonika before he frigidly stated, "You may rise, but the wolf will remain keeling and absolutely *silent*. You two, unbind the wild creature's arms. She won't be going anywhere."

Kulako's breath hitched in his throat even as he and the soldiers obeyed their commands. He stood in a formal attentive stance with his hands behind his back; a shiver ran up and down his spine. The wordless exchange between their eyes lasted for a long, agonizing moment, until the Emperor blinked and Kulako remembered to breathe again.

"I am told that you were born under the name of 'Kulako,' Nightshade. Since we are about to become well-acquainted, I shall use this name. However, you will not address me so informally." His voice was smooth, aloof, and the warmth with which he spoke failed to reach the air between them. He continued, "It appears as though we have quite a bit to discuss, Kulako."

The Emperor snapped his fingers, calling over a servant to pour wine for him, and then disinterestedly waved a hand to dismiss him. "You have been quite a bit of trouble for me, I hope you're aware."

Kulako winced at the accuracy in his statement. Akuko gave a brief smile of numb amusement and glanced at Sonika. She looked away hastily, and interest crossed his features as he drank from his cup. When he set it down again, his expression faded—it had all happened almost too quickly for Kulako to notice. "I wonder what we should do about that. I suppose the simplest and most obvious solution would be to eliminate you and your little companion. However, that poses a problem for me."

"A problem, Your Highness?" Kulako dared to play ignorant.

A cold smile touched Akuko's face again. "But of course. You see, you are one of my best assassins, even given your rank. Your reputation for lacking mercy is beguiling, really. It would be harmful to us both if you were to be taken out of action."

Kulako's voice stuck in his throat again, and so Akuko continued on while giving an open glance to Sonika, whose tension could have been easily plucked from the air, "The wolf is only one woman, if you can call her that. If this is what interests you, I can personally provide you with more, possibly your pick of the population here on Perena. It would certainly be better breeding stock."

Kulako felt Sonika's eyes on him, and finally, he was able to look at her. She wore an unreadable expression, and Kulako, remembering the conversation he previously held with Obito and Daisuke, wondered exactly how far the Emperor would go to ensure her death. The last nine years of attempting her extermination must have cost him enough in resources and skilled men—perhaps he could be convinced to put it to rest. He made sure her eyes were on him. *"You are absolutely not going to like how this sounds—I know I don't. You're also not allowed to kill me afterward, though."*

"Kulako, what—"

"Your Highness, if I may." His heart thudded wildly against his chest as he spoke, though he kept his expressions under control. "Could it not be more beneficial to the Empire if she lived?"

Akuko leaned forward, an eyebrow raised as undeniable interest amounted in his features, though he still restrained against letting curiosity hold him. "I'm listening."

Kulako took a deep breath, pressing on with his approach. "I know it may not sound preferable to you, but if she produced offspring, they would possess the same power as her—if not more—and then you would have those skills added to your ranks."

"The wolves of Othakra are said to be wild creatures—their feral nature unharnessed." The Emperor said at last after he took a moment to think the proposal over. His eyes wandered over to Sonika before pointedly settling on Kulako again. "You *know* how the Empire values obedience."

"It is also said that the wolves are extremely loyal to those who they consider their leader." Kulako knew that wasn't quite how the mindset worked, but as long as the Emperor thought it was the truth, he saw no reason to say otherwise.

Akuko smiled coldly again. "What an intriguing argument. Perhaps your blade isn't the only thing sharp about you; having the Okami under Giahatian control at last could prove to be interesting, and—as you stated—even beneficial. However, this is but one quandary: you have openly defied me. You have ignored orders. You have committed crimes punishable by death. While it is true that the wolf will regard you as her leader if she is bound to you, how could I guarantee that any of her mutts—or *you*, for that matter—would remain completely and singularly loyal to the Empire?"

Kulako remained firm in his response, despite being only barely able to keep his features calm and unreadable. He looked Akuko in the eye, saying, "I don't know any man who would dare to directly lie to his emperor, Your Highness. You have my word that the wolves will be completely under your control and that my own loyalty is unwavering, and I hope that one day you can forgive my weaknesses."

The Emperor's face relaxed with satisfaction. "I accept your word at a high value, Kulako. However, your disobedience cannot go unpunished; if the Nightshade were to act without regard to command, it would only encourage others to do the same."

His eyes flattened suddenly and turned on Sonika. He rose from his seat, gliding across the floor as he went to her. Kulako thought his heart stopped when the Emperor stood in front of her. Sonika's eyes were wide with terror as he gracefully knelt to her level, cupping her chin with long, delicate fingers. "And you, little wolf, have caused such a path of death for those who were unable to apprehend you. My father and I have both been forced to eliminate entire military units because of their failures. If I give you to Kulako, can I trust that this will be our last time meeting in such a manner?"

Sonika mutely nodded, and the Emperor released her with surprising gentleness before he straightened again, retreating a few paces from them both.

Emperor Akuko examined them for a moment, interest disguised as indifference etched into his features. Finally, his eyes settled on Kulako once more as he announced, "As an act of good faith, I will trust you to follow these men and allow you to keep your wolf with you. Within several days, however, you will endure a rather...public punishment before I can return your freedom. Do you accept these terms?"

Kulako thought back to his days at Kurushima, his heart sinking into his stomach at the very idea of it. He didn't know what the Emperor had in store for him, but he could only assume it to be worse than what any of the masters had forced him to endure; he had never done anything quite this traitorous during his training.

He forced these memories and fears away by calmly nodding. "Yes, Your Highness."

"Very well, then." Akuko looked at the two soldiers who had held Sonika's ropes this entire time in utter silence, signaling for them to allow Sonika to rise to her feet. "Please escort Nightshade and the wolf to more suitable quarters. Kulako, I'll be seeing you in a few days."

Eighteen: The Punishment and the Promise

Kulako and Sonika were led down to the dungeons by the two guards, who were oddly wordless for the duration of the crossing despite the few quips made earlier—likely sobered by the Emperor's presence and decisions. The guards escorted them to a cell with nothing but a tiny window and chained by the ankle to walls opposite one another. It was the second of four levels of dungeon cells, which meant they at least weren't near the sewers below and far enough from the screams of the torture rooms two floors above.

Sonika's unrelenting eyes gave off a slight glow with the flickering torchlight. She immobilized him with a long, hard look before turning away, rubbing at the marks on her neck. Kulako sighed before he carefully approached her as far as his restraints would allow him to go.

"In my defense, I *did* say that you were going to hate the idea," Kulako said quietly, crouching to the floor. Even if he ignored proper Okami body language for the situation and how it would have required him to be lower than her, he didn't know many men who sincerely apologized to a woman while standing. He certainly didn't dare risk upsetting her further. Sonika shifted to face him again; she remained silent, and her brows furrowed, indicating that she was calculating what to say. He hesitated at her lack of a response but continued anyway. "There are plenty of places you could go into hiding once we're free—anywhere in the south, Noshe, Okara."

"Okara?" Sonika repeated incredulously, almost as if she were teasing him for the suggestion. "Isn't that the slave region?"

Kulako nodded after a moment, tentative about how she might react to his answer. "Yes."

"Would *you* ever go back?"

"...No."

Sonika rolled her eyes. She spoke slowly, choosing her words as they came forth. "You just swore Okami loyalty—my loyalty—to the Giahatio, Kulako, the very thing my people fought against for ages. They were slaughtered because of it. What was the point to any of that, now?"

"My record for being honest might not be the greatest at this point, but you aren't held to anything. We can get you out of this." Despite his attempt to sound promising, he faltered as her stern expression silenced him once more.

She sighed and got as close to him as her shackles would allow. She could just barely reach his knees when she also lowered herself to the floor, and she stretched out to lightly brush him with her fingertips. She looked away, a strange expression in her downcast eyes. "I'm so tired of hiding, Kulako. I actually quite enjoy my life on Itake. And I...I enjoyed my life with *you* on Itake."

They met one another's gaze, her firm stare holding him just as it usually did. Kulako smiled a little at her, and she mirrored the expression. He told her softly, "I enjoyed that, too."

"Then," Sonika began as she moved away from and stood with Kulako following along. "Perhaps we can make something work."

She closed her eyes to concentrate before a rush of wind swirled around her. Her form became a dark brown wolf with long white patches on the front legs, and the shackle around her ankle shattered from the force of the transformation. Her wolf form was not quite as large as those of the Okami Lords', but it was equally intimidating. She quickly shifted again and placed a hand over Kulako's mouth to stifle his involuntary startled cry, then snickered at his wide-eyed expression. Kulako laughed with her as she withdrew her hand and then threw her arms around his neck. Sonika kissed his cheek and he held her tighter.

"How long have you been able to do that?"

"Only a year or two. I try to keep it to myself." Sonika buried her face in his neck. "I missed you so much. No more lies?"

"No more lies."

"No more secrets?"

"You know I can't promise that."

Sonika retracted a little and their eyes locked again. When her lips parted as if to speak, Kulako took her face in his hands, then kissed her deeply. He felt her press on his back as she pulled him in closer. They kissed again, and Kulako backed her against the wall. Trembling ever so slightly, he slipped his hands beneath the fabric of her shirt. Sonika's skin was soft against his calloused palms; a breathless sound escaped her as he moved from her waist along her sides. He found the lowest tie to her shirt, but when Sonika froze at his touch, Kulako's hands quickly left her skin. She sighed in relief.

Kulako looked away, embarrassed by his lack of control. "Sorry,"

"It's just that, because of Okubo, I haven't—"

"You don't owe me an explanation. You told me to stop, and that's the end of it."

Sonika watched his face, tracing lines along the bridge of his nose, the curve of his brow, then down to his cheeks; she pressed her forehead to his. Kulako's eyes closed and he breathed deeply at her touch. He pushed away thoughts of what might befall him within the next few days and instead focused on the state of mind she reminded him existed. For however long he would be allowed to stay with Sonika, it was the only place he wanted to be. Whether it was only in this moment or until his death—however soon that may be—he was not afraid to face anything, so long as he could be at her side.

Sonika glanced to the floor and then back to him. She gave him an uncommonly shy smile and blushed. "I *did* like what we were doing, and I think I like the direction it was going in. Can we go a little slower?"

Kulako nodded, his face burning. Sonika playfully grabbed him by the shirt and pressed her lips to his again. Helpless against her, he was lost in her, and didn't care to find his way back. A heavy metal door creaked open in the distance, startling them both, and Sonika fled to the opposite side of the cell just before the shadow of a guard cast into view.

The next few days wore on monotonously. Sonika kept her sharp ears alert for any guards outside of their cell. After that first night, they were in constant rotation. On the rare moments when none were present, she would join Kulako where he was restrained; if they were heard, she would retreat before the guard could peek in. In these few times of actual solitude together, they spoke at what length they could about their current situation. Kulako knew if they did decide to share a life, Sonika would often be left alone for weeks at a time, and he relayed such and that it would be a relatively unstable way for her to live. However, to Sonika, it seemed like the most secure existence she had known since childhood—her life wouldn't be threatened, but most importantly and most concise with her Okami beliefs, she knew she would be with someone she loved.

Inevitably, however, these discussions brought a word into the conversation that neither Sonika nor Kulako entirely liked.

Assassins weren't expected to marry until a certain age and number of years into their service for the Empire—a point Kulako wouldn't reach for at least another decade if he lived that long. Even when they did, they usually married a favorite prostitute to have someone keep them company. Sometimes they would raise a child or two. The number of assassins who chose that route was much smaller than the number of those who decided that violence was all they would ever know, and continued the cycle as masters at Kurushima. Assassins eligible to marry still had to have the Emperor's approval, something Sonika and Kulako both concluded that Akuko would never grant them, thus ruling out a Giahatian marriage.

Kulako was relieved that Sonika was as unbothered by that as he was.

On the dawn of about the fourth day of their imprisonment, the heavy cell door creaked open, stirring them both from sleep. A large Giahatian man stood in the doorway, where he glared at Sonika before plodding over to Kulako and unlocking his shackle. Sonika rose from her cot, ready to defend, but stopped upon catching Kulako's eye. Although he looked terrified as the man grabbed him by the lapel to lift him to his feet, his expression soon changed. He inhaled deeply as the man chained his wrists, and a firm resolve washed over his face.

"It's almost over, Sonika."

Before Sonika could reply, the man all but dragged Kulako from the cell, leaving the door open behind him. Sonika tried to follow, but then another figure appeared, slowly approaching her. He stood only about two inches taller than Kulako with raven hair. As he came closer, Sonika could see he had the same pale skin and violet eyes. He stopped an arm's length away from her, and his gravely set face slipped into a clever grin.

"My, my brother's taste in women is far better than I expected." He chuckled to himself as he bent down to release the shackle. Upon seeing that it had broken, he merely shrugged and straightened. He eyed her for a moment, shamelessly amused by her confusion. "You'll be coming with me for a little while. I trust I won't need to pull you along unceremoniously; after all, dogs require leashes, not wolves."

Cautiously, holding back her urge to lash out and hit him in preemptive defense, Sonika asked, "Who are you?"

"Daisuke Akahana," he replied smoothly. At the way she cocked her head to one side, he laughed again. "Yes, I know I'm the better-looking sibling, but we don't have much time to discuss that. Besides, even if I were into women, we wouldn't be a good match. I'm afraid we would burn too brightly and too fast, Lady Okami. Come along, Sonika."

They walked along the damp, chilly corridors of the dungeons for quite some time in silence before Sonika found she could not control her racing thoughts. However, when she opened her mouth to ask the first thing she could think of, Daisuke looked at her from the corner of his eye.

"I take it I must be one of the first other than my brother to use your actual name since your apprehension on Itake. I hope it's a welcomed change. Your title, however, I will only use that once. As I'm sure you're fully aware, it's unsafe for such terms to be used here, no matter how much truth is behind them."

Sonika nodded, not expecting the way he spoke to her. Even if he were Kulako's brother, he was still a spy. She wondered if she should trust him, uncomfortably aware that she had few other choices. She found her voice again. "Where are you taking me? And what's going to happen to Kulako?"

Daisuke's countenance faltered. He grimly pressed his lips together. "Unfortunately, you'll know all too soon. You're to be serving wine to his Highness this afternoon. I'm certain that he believes if you're to be found loyal to him and Kulako, watching this fiasco is the perfect punishment for you and that it should serve as a warning. So, I'm going to escort you to the baths, the maids, and then to the arena to stand by his Highness."

"That doesn't—"

"His Highness, of course, offered an alternative if you do not wish to be in the arena. He said that he could instead visit you later, and you could both have a chat over the effectiveness of fire as a weapon." Daisuke took in the horror that washed over Sonika's features and softened a little. "If you really want to help Kulako, Sonika, you'll do your best to stay strong; it won't be easy."

• • • •

THE GUARD FREED KULAKO'S hands, allowing him to rub his wrists. He was ordered to remove his boots and shirt. The room was still for a few moments as both were taken away; Kulako thought he'd been left there with how quiet everything went, until the guard's heavy scent of sweat returned and he was grabbed by the hair.

The guard pulled back on the length of Kulako's hair, and he felt sharp, merciless tugs at it as the guard ripped through it with a knife to cut it. This was normally a symbol of stripping away one's military rank, but his name held no decorative terms in the first place. He looked at the floor as best as he could with the way his head was forced back, watching red strands fall around his bare feet. He hadn't gotten his hair cut short since he was first brought to Kurushima, now it rested in a shaggy mess against his neck.

"Stand at attention, for Hikari's sake. Don't they teach any respect at Kurushima anymore?" The guard barked when he released Kulako.

Kulako's mind was too blank to argue; he complied, placing his hands behind his back and waiting, unable to process what was beginning to take place. A small window carved into the wall in front of him showed him the pleasant, sunny spring morning waiting on the outside. Kulako involuntarily shivered—a nice day guaranteed that plenty of the Giahatian and Perenin nobility would attend as spectators, along with the successful merchants who slipped into these events. Soldiers and assassins would likely be there, as well. Whatever was about to happen would serve as an example for years to come.

"Recite the four oaths of the hitokiri."

Kulako fought the grimace that nearly formed on his face, though he was sure he hadn't been able to repress it completely; he'd said this too many times in his life. "Honor to the Empire; loyalty to the Giahatio; obedience to the Emperor; discipline to uphold them all."

"Stand at attention." The guard repeated as if Kulako hadn't said anything.

Kulako hadn't moved in the slightest during the exchange. He dared to look over at the guard to question him, but as he did, he got a blow to the ribs. He flinched, as the strike was more unexpected than it was painful. The second hit that followed was much harder, however, and landed in the same spot.

"Stand at attention." The guard struck him again as he tried to stand straight. "We have until noon for you to get this right. Name the principles of the oath."

The guard waited for Kulako to regain his bearings this time. He tried not to think about the wood he heard dragging against the stone floor. "Honor, loyalty, obedience, discipline."

The club swung into his side twice more, this time lower, and on the second strike, Kulako lost his balance.

"Stand at attention." The guard said again as he pulled Kulako to his feet, coiled in pain while clutching his side. "What else does the oath say?"

Kulako now had to fight a little to stand straight. "To deny the Goddess is to deny the Emperor."

"Have you prayed to the Goddess yet today, hitokiri?" The guard raised the club. "Or ever? I certainly hope you have, for your sake."

• • • •

KULAKO SHUDDERED AS the cool, spring breeze touched his bare skin. Shirtless, shoeless, with his shaggy hair brushing against his shoulders in the light wind, he no longer looked like military personnel. He tried to breathe deeply, but air constricted in his lungs as a sharp throb from his ribcage reminded him of the savage beating he'd endured for the last few hours. His entire left side from hip to chest was deep blue and purple with bruising; he was confident in the assumption that he now had cracked ribs, but he knew more was to come. He stood with two guards in a tunnel leading to the arena where ceremonies—graduations including his own, public torture and punishment, executions, and occasionally master demonstrations—were held. The sun was beginning to climb towards noon. Kulako's heart thudded wildly in his chest.

He closed his eyes as the steady drumming of voices grew outside. Consolidating what little courage he had left, he reminded himself that Sonika would live; it might be within an inch of his life, but so would he. Someone announced the Emperor's presence, and the three men stepped closer to the opening as the sound of a gong reverberated throughout the arena. Although they'd shackled his hands behind his back once more, the guards insisted on grabbing Kulako by the arms and fiercely dug their fingers into whatever pressure points they could reach.

They escorted him out into the open area. The hum of voices burst into a roar, but Kulako didn't acknowledge any of them. He looked to the high dais where he could see Akuko's figure sitting comfortably in the shade, his ordinarily expressionless face alight with amusement. At Akuko's side, he saw Sonika dressed in a Giahatian kimono, holding a serving tray. Their eyes met before the guards turned him to face the rest of the audience.

The herald began to speak again, but Kulako couldn't concentrate on what was being said. He could only look from his periphery to glimpse at what awaited him. His stomach flipped in horror as his heart continued pounding in his ears. The guards who had been standing with him meddled with a pile of glowing, hot coals and iron rods. Kulako's jaw clenched as one of them returned to his side to adjust the bindings on his wrists and the other picked up whip from beside the coals. He already knew all too well how badly this was about to hurt.

• • • •

SONIKA STOOD AT EMPEROR Akuko's side as her eyes anxiously scanned the arena below. The Emperor barely noticed her; quite possibly, he didn't know she was there, even when he set his wine glass down to be filled. Sonika was relieved. She fought with her emotions enough as it was, desperate to hold onto her bravery, no matter how heavily her fears weighed on her. She could barely face Kulako when he looked up at her. He didn't deserve any of this, especially not for her sake. She'd been so terrified when they met with the Emperor that she hadn't been able to find her voice to defend him.

She glanced over at the Emperor, hoping if there was perhaps the slightest bit of humanity she could appeal to.

"Your Highness," she whispered, avoiding the notice of the attendants or other guards who busily flocked the balcony; she hated the submissive words as she spoke them. To her surprise, Akuko's head tilted toward her, but his eyes remained firm on the speaking herald. Sonika's heart leapt into her throat. "Please don't do this to him."

A cold, hateful smile cracked the Emperor's face for only a fraction of a second. Genuine, cruel amusement at her plea. "The price one must pay for weakness is great, little wolf, and a seductress such as you must also learn what that looks like. As I understand it, you wolves are very sensitive creatures to the pain of others, most of all those you love. His will be yours. Hitokiri Nightshade was immovable before he was sent after you. Whatever you did to ruin my best assassin, you will both pay for it here."

Sonika swallowed as her eyes fell on the arena below again before they flicked up to the sky. *Help him. He doesn't deserve this.*

• • • •

KULAKO'S ANXIETY ONLY continued to build as the herald listed off the charges the Empire had brought against him. Intense silence followed when the herald finished his speech as everyone—guards, nobility, assassins, and soldiers, almost anyone Kulako could think of; he had been correct in his earlier assumptions about who would attend—shifted their attention to the Emperor.

Akuko stood fluidly, looking at the assassin once before acknowledging the mob and pronouncing, "Guilty as charged."

He spoke solemnly, expressionlessly, the last syllables leaving his lips on a ghostlike breath before he sat again upon his throne. The crowd roared at the Emperor's decision. Some shouts calling for Kulako's life were distinct over the rest of the noise. The chains securing Kulako's wrists were secured to a post, ensuring he wouldn't be able to move, and the man who had been beside him roughly hit him in the back of his head, driving his cheekbone into the wooden support. A whistling noise cut through the air. Only seconds later, Kulako felt the first sting of the whip as it crossed his back.

The collective bellow from the gathered was deafening, the encouragements and obscenities only seeming to incite a harder flogging with each strike. It continued relentlessly until Kulako's body begged for relief, and his shaking legs collapsed. His bindings to the post were the only thing supporting his weight, as he no longer could. He was struck three more times, then heard one guard relay to the other to be finished. They released his chains from the post, throwing him onto his back. The manacles hit him in the face carelessly and the fresh wounds tore open even further. One of the men, who easily outweighed Kulako, pinned him by the chest with a strong forearm and forced his mouth open by holding pressure points in his jaw while his partner took one of the burning hot coals with a pair of prongs and shoved it down Kulako's throat. Kulako struggled against the man as ice-cold water chased after the coal. They allowed him up as he heaved, then violently vomited blood and bile.

Kulako blacked out, but it must not have been for long. He was barely conscious as one of the guards grabbed him by the hair and dragged him back to the post before restraining him. A soft glow appeared at Kulako's side, and a white wolf sat beside him while he watched the branding irons being prepared. He vaguely recognized the characters to be engraved into his skin as "discipline" and "loyalty", permanent reminders of the lessons learned on this day, forever reminding him that his oath to the Empire came first.

"I cannot stop what is happening," the wolf spirit said softly. Kulako's vision blurred as the agony he already felt began to fade. *"But I can stop you from feeling the worst of it."*

"We both will." Takeo's voice came from his other side. Even though he was aware he wouldn't be seen, the wolf exposed his fangs and growled as one man passed his brand over to the other. The first guard knelt beside Kulako, holding him down with an elbow to his bruising.

They forcibly bared Kulako's left forearm beneath the symbol for "discipline" and aligned "loyalty" with his heart. Kulako watched the white-hot irons sink into his skin. As the wolves promised, he felt nothing. He closed his eyes, willing the world to go black again.

Nineteen: The Glass Gardens

Though Sonika had kept control of herself through the process of the Emperor dismissing her, bathing again, and redressing in her everyday clothing, once alone in an antechamber, she was unable to prevent herself from crying. She had never seen such a display of cruelty in her life. It shook her to her core. The Giahatio had spared even the Okami from torture.

Daisuke found her in this moment of helplessness. His original intent had been to escort her back to the dungeons after she completed a final task designed by the Emperor to affirm her loyalty. Instead, when he approached her and heard her soft cries, muffled by nothing more than a hand over her mouth, he sat beside her to try comforting her.

Daisuke now quietly padded alongside Sonika through the Palace.

Upon seeing Kulako's bruising when he was first brought into the arena, Daisuke did not want to witness more and excused himself from the rest of the afternoon's event; he was incapable of keeping the strength he had asked of Sonika. It was a painful reminder of the absolute fear and heartbreak he had experienced the only time he'd tried to visit with Kulako at Kurushima. When Daisuke saw his younger brother pinning another boy, about to drive a knife into the other child's stomach, Daisuke immediately requested to leave with his own master before Kulako was ever aware he had been there.

He didn't like to think of that particular moment and avoided it as often as possible; he hated the cowardice he'd displayed at the time. When Master Ewah assigned Kulako to Obito's command, Daisuke kept an eye on his brother before their eventual attempt to reconnect. Obito had been a friend to Daisuke since his earliest days as a spy, and their relationship eventually blossomed into a romantic one. Though they tried to stay out of each other's official dealings, after hearing rumblings from his superiors about Obito's incompetence to resolve the issue, Daisuke chose to entangle himself in the mess Kulako had created by volunteering his skills for finding correct information.

Daisuke had never held anything personal against the Okami, but things would have only been worse for everyone involved once the confusion of what really happened bubbled over and revealed the truth.

He looked over at Sonika, who didn't seem to mind that he'd placed himself in charge of her to assure her safety in the Palace. Lost in thought, coupled with Sonika's heavy silence, Daisuke had nearly forgotten she was there. She was free to roam in certain areas without anyone treating her as a prisoner, so he thought it wise to allow her that freedom for a few hours before she saw Kulako again. He would need time to rest as it was.

He had been able to encourage her to eat a little and sip at some tea, but sensing her restlessness, he decided to change their scenery, and they currently wandered through a hallway where Sonika stopped to stare at a large, marvelous painting of the mountain range visible from the city. The sun was rising in orange streaks behind the mountains, and the unknown artist had captured the glistening of light on the snowcapped peaks. Daisuke watched her for a long moment, silently thanking her for being able to soften his brother's heart as she had. He'd spent years quietly worrying about the assassin and man Kulako was becoming, and she had interrupted the cycle of violence in his life. That interruption was necessary for Kulako's sanity and for keeping the darkness out of his soul.

Daisuke sighed as he remembered the Emperor's final test.

"You must be exhausted." Daisuke said to her softly, thinking he might startle her if he spoke too suddenly or loudly. Sonika looked at him, the very essence of exhaustion etched into her features. "But, I'm afraid that I need to ask one more thing of you this evening."

In an attempt to feel better, Sonika tried a bit of wit. "You'd better not be asking me to serve you wine."

Daisuke chuckled. "Maybe not today, but I'll convince you eventually. Try not to be too surprised by my next question, since what I know about you mostly comes from secondhand reports. Is it correct that you're the local medic on Itake?"

She blinked, clearly not expecting that to be what he'd want to know, but nodded. "What of it?"

"The Healers or medics here are generally instructed to stay away from those who end up in a mess like this," He told her slowly, waiting for when her eyes would widen in horror. He continued when they did. "Fortunately for my idiot brother, His Highness knows that Kulako dying of infection would be a waste of necessary manpower. Don't get me wrong, someone *will* stop by, but it's anyone's guess as to when."

"But," Sonika paused out of shock. "Those wounds can easily become infected. He might not be able to wait."

"I thought you'd agree with me. Come on, then. I'll show you where you can make one of your medicines." Daisuke noted the worry that flickered in Sonika's eyes at wandering into private areas of the Palace. "There won't be any trouble if someone sees you. You're with me. It might not be much, but it's better than being considered a prisoner at this point."

It was quite late by the time Sonika finished producing the salve she thought would best treat Kulako's wounds; she decided to make two batches in case another application would be necessary. She tucked the small jars away into a hidden pocket in her shirt, which usually stored weapons, before turning to Daisuke and relaying that she was ready. When they came to the familiar cell door, Sonika hesitated as he slipped a key into the lock.

"Sonika?" Daisuke bent down to her level. She looked at him warily. "Make sure he writes me when you two get home won't you, dear sister?"

Sonika was surprised at first, but then smiled and nodded, which reassured him enough to give her one last mischievous grin. Daisuke pushed the door open and ushered her in before closing it behind her.

Sonika glanced back briefly before her eyes fell on Kulako. Her breath hitched in her lungs, but Kulako did not stir as she entered. Shackled again by the ankle, he'd settled in the far corner of the cell where the lash marks across his back would be the least agitated, and where he could be away from the torchlight. His skin exposed, she could easily see the shadows of the injuries along his body. His breathing strained and shallow, Sonika could only imagine the pain he was suffering. He was shaking from it. Softly, she went toward him and knelt before him. She gently touched his right temple, and he slowly raised his reddened eyes to acknowledge her. Sonika brushed the hair away from his face and pressed her forehead to his. Relief washed over both of them at being reunited.

When he tried to speak, only a strained, hoarse grunt came forward. Sonika put a finger to his lips to stop him from doing it again, afterwards nuzzling his neck in a wolf-like manner, hoping she could comfort him. Sonika retracted and pulled one of the small jars of balm from her shirt. She helped him move further away from the wall so she could slip in behind him. She placed a hand over her mouth, stifling her reaction to the mess of long, open wounds layered over older scars of the same shape, still highly visible against the pallor of his skin. Pushing this aside, she opened the ointment and set to work. Kulako made a pained noise and pulled away only initially, soon settling in again.

The familiar, rich aroma to Sonika's medications reached Kulako's nose and he closed his eyes. He lapsed comfortably against the expert labor of her hands as the formula worked to temporarily soothe and numb the open wounds. She shifted around him to apply it to his bruising and gently rub some on his throat, pausing when she looked to both of his brands, unsure of which to tend to first.

"I can't believe they do this to people," Sonika said quietly as she took his left hand and extended his arm to expose the character now permanently engraved into his skin before carefully rubbing the medicine on it. "And they called the Okami savage and barbaric."

Applying the last of the remedy to his chest, she sighed and sat down cross-legged in front of him. Kulako reached out to touch her cheek, the action startling her, as she jumped before meeting his gaze. Unable to use normal speech, he gently pressed against her consciousness with his own. *"Thank you."*

Sonika rose from her spot to bring over the shirt from his cot, draping it across Kulako's shoulders. She settled in beside him and glanced at him sternly. "You are never, *ever* allowed to save my life again."

It was close to midnight when Sonika was pulled from sleep. She knew she was still in her cell, but she had somehow shifted into the corner. Kulako slept heavily, with his head on her chest. His eyes fluttered open soon, however, and they looked at one another in confusion as he pushed himself up. She had heard of this rare phenomenon before, but up until now had highly doubted its existence. Like Mindspeak, two linked through such a connection communicated through dreams just as they did thought—the Okami called it Dreamspeak. According to her people, Lord Kohaku and his partner Lady Ayame were among the few known to use it well.

Kulako seemed as though he was about to speak, but a blur from the other side of the cell caught their attention, and they were staring at the large figures of the five Okami Lords. Sonika gasped as she recognized Takeo, shock preventing her from moving as he began to approach her. He stopped briefly to glance at Kulako and gave him an approving flick of the tail while dipping his head. Kulako smiled a little. Takeo turned to his daughter once again, his tail now shamelessly wagging like a puppy's when she tightly hugged the wolf around his neck. The Okami Lords all gave a nod of assent to the pair and dissipated as if on a wind that did not exist, taking Takeo's form with them.

Sonika looked down at Kulako as he settled against her, this time with a conflicting mixture of curiosity and understanding. *You really are the strangest wolf I've ever met.*

• • • •

GUARDS CAME TO RETRIEVE Kulako and Sonika four days after his sentencing, this time without manacles or ropes. The summons surprised them both. Kulako ambled about stiffly, and his voice barely worked. His spirits seemed to be returning to their usual demeanor despite those things, and Sonika felt relieved. They followed several opulently dressed guards who encircled them entirely in a fluidly moving formation. Kulako recognized the path to the throne room from the week prior.

After being ushered through the ornate doors, they now stood mostly alone with the Emperor. Kulako could sense the presence of a few hidden spies; he was sure Sonika had picked out their scents. Velveteen curtains of mottled gray draped across long windows hung in the perfect way to keep the room comfortably dark against the late afternoon light. Akuko was dressed in elegant gray robes, leaning on an arm of the throne. It was a much different atmosphere than when they first met with the Emperor.

However, he straightened when he saw them, making his figure loom as he gestured for them to come forward. Sonika moved so that she could hide behind Kulako as they obeyed the silent command, knowing this was not the place to be brave. The Emperor's exterior was the usual shield of cold indifference, but Kulako thought he felt something more ominous in the air as he did his best to stand at attention.

Akuko relaxed on this throne after a moment. "I trust that you are well enough to travel, Kulako?"

Kulako nodded and replied raspingly, "I believe so, Your Highness."

Akuko shifted his gaze to Sonika curtly, drawing her forth from what little protection Kulako could provide. His Highness keenly observed the way she looked to the assassin before speaking, deferring to him first, and he forgot to hide the curiosity flickering in his eyes. "And what about you, little wolf? You appear malnourished. I've spoken with some of the most trusted midwives in the city and have been led to believe that such a skinny form is hardly good for bearing sons—after all, it is *male* offspring that we are looking for to carry Kulako's talents and the gifts of your ancestors."

"I'm well, Your Highness, and able to help Kulako continue his recovery." She relayed. The Emperor nodded in satisfaction with her answer before turning his attention back to Kulako.

"Consider yourself furloughed for the next few weeks while you fully recover. At the end of this time, I expect nothing but a replica of the performance you have given in the past—an improvement, even. I believe Itake has missed having a reliable medic, and I do not wish to send a Healer to take your place, little wolf; they're far too expensive to pay when off in some horrendous little area such as that. Besides, if Magistrate Tomio's health truly is failing as I've heard, then his replacement will soon be able to keep an eye on you two." Akuko stood before he snapped his fingers, and a pair of servants appeared, each holding one end of Kulako's sheathed katana and carrying the knives he'd brought with him when he had been arraigned.

The servants held out Kulako's weapons for him to take, which he did only after waiting for Akuko's nod of approval. To both of their surprise, the servants also handed Sonika her beaten leather case. She accepted it nervously after repeating Kulako's process for permission and held it to her chest rather than arming herself.

Sonika looked at Kulako while he put his weapons back in their assigned places among his clothing, and then back to the Emperor. She dared to speak. "Your Highness, we *are* allowed to return to Itake?"

Akuko raised his eyebrows at her, though no true expression touched his face. Sonika shrank behind Kulako again, peeking from around his shoulder. "Did you think I wanted to keep you in my dungeons? Frankly, little wolf, I cannot be sure *you* are even human; you might have to sleep with the hounds if that were the plan. It would be one thing to keep you both alive after effectively punishing you, but to keep you both alive and in my city? I'd rather not deal with the political scandal, especially once you *do* have a child. I would not be able to guarantee the child's safety—after all, Kulako here has proven to me that my assassins can only be controlled so tightly. If I cannot do that, then this experiment is a waste of time, which would make me look foolish for not eliminating you both, as I should have. Itake would be a safer place for you to raise your little half-breeds before you give them to Kurushima."

Kulako wanted to say something, but the words were lost on his tongue when he opened his mouth.

"In any case, I regret this shall be the last time we meet for quite some time. You will leave through the tunnels and the glass gardens. However, those gardens are where Ewah's elite like to train; they tend to set many traps for unwanted visitors with the aid of Kuro's priests and their enchantments. They will not be made aware of your lawful release or told to disengage their snares before you arrive—to do so in such a short amount of time would be simply impossible." Akuko smiled cruelly. "With that said, if you can make it out alive and together, you will have earned your right to my decision to allow you to live on Itake. If one or both of you fall, you were never worthy. Hikari's blessings, Kulako, little wolf."

Kulako gestured for Sonika to copy him again, and they both bowed at the waist as Akuko gave a slight dip of his head to dismiss them. The guards who had guided them to the throne room opened the doors and, with synchronized movements, surrounded them once more to lead them away from the Emperor.

The tunnels Akuko referred to were nothing more than abandoned hallways on the ground level of the Palace, thick with dust and cobwebs from years of neglect. Though they were not the only way to the glass gardens, they were the most secretive path. Kulako and Sonika stood at the entrance to the gardens at dusk, then the heavy iron door slammed and audibly locked behind them once pushed outside.

Sonika took surveillance of their surroundings while she secured the leather case around her right thigh. As far as she could see, there were tall hedges lined with what she recognized to be poisonous flowers—iris, lily of the valley, even tulips, but their typical aromas were different somehow; Sonika couldn't smell any of them. It was suspicious, yet night encroached on the pair, and Sonika realized that if what Akuko had claimed about the spies was true, they had to move no matter what. She didn't like how quiet things were, and would have to rely on her nose and sight.

"Do you know the way out?" Sonika stepped in close to Kulako and stole one of his kunai without any protests.

Kulako was healing, but he hadn't expected the Emperor to call for them and had spent most of the day before their summons moving around in the cell to ensure his health. His face betrayed his level of discomfort. "I've never been here before, but we need to go toward the wharves."

"The wharves? I can lead us out of here."

"I know."

The ocean seemed to be the only thing she *could* smell. Sonika beamed at the trust he placed in her and began to lead the way by scent—her eyes easily adjusting to the deepening night. As they wandered through the gardens, Sonika understood why they deserved their name. There were large glass statues to mark every corner in the hedges; some appeared to be previous emperors' likenesses while others were more abstract. At their edges, the figures were lined with a pink, pastel glow.

"They're enchanted," Kulako said abruptly, startling her. When she turned to him, he was visibly concerned. *"This is what His Highness meant. The priests made the statues, and their enchantment is probably why sound is so off here. Keep your guard up."*

They walked in silence after that, until Sonika's sharp hearing caught the whistle of a knife cutting through the air. She grabbed Kulako by the sleeve and jerked him out of the way just in time, as the sound had been so distorted, and the kunai landed just inches from where Kulako had been standing. Sonika's eyes wildly scanned the area, but she saw no one. There were no scents to trace. She felt Kulako's back against hers for as long as he could bear it, and he pushed a little, forcing her to continue walking forward as he guarded the steps they had already taken.

Kulako's left hand suddenly shot up, and the delayed ring of clashing weapons rose into the air. The subsequent groan of pain Kulako made at the quick movement was also belated, emphasizing how much the hedges and the enchantment muffled sound. Looking down, Sonika was finally able to catch the glint of a hidden wire in the rising moonlight. She sniffed at the air again. They were almost out.

Sonika grabbed Kulako's arm again, this time sprinting forward, the kunai she had taken from him held in front of her to guard. The last turn toward the sea was sharp and the tunnel was narrow. Sonika pushed herself to go faster, never releasing Kulako. Large spikes closed the gaps behind them from both sides of the hedges, barely missing them and making no sound when they connected—the reactions of the traps were fast, but with Sonika's speed, she and Kulako were even faster moving as a unit. Sonika could see the drape of vines covering their escape.

Their breathing had been the only detectable sound for so long that the rumble of sliding rock caused Sonika to freeze. The exit was only feet away now. Two sheets of crystal with the same pink glow as the enchanted statues were sliding toward them on either side. If the crystals came all the way through their places in the hedge, they would be trapped, and the back crystal was already in place. When the front crystal slid forward, they would be crushed between the two plates. This time Kulako pushed Sonika out of the way. She kept her grip on him, ready to yank him away from danger. The crystals settled and their glow faded. Sonika backed into the vines only to discover that they were no longer there, and she fell into an abandoned street where the Palace loomed in the distance. She recovered from the blunder gracefully with a backward roll, though she felt less than elegant when she pulled herself to her knees, and a frustrated howl—wolf-like or hysterical, she wasn't sure—burst out of her.

"What the fuck was that?" Sonika barely remembered to keep the pitch of her voice in control as Kulako helped her up again. Her eyes were wild when she looked up at him, but Kulako was oddly calm, even for him. "Did you expect that?"

"Not quite that, but His Highness isn't exactly known for making things easy." Kulako winced in pain. "You were leading us, anyway. I didn't see a reason to panic."

"No reason to panic? We almost died, and—"An involuntary growl at his nonchalance interrupted Sonika's speech. She pinched the bridge of her nose in exasperation and sighed, unsure what to do with her burst of adrenaline.

"It's too late for us to leave tonight," Kulako told her as he began to walk, clearly not wanting to discuss what just transpired. He was slow enough with his movements that Sonika could easily keep pace with him even after she waited to follow. "The Spring Festival is soon, too, so the inns are probably full."

Sonika cocked her head to one side but said nothing as they continued on their way. The abandoned street connected to another with heavier traffic, and they were nearing where the roads intersected. Both oil and paper lamps lined the sides of the main road. She was surprised to see how many people milled about when they came to the edge of their darkened street. A man passed by without taking notice of them, soon followed by a woman who seemed to keep her pace measured as to stay behind him. Sonika at first dismissed the observation, thinking it too strange to *purposely* trail one's significant other, but when the man stopped to point at the Palace's threatening silhouette in admiration, his companion did the same. The woman said something Sonika no longer had the energy to decipher, and the couple moved on. Sonika glanced up at Kulako.

"Different cultures, I suppose. Do I have to do that?" Sonika gestured vaguely at the pair that had gone by.

Kulako laughed. "If I said you did, you probably would try to kill me. Come on. It's still early enough that most of the others should be out."

Sonika felt relieved when she and Kulako stepped onto the street and she knew she could remain at his side, though her anxiety returned at them being in the open and at his last comment. "'Others?' What do you mean?"

Kulako looked away for a moment, not liking his answer. "The other hitokiri. I still have a flat in the assassins' quarter until the festival is over."

Sonika bit her lip and distracted herself with the ongoing activity around them. She had never seen a city as large as the Capital before—the town Makoto had lived in was probably the most extensive settlement she had seen until now. There was much to look at. It was decidedly too much, as she found herself becoming overwhelmed by the crowds of street performers and patrons to vendors. She noticed that Kulako was beginning to slow again.

"Sonika, can I—" He fell against her, too sore to carry himself properly anymore.

Sonika smiled and moved so that his arm could be around her shoulder. "Always."

• • • •

"AKAHANA? WHEN WAS THE last time you brought a woman home?" A man slurred from one of the higher levels of flats. Kulako stopped briefly to look upward; Sonika felt her face turn hot, but she didn't acknowledge the other assassin. "Can we share? I'm too drunk to find my own whore tonight, and this one's got nice legs."

"Care for a knife in your throat?" Kulako's roughened voice called up to the swaying man.

The man grunted in response before he slumped against the outer wall of his home and took another swig out of an unmarked bottle. Kulako rolled his eyes in annoyance, and walked a little faster toward his own residence on the ground level a few doors down.

Kulako paused after he pushed open the door to his flat, waiting to see if anyone had rigged the entrance. After nothing happened, he opened the door the rest of the way to bring Sonika in. There was a lamp near the door which he lit upon entry, and Sonika looked around while Kulako went into the next room, one of his knives leading the way.

Sonika wasn't sure what she expected from an assassin's flat, but it was even barer than she originally imagined. The only decoration on the walls was a required banner with the Empire's seal. If not for the small stack of papers she could see on the table in the kitchen, she would have assumed the flat had never been lived in. Sonika cautiously went in further, where she saw Kulako in the main room, lighting another lamp before he knelt next to the neatly folded futon.

Sonika knelt beside him to help with the bed. When it was ready, she flopped into the center of it, stretching out, grateful for an actual bed for the night. Kulako laughed at her, and she pulled him down to lay beside her, padding his landing with her free arm, embracing him in softness.

Twenty: Admonition

Kulako was awake and on the move early in the morning to search for a ship departing for Itake that day. He had practically begged Sonika to remain in the flat while he was gone, the tone with which he'd asked her to stay in one place was all Sonika felt she needed to know about the assassins' quarter, and so she abided, though she was horrendously bored within an hour.

Without someone to talk to, Kulako's flat seemed even more barren than it had the night before. He owned no books or scrolls to thumb through as she waited, and though the day was pleasant and warm, all she could do was open the windows to enjoy the breeze. Sonika wondered if Kulako had ever spent much time in one place, which seemed unlikely, and she questioned if he would adjust well to living on Itake. She shook her head. If Kulako hadn't wanted to leave for Itake with her, he wouldn't have planned on it.

Kulako returned not long before noon, irritable from trying to use a voice that still hadn't found enough strength for full conversations, but proud to announce success in securing a way home. Sonika was nearly out the door when he urgently added that they wouldn't be leaving until evening.

"Evening?" Sonika repeated, trying to conceal her disappointment. Kulako nodded.

Sonika mulled that over while she looked out the window and wondered at the best way to pass the time. The Capital was overwhelming, so she didn't feel up to exploring the city, and she doubted Kulako would enjoy the activity, anyway, injured or not.

"Is there a bathhouse nearby?"

"At the end of the street," Kulako answered.

Sonika wrinkled her nose at him playfully. "Good. We both need one before we leave."

The bathhouse was unoccupied, which Sonika was thankful for. If anyone else had been in there, she likely would have chosen to skip it altogether, which was far from her preference, as the bathhouse on Itake was at least a week away yet. When steam began to rise from the adequately heated bath, and Sonika reached under her shirt to undo the first set of ties that secured it, Kulako decided to retreat. Sonika stopped what she was doing and caught him by his shirt collar to prevent him from escaping. He'd nearly forgotten about her quick reflexes.

"In the bath with you, too." She commanded.

Kulako flushed. "There's another one just down the hall,"

Sonika rolled her eyes and opened her shirt the rest of the way to pull the spare jar of ointment from it. "How can I help you with this if you're in there?"

Hikari's sake, Kulako averted his eyes, trying to be polite about the situation.

He looked at the jar, back to her, and then repeated the motion once. He hadn't wanted to protest much in the first place, especially if she was offering, and he now had even less of an argument to stand by. Moments later, Kulako found himself leaning against the edge of the bath. After applying the medicine to the branding on his outstretched arm, Sonika left the open jar beside him. He closed his eyes and sighed as Sonika carefully poured warm water over the healing wounds on his back. Sonika's hands were as gentle and firm as she was, and the way she worked lulled him into a relaxed state of mind.

Sonika leaned forward to reach for the ointment. Kulako jumped when he felt her body against his back, though it hadn't been out of any agitation to the lash marks. He may have been facing the opposite way, but he could practically see the grin he was sure she was wearing when she much more deliberately pulled back.

"Did you forget I was here?" She teased. He tensed when he felt her move against him as she leaned over to try looking at him.

Kulako put his head down. *"Not exactly."*

Sonika snickered and pulled herself to his side. They spoke little from there, but found they didn't need many words to fill the space. Warm skin touching warm skin, contented silence to wrap around them like the steam of the bath, the outside world no longer existed, and the moment felt whole. Kulako thought that was especially true when Sonika interlaced her fingers with his and rested her head on his arm.

••••

CITY WORKERS WERE IGNITING streetlamps when they left the assassins' quarter near sundown. As they approached the wharves, Kulako began to feel uneasy. Exposed. Sonika must have sensed this, as well, as she gripped his sleeve in a sudden manifestation of worry. Unable to explain why, he pulled her off into the shelter of an alleyway created by a moored ship and a mountain of crates as a dense evening fog began to roll in from all around, the lamppost nearest to them now their only viable source of light.

Kulako was only given a moment to examine their surroundings before he had to push Sonika away as a figure lunged at them. He threw a knife at the attacker, who withdrew, and heard it sink into the dock rather than its intended target. He positioned himself in front of Sonika, ignoring how his recovering body protested the action.

Ewah's form materialized from the fog, his eyes gleaming ominously as they caught the last bit of sunlight through the mist, and he pushed back the hood of his cloak. He stooped to pick up Kulako's knife before throwing it back at him. Kulako caught it by the pommel before it went too far past, unable to decide whether he felt more fear or suspicion as he concealed his weapon once again.

"After all that, and you would still attack a superior for that beast?" Ewah mumbled as if to himself, though he kept a vicious, level gaze on Kulako as he spoke. His fingers swept over the delicately crafted hilt of his katana. In one fluid motion, he drew it, advancing again.

Kulako nudged Sonika to retreat, handing a knife to her as he attempted to draw his sword. With Kulako still too weak to defend either himself or Sonika properly, Ewah slipped past with ease, the point of his sword first stopping a paper's width from Kulako's jugular. He dipped it down toward Sonika's heart. Kulako felt terror explode in his chest as he heard the breath catch in her throat. Ewah glared at her balefully, not satisfied until she shrank away.

"You are a very fortunate man, Akahana, to have slipped through the system in such a manner. I can assure you that had it been my decision to make, your fates would have been very different." Ewah's countenance tightened with anger. "You've given me much trouble—you and that repugnant...*animal.* Unlike the others, Akahana, I am *not* slow. I'm fully aware of how far you would go to protect *this.*"

Ewah's katana retracted as he prepared to make another feint for her throat, but Kulako thrust his forearm out in front of her. He spoke as strongly as he could manage. "Enough."

Ewah growled with distaste as he decided to sheathe his sword. Sonika tightly gripped the kunai Kulako had given her, baring her canines as she pushed past him and prepared to use it, but Ewah grabbed her firmly by the jaw, bearing down on pressure points with little mercy. Sonika struggled against him.

"None of that, little *mongrel.*" He spat the word with such maliciousness and hate that Sonika involuntarily let out a canine-sounding whimper.

Kulako shook with fury, and a slight smirk pulled up at Ewah's lips as he noticed the rage building in the assassin's eyes. He knew that Kulako was aware that there would be dire consequences if he chose to react. He released Sonika, pushing her head back forcefully as he did so, and she retreated behind Kulako again.

"Perhaps it's fortunate that you're still mostly unable to speak; I want you to remember how you feel—how that *wolf* feels—in this moment, hitokiri." He pulled a black envelope from his clothing. "You will not disobey my command again. Any other moments of weakness from you, and you shall find that this letter awaits you."

Ewah pulled his hood around his face again and inclined his head curtly before turning on his heel to leave, his cloak billowing behind him as he faded into the fog as suddenly as he had appeared from it. Kulako swallowed the anger rising in his throat like bile as he clutched the letter tightly in his hands. He quickly scanned the order with the assistance of the nearby lamplight as soon as he was sure Ewah had gone.

It called for him to take Sonika's life, and the lives of any family they may eventually have.

"That demented bastard." Kulako croaked, glaring down at the paper before rolling his aching shoulders back and making his way to return to the ship they needed to board. Sonika followed after a second of hesitation, more frightened by the look in Kulako's eyes than she had been at the intelligence master's threat. She suppressed her fear, reaching out and firmly touching his shoulder. No matter what the circumstances, she knew that Kulako would never hurt her.

"Kulako," she said calmly, yet resolutely, forcing him to stop and meet her gaze. The growing crowd took no notice of their interruption of traffic, instead skirting around them. "It's over."

After a moment, he visibly relaxed and his eyes softened, as if he had forgotten where he was. He sighed in resignation, looking away from her to adjust. "I'm sorry, Sonika. We won't be seeing him again."

"Let's get home." She encouraged as she tugged on his sleeve, relieved he shifted back to his normal behavior. Kulako nodded.

"By the way," he began, his voice dry as they fell in line with other passengers preparing to embark on the same vessel. "What did you end up doing with my knife?"

Sonika smiled at him impishly, an expression he knew to be wary of; he was rolling his eyes as soon as it crossed her lips. She stood on her toes and said to him so that no one else could hear, "You can look for it later if you're up to it."

Kulako's face turned red.

Twenty-one: Alone Together

Maru looked at Kulako critically as he finished a delicate bit of metalwork. The two men stared at one another in solemn silence, Kulako growing increasingly uncomfortable at the uncharacteristic seriousness in the blacksmith's face. Not long after returning to Itake, Kulako had received a package from Daisuke and Obito. It contained a couple of personal belongings he had forgotten about and gold coins that should've been paid to him before his meeting with the Emperor—the Treasurer had put everything on hold until a decision had been reached; there was no point in paying a dead assassin. The note sent along with the parcel called it a wedding present. Sonika had taken the opportunity to remind him to write back to his brother, who had lovingly signed the letter with ghastly-looking doodles only Daisuke could—rather, couldn't—draw.

Kulako, able to afford it and on forced leave, took up a project he felt of great importance, but he needed Maru's help to finish it off. Maru had been hesitant to assist but eventually agreed, though he only worked with a tense quiet. At last, Maru glanced away, and Kulako softly released the breath he had been holding.

"This is a pretty unusual request, at least from your kind." Maru finally said as he handed the completed project over to Kulako. "When you first asked me, I was thinking knives, maybe even your sword needed repairs, but not this."

"If we're being honest, and I really hope that we are, this is *all* pretty unusual for my 'kind,' Maru." Kulako replied quietly, brows furrowed at the implication as a sour expression lined his mouth.

It came as no surprise, but Maru wasn't the only one who withheld a friendly demeanor toward him. The village hadn't exactly greeted Kulako's return with open arms, particularly upon learning about his true identity as an assassin, which only seemed inevitable with the retelling of where Sonika had disappeared to in the captivity of Giahatian men. His relationship with Sonika appeared to be the only thing that prevented him from being a complete outcast.

Though the wary and even hateful glances thrown his way as he walked about in the village were unnerving, Kulako understood the suspicions held by the locals—hitokiri were generally unwelcome, even in their own circles in the Capital. However, despite all the negative energy surrounding his permanent relocation, the people of Itake were more than happy to have Sonika back, and therefore at least tolerated his accompaniment. Kulako marveled at the way people flocked to her; she did good things for her community, but Kulako thought it had more to do with the warmth and certainty that she projected.

"Do you actually love her?" The smith snapped; the tone in his voice startled Kulako and drew him from his reverie. "The Okami take this very seriously, and Sonika's been through enough in life. An empty marriage would crush her."

"I don't think 'marriage' is the right word to use," Kulako laughed a little. "But I *do* know how I feel about Sonika, and our lives together."

Maru relented a bit after trying to determine Kulako's seriousness for himself. "She's my friend, Kulako. Please take care of her. Do that, and I'll pray she doesn't drive you *completely* insane, deal?"

Kulako paid Maru for his work and stood as he prepared to leave. He thought briefly of the absolute whirlwind that had taken place since he had first arrived on Itake eight months ago and smiled. "Considering it all, it might be too late for that."

The short walk home from the forge seemed to last forever as he contemplated what he should say to Sonika and the folded cloth tucked away for safety. He hesitated before taking the three short steps into the house, only to find an empty front room. Curious, Kulako searched through the other rooms of the house. When he came to their room, he noticed the leather case containing her weapons was missing.

"I should have known." He said into the empty room.

He wandered through the forest until he came upon the glade where Sonika liked to train. He stayed by the bushes and leaned against a tree as he watched her practice forms. Her movements were both swift and strong, and her eyes were intense with an almost predatory focus. When Sonika settled into these routines, Kulako could sense the power in her Okami blood rise, and he thought she had to be the strongest warrior he would ever know.

She took three throwing stars from hidden pockets in her clothing, and he knew the pattern that followed. She turned to a tree and unleashed them all in one fluid motion, as if it were a dance—one sent for throat level, one for the ribs, and one for the inner thigh. He was familiar enough with this set of attacks to dodge around them. If any of those projectiles landed, Kulako knew it would be a deadly encounter.

Sonika turned with more weapons at the ready, startled when her eyes landed on him. The knife left her hand with a surprised jump upon seeing him standing there, and he had to take cover behind a nearby tree to miss being caught in its path of trajectory. Sonika swore under her breath and went over to where he poked his head around to check for safety, a stream of worried questions already on her tongue as she rushed toward him. Kulako picked her knife up from the forest floor and handed it back to her.

"I wasn't planning on losing my head today," he laughed.

"You're an assassin, don't you know better than to be in the way like that?" She teased, relieved that he hadn't sustained any injuries. "Or is something else on your mind?"

"Well..." He trailed off, not knowing how to approach the subject. They looked at one another for a long moment, Sonika now able to sense his troubles. Finally, he suggested, "How about a walk?"

Sonika tilted her head to one side, but then nodded in agreement. They picked up her scattered weapons before setting out.

Sonika's usual spot on the cliffs was marked by the end of a mostly overgrown game trail relatively secluded from the rest of the scenic overlook to the ocean by bushes and leaning trees battered by fierce winds during storms. Laughter and varied conversations could be heard in the distance, barely audible over the crashing waves below. Kulako glanced toward the water and, for a moment, wondered if this was an ideal location. After all, she could throw him from the cliff.

Sonika repeated her previous question, "What's on your mind, Kulako?"

He mulled over the words in his mind, trying to get them as straight as he could, and plunged ahead. "I know we've talked a lot about where we should go from here—we've beaten the subject practically to death. I also know that we agreed that a *Giahatian* marriage would never be possible."

Sonika looked at him solemnly for a long moment. She told him slowly, "We don't *need* to be married to make this work. It's honestly something that I never gave much thought to, anyway, and I'm sure you haven't, either."

"That is true, but I might have a better idea...if you think it's acceptable."

Kulako carefully handed over the piece of folded white cloth. After giving him a suspicious glance, Sonika cautiously took it and gently placed it on her knee before peeling back the fabric. She let out an involuntary gasp when her eyes fell upon the contents of the package. She looked at Kulako in disbelief as surprise and elation overwhelmed her. Nestled in the soft material were two necklaces—one beaded with blue glass, and the other with molded blue stones, and each featuring a bright gold pendant.

As Kulako lifted the delicate glass-beaded necklace from her lap, the beads caught the sunlight and refracted blue freckles spread over his hands. He smiled nervously as their eyes met again.

"I don't think 'marriage' really describes what we should have between us, anyway."

Sonika moved the length of her hair away from her neck as Kulako leaned in and secured the necklace in place with the delicate clasp finished only hours earlier. She beamed with pride and joy as she felt the weight of it on her skin and examined the careful craft. After bare moments, she latched the other necklace onto him and pulled him tightly against her.

"And here I was sure you were only passively listening to me all those times." She said quietly, laughing a little as Kulako held her closer. "You're suggesting an Okami union, aren't you?"

"Would that work for you?"

Sonika nodded wordlessly, too overwhelmed by emotion to speak properly.

The Okami did not support traditional marriage in the Giahatian sense of the word, instead forming permanent unions with their bonded partner at a time of the pair's choosing. To Kulako, this was the only way he could imagine sharing his life with her and asking her to do the same with him. Even the way they had exchanged their necklaces was a tradition of the Okami—alone together, the only witnesses needed being the elements of the earth surrounding them. Despite being a culture that loved festivities, this was a very intimate moment to the Okami, and Sonika was overcome that Kulako had been able to honor that so perfectly.

"I'm so thankful you see me the way you do," Kulako whispered. "I love you."

"I love you, too." Sonika gently touched her forehead to his. She gripped his sleeves and stood, bringing him up with her. She grinned mischievously. "The village might not appreciate if we had the traditional bonfire that follows, but there are some other things we can still do."

Kulako twisted a lock of her hair around his fingers as she leaned in to kiss him. "What did you have in mind?"

Sonika's stomach growled loudly and she flushed. Kulako laughed. "Apparently that's what."

• • • •

SONIKA'S SEARCH FOR food was slightly impeded. The village's main road was busier than usual as travelers began to leave the docks and make their way toward the inn, which made it unsurprising when someone bumped into Kulako's left shoulder, though the texture of paper in his hand afterwards told him it hadn't been an accident. He paused to look at the black envelope between his fingers, temporarily forgetting that he was no longer in the Capital and that Sonika was beside him. Kulako glanced over his shoulder to see if he could find the one who'd made contact with him, but no one stood out.

"What is that?" Sonika peeked around from his right side and tilted her head curiously.

"An order," Kulako wasn't sure if she should know what the envelope contained, as even most soldiers were unaware of how the hitokiri received assignments, but he doubted it really mattered. Though Kulako was desperate to avoid a third brand, he thought Sonika was less likely to rip one up than he was.

"Already?"

"To be honest, I'm surprised one didn't come sooner. I've been healed for a while, now." He glanced at her; Sonika's eyes were on the ground. "What?"

"I almost forgot you would have to leave when those come." She confessed. "You know, it gets really quiet around here without you."

Kulako smiled as Sonika touched her forehead to his affectionately. "I promise you're the only one who feels that way, wolf."

Twenty-two: Friend nor Foe

Kulako shifted his sword so that it rested against his left shoulder, watching the man he sat across from with undisguised calculation. Teiji's story was strange, but it was in accordance with the order that sent Kulako to the northern archipelagos of Oshosha. An opium dealer had supposedly issued a death threat against the lord of the islands, and Kulako had been ordered to protect the nobleman. Lord Haruya had a history of financial support to the Empire and of personally executing traitors, a decorated way of describing the slaughter of natives who refused Imperial rule.

However, Teiji was the only one present in the household other than a handful of the staff, and Kulako thought there were too few of them for a rice plantation. His instincts told him that perhaps even the Empire only knew half of what was really happening, and he tried to discern the rest of the story from what Teiji was telling him. As he listened to Teiji drone on, however, Kulako observed that such a task would be more complicated than necessary. He bit back his annoyance.

Teiji had been rambling for a while now—somewhat intoxicated, as indicated by the half-empty wine bottle on the floor—about how he had initially been assigned as a bodyguard to Lord Haruya, and through faithful service been granted access to the house, servants, and women. Women were the topic he seemed fixated on at the moment; he had been jumping around between these subjects for a while.

"All's a woman's good for to a man, anyway, is getting his dick wet and waiting on him hand and foot." Teiji slurred. "Fuck 'em and leave 'em if you can. Not that you'd understand; you never *were* much of one for the whores, but damn, did they ever like you."

Kulako's face involuntarily formed into a disgusted scowl at the crudity with which his fellow assassin spoke, and Teiji laughed, teasing him for his sensitivity as wine spilled over the rim of the glass. Kulako's expression soured. Teiji chuckled again. Kulako leaned forward in exasperation, silently wishing his counterpart had waited to start drinking until they solved the current problem. The other hitokiri grabbed at the necklace that fell out from beneath his undershirt as he bent.

"You've been collared," Teiji said, blinking several times as he grasped for understanding. He smirked. "Who the hell could have collared *you*, Hitokiri Nightshade? I was sure for a while that you didn't even like women."

"Never mind that," Kulako growled as he jerked the necklace from Teiji's hands and placed it back where it originally sat against his skin. "Look, your story doesn't make much sense, Teiji."

Teiji took a long drink of his wine, not taking his dark eyes off his counterpart, his interest piqued. "No? Then tell me what you think."

"You weren't an easy opponent in the sparring rings, I remember that, and because of it, you were sent here almost immediately after graduation. Surely your skills aren't that dull after only three short years to need another assassin's help, so why would Lord Haruya ask for one?" Kulako paused for a long moment, watching the way Teiji's eyebrows arched and betrayed a small hint of surprise. He then asked bluntly, "Did you kill Lord Haruya?"

"No, not me, the poison I gave him did."

"What kind of argument is that?" Kulako yelped a little in surprise when Teiji's knuckle was driven into his forehead.

"Shut up. I had to make it look somewhat natural. The lord had no heir and was so appreciative of my services that he set me up to inherit the land. How could I resist if he was going to insist on being so stupid? It's not like the Empire knows—I still sign with his seal. I'll be sending word of his death and my inheritance soon enough." Teiji grinned. "Should I *want* to go back to Kurushima in a few years as a master? Whatever, you and that damned brother of yours always know too much, even if *you* find out by dumb luck. What's your next step, Nightshade?"

"What I *should* do is walk away and let this opium dealer's thugs get their hands on you, especially with how useless you are right now." Kulako sighed. "But I think I'll follow my orders—I've been in enough trouble lately."

"So I've heard." Teiji sneered again. "Everyone else was selfish and spared the gritty details. Care to show me those brands?"

Kulako narrowed his eyes dangerously, but when it seemed as though Teiji was about to reconsider the decision to agitate him, Kulako heard voices from just below the open window. He rose from his spot on the floor and moved toward the window in a fluid motion, keeping low as he counted the number of hushed voices conversing into the darkness of night. Eight, maybe nine men in total stood to collect Teiji's life.

"Tell me," Kulako said quietly, turning his head to look at Teiji once more. "What exactly would an opium dealer want with Lord Haruya in the first place?"

"When I first came to guard Lord Haruya, I killed a few of the dealer's men accidentally, thinking they were intruders. Lord Haruya never apologized for it or compensated him for the losses. In fact, he ordered me to be as ruthless as possible if more came without product."

"'Compensated?'" Kulako shook his head. "'Product?'"

"You heard me. Lord Haruya had bad joints—he used the opium to help. Not sure if it did or not, but it definitely made him easier for me to poison. I guess the dealer finally got tired of waiting for someone to pay him back." Teiji stood, wobbling slightly, and Kulako rolled his eyes in frustration, thinking his time could have been spent better than correcting a nobleman's mistakes. Teiji hiccupped. "Should I help?"

"Don't bother," Kulako replied, his voice thick with annoyance as he began to leave the room. "You'll only be in the way."

Kulako slipped out through a hidden exit in order to position himself just outside of view from the small troop of eight. From what he could tell, their readied weapons consisted of daggers and spears, all of which were easy enough to avoid. He pushed up on the guard of his sword with his thumb, drawing it slightly as he prepared to attack. He descended upon three of them, felling them with a single strike. He turned on the others—two upward strikes, a parry and thrust, and a quickly-drawn knife to the seventh man's throat finished all but the leader of the group, and Kulako was only now visible to him in the moonlight.

"This isn't even skilled enough to be called assassination," he muttered to the trembling man. "This is slaughter."

• • • •

TEIJI WALKED ALONGSIDE Kulako with unusual quiet as he guided them toward the docks. Teiji glanced over at his comrade once and then shuddered from a chill not caused by the weather. The night was warm, and a pleasant breeze floated through the air along with the songs of frogs from a nearby pond.

Still, Kulako did not speak as they moved through the long grass, and Teiji felt his anxieties grow as the pressing silence continued between them, though the silence wasn't so strange for Kulako—his introversion was one of the first things Teiji had picked out about him when they were young. Teiji thought that he seemed determined to get on a boat as quickly as possible, which wasn't altogether unusual, either, but he saw something odd in Kulako's eyes. Was it worry?

Teiji remembered when Kulako was still a new student at Kurushima; worry was an unusual expression for him to wear even then.

Kulako was three years younger than Teiji, yet he had still managed to graduate the same year, which to Teiji had seemed unlikely. He remembered the small red-haired boy who had always ended drills with multiple bruises. Unlike him or most of the others they trained with, Kulako's aura was unimpressive and unthreatening. Teiji assumed a lack of physical presence intensified that, which had often led Kulako to avoid confrontation with Teiji at all costs—even when at one point Teiji had made it a daily habit of beating on him for a good month or so. Because of this, Teiji had little reason to expect the brutality with which Kulako fought against opponents. Until witnessing the way he'd cut down the men the opium dealer sent after Lord Haruya, Teiji had nearly forgotten exactly how cold Kulako could be with a katana in his hands. Those men were practically defenseless against an assassin, and still, their lives were ended before they had a chance to process their impending deaths.

"Teiji," Kulako suddenly spoke, breaking the spell of his thoughts. He was holding the order that sent him to Oshosha in the first place. Protocol required orders to be destroyed after reading, but Teiji saw no reason to remind Kulako; he was more than aware of the policy. "Did you hear about the royal family on Iki?"

"You must have received word around the time I did," Teiji said after a moment; he'd needed time to allow his mind to focus on the present once more.

"Do they know who was responsible?"

"They won't say the traitor's name. They fear that by making him known, people may seek to join him in slaughtering other highborn families." Teiji paused and looked at Kulako directly. "Do you remember the execution we went to in the Old Square when we were still students?"

"I might need more than that; we attended a few. The masters liked to make sure we knew what happened to traitors."

"Amazing that you still fucked up, then," Teiji muttered before continuing, ignoring the annoyed expression on Kulako's face. "I believe I was about twelve at the time, which would have made you only nine."

Kulako stopped walking, as did Teiji when he realized his counterpart had fallen behind. Kulako recalled the day. The masters herded from their regular training routines and ushered them into the city, bound together by chains to ensure that no one could stray from formation.

Kulako remembered the crowds and the scornful ways people looked at and spoke to them as they trudged through to the square. The man on the scaffold had been in the dungeons for years, subjected to torture following an accusation of bedding the empress. The empress died in childbirth with Akuko later that same year, but the man hadn't been caught until four years later. Kulako remembered Akuko's face being detached even then, no different from Emperor Akuwara's, who stood beside the former assassin about to be hanged. Kulako had looked away as soon as the noose was secured, though when the masters noticed, they forced his eyes forward, grabbing him by the pressure points on his neck. They starved him for a week for insubordination after that.

"What about him?" Kulako asked, shaking the memory.

"He was thought to be a *very* busy man. He had a political following that could have become a problem for the Empire, had he ever chosen it, but he met an Okami woman not long after screwing the empress when sent to Othakra for a protection assignment during one of our last peaceful occupations there. Supposedly, he actually married that woman and moved her to Perena. No one knows much about her, but they had a son who was found during a recruitment event for Genjing. Not long after the son was born, the father was called back to the Capital, which is when he was arrested. They kept him in that dungeon for *years*." Teiji scratched the stubble on his cheek. "I know, it all sounds extremely unconnected, but intelligence has reason to believe that the assassin who killed the royal family on Iki is that man's son. Dispatch records haven't confirmed anything yet. Either way, they're both traitors—there's *definitely* a connection, there."

Kulako rolled his eyes. "If you ask me, it sounds *paranoid*, not connected. Leave it to both you *and* the higher ranks to make it that way. That boy would have never known his father if your timeline is even close to accurate."

Teiji gave him a sour look and shuffled his feet a little. "I said it was inherited."

"I think all this time to yourself is starting to go to your head. I highly doubt rebellious behavior can be passed on." Kulako grinned at the obvious annoyance on Teiji's face. "Plus, there's something else wrong with your story."

"You just love pointing out my narration issues." Teiji sulked, and Kulako smirked again. Sometimes he had to make his own fun. "First, you doubted my story about Lord Haruya, now this one, which isn't even mine. Why don't you trust an old friend?"

"'Friend' is a very strong word to be used between us, Teiji, and you know it."

Teiji ignored that and threw his hands up in exasperation. "Fine, what is it *this* time?"

Kulako paused, looking toward the crescent moon in the sky. "The other problem with that story is that the Okami never willingly left Othakra, so why would one of their women just move to Perena? Married or not, they usually stayed in their homeland."

Teiji hesitated and then shrugged, having no real answer, but then his expression grew suspicious as he looked over at his companion once again. "You know, that isn't entirely common knowledge about the Okami—but then I guess nothing really is anymore. When did you hear that? Hell, since when do you know two bits about the Okami?"

Kulako also shrugged and continued walking toward the docks. "Not that you really need to know, but my partner is Okami. I miss her, too, so can we get moving?"

Teiji quirked an eyebrow and followed Kulako. His voice then adopted a sly inflection and his face an equally shrewd grin as he sidled up to him. "So, those brands?"

"Let it lie." Kulako grumbled.

Twenty-three: Onyx and Gold

Sonika watched from her bedroom window as dark clouds began to roll in from the western sky. When the scent of impending rain had touched her keen nose, she'd ended her training session early and was now stretched out on the bed on her stomach, feeling as if she could drift off at any moment.

Raindrops began to patter at the window not long before she heard the front door open. Sonika's heart fluttered with excitement when she registered Kulako's familiar scent in the house once more. She looked over her shoulder, ready to greet him when he entered the room, turning halfway over to see him.

"That tired already?" he teased her as he removed his shirt; the rain had barely begun, but he was soaked from his walk through the village.

"Some greeting," Sonika laughed. "Am I not allowed to relax?"

Kulako sat near her on the edge of the bed, and she shifted onto her back, propped up by her elbows. He smirked at her, and her eyebrows knitted with suspicion. "I guess I could just let you sleep."

She tilted her head curiously. "Did you have other plans?"

"Not if you're ready for bed, no."

"You *did* just get home, and I *could* probably stay up for a little longer. If you can convince me to, that is." A knowing, teasing grin flashed across Sonika's face, revealing one of her pointed canines. Kulako knew to be wary of the mischief that followed the expression. She scooted closer to him and ran the tips of her fingers delicately along his jawline.

"Convince you? How—?" Kulako's next question ended abruptly when she pressed her lips against his. Slowly at first, but when he enfolded her in his arms, her kiss became more fierce.

Sonika broke the kiss as suddenly as she had initiated it, allowing her teeth to drag lightly across his lower lip before she leaned back on her elbows once more, her eyes full of mischief. Kulako grinned at her and shifted so that he could lean over her. She rubbed her nose against his, and he slipped one of his hands under her shirt, finding the first set of ties that secured it and unfastened them with ease. He paused when he came to the second set, allowing his hand to linger near her breast before he pulled on the ties slowly, gently brushing her skin and purposely tracing his thumb over her nipple. She inhaled sharply.

"How would I convince you?" he asked her again as her shirt fell open.

Sonika ran her fingers through his hair, playing with the ends of his bangs, that mischievous look never leaving her features. When she kissed him again, her tongue moved into his mouth with little effort and danced around his. She pulled away even more slowly than she had the last time, dragging her lips along his neck and shoulder before gently biting his collarbone.

"I think you know exactly how." Sonika's voice was low. She was teasing him, now. Kulako ran his hands through the length of her hair before he pulled her shirt the rest of the way off. He kissed both of her breasts, licked and sucked each of her nipples as he pulled down her shorts with her assistance. He kissed her stomach, her navel, and her inner thighs.

Sonika's back arched and a heavy, pleased sigh escaped her when she felt his tongue between her legs. She closed her eyes and stretched her arms over her head as the warmth of his mouth met with her body over and over again. When his speed increased, her knees involuntarily tightened around his head, and her nails went to his hair. She felt his nails dig into her thighs as her breath quickened. When she came, an involuntary cry erupted from her throat as she desperately gripped the sheets at her sides.

Sonika didn't notice when Kulako slid his own pants down—normally she would have helped—but she felt him against her when he leaned over her again to kiss her. She nipped at his ear as she dragged her nails along his back before pushing her hips against him. She pushed him down onto his back and climbed on top of him. She traced the character for "loyalty" permanently etched into his chest and then kissed his throat, allowing the sharpness of her canines to linger, and then his lips. Kulako's eyes never left her the entire time. He lovingly watched everything she did.

Kulako's hand took Sonika's, and together, they guided him inside of her. She worked slowly at first, only putting weight into one of her hips, but as Kulako's hands busily explored the rest of her body and her nails dug into his chest, she soon moved more confidently. Each curve, each bend, each inch of her belonged to him in these moments, but only because she said that it could be as such; Sonika knew that if she changed her mind at any moment, she could do so safely. Close to climaxing again, she allowed herself to let go.

Kulako could barely keep up with the rhythm Sonika set. Her hair hung around her face, tenting them both from the outside world as thunder accompanied the rain. He feared he would be finished too soon, and as she bent to kiss him, he used his weight to switch their positions. Grabbing her by the hips, he pulled her against him. He caught his breath as he ran his fingers again through her hair and along her spine, careful to avoid touching her scar. Sonika bit her lip and looked back at him, another mischievous grin planted firmly on her face.

Kulako spread her legs apart with his knees, gently pushing on her back to bend her further. He cupped both of her breasts in his hands, playing with her nipples again as he thrust himself into her. The next moments were a blur. Sonika was moaning, and so was he. She pressed against him to try and get him in further, and suddenly Kulako couldn't control his pace anymore. He braced against her and held her tightly as he came, shuddering and gasping for air. He buried his face in her hair. Sonika rested her face on her arms, her knuckles white from gripping the bedding.

Kulako finally found himself a little and reached around to turn Sonika's face toward him. He kissed her deeply, wordlessly thanking her. She smiled a little when he pulled away, pressing her forehead against his before they both collapsed forward again.

"Was that convincing enough?" Kulako laughed.

Sonika snickered, her face as flushed as his. "I'd say so."

Silent, contented bliss filled the room as they listened to the rain and thunder; Kulako was nearly asleep on Sonika's chest. There was nothing, and there was everything. Uninterrupted peace.

A distant, anguished bellow suddenly rose from above the sounds of the weather outside, though Sonika was the only one to hear it. Kulako wouldn't have noticed anything was wrong were it not for how her heart pounded against his ear. He still couldn't hear it, but when the cry repeated for a second time, Sonika's expression changed to one of worry and fear.

Sonika jumped up to locate her clothes and redress. Kulako blinked tiredly as his eyes followed her around the room, eventually realizing that he should be doing the same. He might not have understood why her actions had changed so drastically, but they were enough to make him move. Sonika glanced at him just as she was preparing to leave the room.

"Leave the katana," she said, but after a moment added, "Bring a few knives."

Kulako did as he was asked, though he still had no idea what was going on. "Sonika, what—"

"You can't hear that? There's someone out there. They sound hurt." She explained once in the front room and pulling a cloak around her shoulders. Before he could retort, she wrapped one around him as well and kissed him. "Let's be quick."

The warm droplets of rain soaked them not long after they stepped into the slick soil. Her eyes sharp with the gifts of her ancestors, she fought against the wind and rain while trying to catch the smallest hint of an unfamiliar scent or the slightest noise that did not belong to the forest. Enthralled in her endeavor to find the source of the haunting calls, Sonika lost her footing. Kulako quickly reached out and caught her to steady her again so they could continue on their way.

Sonika took a moment to rest against a tree. She listened to the rain as it fell on the leaves above her and splashed to the saturated forest floor. Cautiously, she began to tiptoe around the tree, sliding her hands along the rough bark. She stopped suddenly, surprise catching her as her fingers brushed against a large, deep gash in the tree's trunk. Slowly, she glanced to her right, and noticed more trees afflicted in the same way. If nothing else, they created a new path for her to follow.

"What did this?" She asked Kulako, who was also touching the injured tree trunk.

"Madness." Kulako had watched enough spirits break at Kurushima to know what he was looking at. He didn't want to tell her, but he worried that the person Sonika was so determined to save may have already fallen on their own sword. He looked at the shredded bark again. He didn't like what it implied about the unknown person.

Sonika leaned against Kulako and breathed deeply. She tightly gripped his hand; with his support, she had the courage to continue onward. As they continued along the twisted route of slashed trees, she noticed smaller victims that had either been broken or sliced nearly in half, and a shudder not due to the soaking weather passed through her. Still, she pressed on, ignoring the ominous sense surrounding her as her sensitive ears caught the sound of a strangled sob, nearly drowned out by the wind.

She followed the destroyed trees to a clearing, leaning against a large rock to try and refocus her resolve. A snarl came from the darkness before her, though it was quickly cut off by a pathetic whimper. She approached only a few paces, carefully and quietly, until her eyes could see the outline of a curled human form on the forest floor. Kulako put his arm out in front of her to keep her from moving forward, and they waited to see what would happen. The form attempted to move from its fetal position with a lurch before it collapsed into its flooded spot on the forest floor.

Sonika ignored her instincts, which ran with fear, and Kulako's call for her to come back as she ran to the other human. She dropped to her knees as soon as she reached him, absorbing the image of the young man haunting the woods. His sopping boots and clothes were tattered beyond repair, he had small cuts all about his arms and face, and one particular laceration on his left forearm that appeared to be deeply infected. Even with the dirt and filth caked around it, Sonika thought she could make out something beneath the injury. She examined his face; his will to live seemed drained from him entirely. When she gazed into his sunken dark eyes, however, there was an incredible amount of hatred burrowed into them.

"You'll be safe, now." She told him quietly as she placed a hand on his fevered forehead. He stared back at her blankly, and Sonika wondered if pain beyond his physical afflictions tormented him. She had to ignore it, at least for now. Her glowing eyes found Kulako standing on the young man's other side. "We have to get him home."

The young man mumbled something incoherent, and suddenly his eyes locked onto her menacingly. Sonika froze, but Kulako's knife was already drawn and at the ready. Lightning streaked across the sky, and shock swept Sonika's features as his obsidian eyes melted into a golden gaze. The lightning faded, as did the color from his irises, and Sonika released a sharp exhale. She looked at Kulako again to determine whether he had seen what she just had, but it appeared he'd missed it. Another moan of pain escaped from the stranger, and Sonika's heart twisted in sympathy.

Sonika moved to lift him and Kulako did the same, though they both stopped at the sound of knives scraping together from inside his ruined clothing.

"Are you sure about this?" Kulako asked her reluctantly.

When she nodded, he sighed and helped her move the young man to his feet. In another flash of lightning, the katana Sonika's new patient had been holding became visible, but disarming him was effortless. Kulako tied the hanging cord at his belt before shifting so that he and Sonika could continue for their home with the injured stranger in tow. A whine of agony came from his lips. Kulako glanced at Sonika, and they came to the unspoken agreement that whatever military status he held no longer mattered. He needed help.

"Kulako, the box with the red ribbon in the closet, can you please grab it along with some water?" Sonika's orders began the moment they had him laid out on the bed in the spare room. Kulako dutifully followed her instructions.

She braided her hair back quickly and stripped the soaked, ruined clothing from her new patient's lanky form before toweling off what she could and wrapping him in several layers of blankets, leaving his left arm exposed. She cleaned the frothing infection, scrubbing the rest of the dirt from around it, and stitched the wound once she was sure the treatment from her medications had begun to take effect. She curiously tilted her head to one side as she looked at the closed wound, wondering again at the contorted marking beneath her sutures; it almost looked like the character for "honor." She made another fluid she could guide down his throat that would help his fever and pain, and then set a damp, cool cloth against his forehead.

The young man was not Giahatian, but Perenin, and only Perenin. From what she understood, that was an increasing rarity except in rural areas on the mainland. His sleek features, impressive height despite his young age, and dark skin confirmed that. His mess of choppy black hair gave off an almost bluish shine, even in the light of the oil lamp. It looked as though he had tried to hack away at it himself; some spots were nearly bald. Sonika guessed that he might be around fifteen years of age, which made her even more curious. During their journey back to Itake, Kulako had clarified things he had once said to her while under the guise of being a soldier, one of those including his own training history. Kulako had told her during this conversation that assassins often didn't leave training until they were at least nineteen. He had been an early graduate, but Sonika knew that was an uncommon event. What were the odds that she would meet two such hitokiri in her lifetime and still be alive?

A sharp twinge of pain in her back where the scar marked her old injury brought her from her musings. She rose stiffly from where she had been crouched beside the bed. She shuffled to her bedroom to change into dry clothing, having forgotten about herself in her rush to tend to the young man. Kulako had already set up a makeshift clothesline in front of the fireplace and lit the hearth. She carefully lowered herself to the sofa after hanging up her wet clothes, attempting to ignore her pain and clear her mind from the evening's events, the latter of which she quickly found she was unable to do.

"Who do you think he is?" she asked Kulako when he stepped into the room. "Have you ever seen him?"

"No, I can't say that I have." He handed her a cup of tea and sat beside her. He placed his hand in the center of the scar and traced his fingers slightly to the right of it, where he gently rubbed at her agitated nerves. Kulako thought of his previous conversation with Teiji. "But I know someone who apparently does have a little information on him. Teiji's facts are a little confused and slightly off from what I originally read—probably *because* of Teiji—but he made it sound like they've been looking for a defector from Genjing for a little while, now."

"Genjing?" Sonika had been gazing into the liquid in her cup while enjoying the back massage, but quickly turned her attention to Kulako.

He nodded. "It's another training facility in northern Perena. It recruits from surrounding villages and takes the overflow from Kurushima, where I was raised. When I was brought to the Capital, most of us were sent to Kurushima, but the rest went to Genjing. It's supposed to be absolutely brutal to survive there."

Sonika's stomach churned a little at the idea that there was something worse than the environment Kulako grew up in. "Isn't...Kurushima supposed to be terrible, too?"

"Genjing is rumored to be worse, from food rations to weather. Their graduation ceremony is more violent, too, but if they live through it, they're given preference in assignments and rank over anyone else." Kulako sighed, and Sonika curled up close to him with a shiver from the weather after setting her tea off to the side. "Sonika...you know that I *am* obligated to report him, don't you?"

"Are you going to?"

He couldn't see her face, but she sounded worried about his reply, and to make matters worse, Kulako hesitated to answer her. To commit the level of treason as their new lodger allegedly had would mean a life of slow, agonizing torture for him the moment he arrived in the Capital, and they would stave off from killing him for as long as they could. Kulako didn't think he could willingly and knowingly subject anyone to that. However Sonika had anticipated him to reply no longer mattered, though, as during his internal debate, she had fallen asleep and sank into a heavy slumber already. Kulako shook his head and shifted so that he could pick her up and carry her to bed.

He watched their bedroom door for a while before he was also comfortable enough to lie down beside Sonika. It wasn't so much the stranger who concerned him, given the condition they'd found him in, but the possibility that he'd already been traced to Itake. He pulled Sonika's sleeping form to his chest, holding her close to his heart, trying to calm himself. They weren't in the Capital, and Teiji had confirmed that the Empire hadn't found their missing hitokiri.

Kulako groaned. *It never ends, does it?*

Twenty-four: Hikaru

Sonika awoke with a start to the pale light of dawn. The gentle drumming of a softer rain could be heard against the roof, and all at once, Sonika remembered her patient in the next room. She attempted to move quickly as she unfurled herself from the covers, but the dull soreness still burrowing into her back forced her to keep a steady pace. She glanced over at Kulako's sleeping form, and decided to leave him there and allow him to rest.

She slipped into the young man's temporary room with cautious quiet before going to his unconscious form. He did not stir when she carefully placed a hand to his forehead to see if his fever had lessened, but when she gently touched his forearm to check the wound she had stitched, he mumbled and jerked away from her, like someone who didn't want to be disturbed. Sonika sighed as she went to her medicine box and prepared another dose of the pain remedy she had given him the night before. Sonika paused when she thought she sensed a disturbance in his subconscious, remembering the flash of gold that had appeared in his eyes. She returned to his side and reached beneath his neck to support him. At the same time, she poured the treatment down his throat.

A sudden burst of speed caught her wrist in a powerful grip as she began to pull away once the medicine was in his system. Sonika gasped and looked down to his eyes, bright gold glaring at her through incoherent fog. However, when she curled her arm inward, she easily freed herself and fled the room as he sank back into slumber. Her heart pounded wildly against her chest, and she glanced at the throbbing ache in her right arm where a defined imprint of his hand was already visible in her skin. Seeing that Kulako was awake and standing at their door across from her, she wordlessly went to him.

• • • •

OBSIDIAN EYES OPENED to the warm light of afternoon. A comfortable breeze sailed into the small room through a slightly open window, and Hikaru swallowed against the dryness in his throat. He had longed for death, but he clearly wasn't in any of Kuro's Hells; he didn't know where he was. Perhaps one had to wait on a bed between life and death until Kuro welcomed their soul to hell. He flexed his hands at his sides, wincing at a pulling sensation from his left arm, and accepted that he was still in the land of the living. He grunted in pain as he shifted to see what had caused it. His eyes struggled to focus on the pattern of sutures along the gash he had created to cross out the brand burned into his skin.

Exhaustion pushed his head back again. He tried to gain his bearings, but the silence of the empty room was becoming increasingly unsettling. It was too quiet to him, and Hikaru was more fond of silence than unnecessary noise. Herbal scents came to him, and he glanced over to see a medicine box with a red ribbon tied to the latch laying on the floor beneath the window, unopened and unattended. Beside the box, a chair held a pile of folded clothing, and Hikaru's head swirled with confusion. The blankets swaddled around him were warm and soft. Hikaru's eyelids were drooping, though he wasn't ready to lose consciousness—sleep could be dangerous.

Where am I, Hanako? He wondered to the ghost of the woman he'd thought he loved. His heart ached when her face appeared before his eyes, and he forced a sorrowful wave of memories away. He choked down a sob, and his mind sank into a state of haunted dreams once again.

Hanako cooed Hikaru's name sweetly from beneath the bubbling surface of a pond. When Hikaru dashed in after her, the water darkened red with every step he took until he was up to his waist in blood. He panicked and tried to splash the blood away, but it clung to his skin. Hanako's voice called him again, and he looked down at his reflection. Her face gradually replaced his. The bloody water began to rise until, shrieking, Hanako erupted from the surface and grabbed Hikaru by the face to pull him under with her. Hikaru did not struggle against her grasp; he wanted to be with her, he'd wanted to die from the moment she had passed from the living world. There was a bright flash from the sky over the pond, and Hanako stopped pulling Hikaru down. Golden eyes suddenly appeared when Hikaru looked over his shoulder. He reached toward them.

Hikaru awoke in a cold sweat to the dusty light of dusk, hardly aware that he had drifted off. He tried his strength again and found that he was at last able to force himself upward. He dully examined the room once more; the medicine box had been removed, and the window had been closed even further so that just a tiny slit kept air fresh air flowing through. Hikaru lurched forward and turned, planting his feet firmly on the floor before deciding to use the atrophied muscles in his legs to stand. He stared at the pile of clothing warily for a long moment, calculating. Hikaru wanted answers, but knew he was too weak for a fight if he was about to walk into one.

• • • •

KULAKO SAT ACROSS FROM Magistrate Tomio on the floor beside the ailing official's bed. The old man looked exhausted. Though Sonika had been trying for months to keep him healthy, there was only so much that medicine could do, and at this point, Kulako doubted a Healer could have reversed the advancement of his age and disease. He avoided looking at the bin full of bloody linens beside the Magistrate.

"Just the poison, then?" Kulako confirmed, uncertain about following through with what had been asked of him only a few days prior when he'd been out to collect some supplies for Sonika, as she'd had to restock some of her ingredients after using them on the injured stranger.

The magistrate nodded. "It won't be detectable."

"Sonika could have made you something better than I did—I barely got through poisons training at Kurushima."

"Lady Sonika would refuse to do it." Tomio smiled weakly, yet fondly, and Kulako knew he spoke the truth. "Lady Kiki would have also refused. But I'm ready. After my death, my son will take my place and become the magistrate here. Make sure Lady Sonika keeps him in line."

Kulako got to his feet and placed a vial in the magistrate's hand. "Drink it before you lie down tonight, and you'll be sleeping too heavily to notice when your lungs stop. The Giahatians and Perenins would ask for Hikari to watch over you, the Nomads would wish you peace in the afterlife, and the Okami would pray for wholeness in your spirit—I'm not sure which one to give you."

"Do you think it would be greedy for me to take all three of those with me?" The magistrate chuckled a little when he received a confused shake of the head in response, and Kulako gave him a halfhearted smile. "Then allow me to wish you and Lady Sonika a blessed life together, Hitokiri Nightshade."

• • • •

SONIKA CALMLY SIPPED at her tea while she waited for Kulako to return from the errand he'd said he had to run. Her slow, meditative breaths were likely the only reason she was able to unwind. She'd had an active day in the village: between two children who had fallen from a moving cart, a man kicked by his cattle, and her usual rounds to a few of the more elderly residents who lived near her, it had been an exhausting day. She'd wanted to check on Magistrate Tomio, as well, but she'd simply run out of time after looking in on Mitake, now heavily pregnant and due any day. Sonika *could* midwife, it had been part of her education with Lady Kiki, but her lack of experience made her feel less than competent.

A slow, laden shuffling reached her ears, and she felt the house shift beneath her. Sonika watched the fire for a moment longer, biting her lip anxiously. Given how busy she had been throughout the day, she had forgotten the patient she kept in her home—Kulako had removed the medicine box for her earlier, but she hadn't been in to see him yet. She hadn't told anyone else about the strange young man yet, either. Her heart raced at the idea of the unknown assassin being well enough to move about on his own; perhaps he was still too weak to become physically forceful. When his looming figure appeared in the entrance of the sitting room, she held her breath, waiting, wishing she had at least one of her kunai available to her, but her leather case was tucked away in her bedroom.

Hikaru halted as his eyes settled on the figure in the room before him: a small, rather thin woman who was probably as fragile as she looked. He couldn't disguise the confusion that etched into his features. Originally, he'd planned to use any amount of force necessary to get information from those who had captured him, but now, he was unsure what to do. He could easily kill her, but that wouldn't help him much. She cleared her throat delicately, and Hikaru growled at her, wondering if she could perhaps read his mind, given her perfect timing for breaking him from his reverie.

"My name is Sonika." She told him quietly and carefully, not wanting to startle him. "It looks like you've recovered well—it's been a few days."

"Hikaru Hinatako," he introduced himself in a dry, cracked voice, not expecting the politeness. He coughed with the hope to moisten his throat and changed his voice to sound more authoritative, allowing his Perenin accent to come through. "Where am I?"

When she moved to stand, Hikaru caught the glint of gold from around her neck as he retreated from her, and he narrowed his eyes, shifting his stance. She stopped immediately, placing her empty hands in front of her to show that she would not harm him.

His eyes fixed on her dangerously and his second inquiry came out just as harshly as his first. "You're married?"

"In a manner of speaking," She admitted. "But what does that—"

"Your husband must be the medic who tended to me, then. Where is the bastard? I'll get my hands on him before he can return me to Akuko and the Giahatio."

"Akuko? Why would—"

"Don't play dumb with me, woman. Akuko, *your* Emperor? Surely my death warrant has been sent out by now." His eyes were frenzied as they scanned every inch of the house currently visible to him.

Sonika's stern gaze settled on Hikaru as she paused, taken aback by his demeanor. Despite the firmness in her tone, she approached him as if she were reaching out to a timid forest creature. "I may not have vows of my own to the Giahatio, but you've no right to speak to me in such a manner in *my* home."

Hikaru growled, the sound as low and wolf-like as Sonika could manage. "Enough of this. I *demand* to see the man of the house. Where is he?"

"Out at the moment." Sonika's eyes narrowed and her stance shifted protectively; her fluid movement betrayed her experience with training, which didn't go unnoticed by Hikaru. "I want to make it very clear that when he does come home, you'll make no demands of me, or us. We have no intention of turning you over to the Empire, but we also won't force you to stay here."

Hikaru watched her for a long moment as his aching head reeled from the confrontation. When a grin began to play at his lips, she growled at him defensively. "You're a strange one, aren't you, woman? Tell me, if your husband was not the one who stitched me up, then who was?"

Sonika felt her guard slip at the question and she straightened a little, hesitating before saying, "That would be me."

Hikaru snorted derisively. "I'm being serious."

"So am I." Sonika rolled her eyes in undisguised exasperation, the light from the fireplace catching the honey-colored hue in them.

Hikaru stiffened, truly noticing them for the first time. While in the throes of his fevered nightmares, he had seen those very same eyes attached to a forbidden figure of Perenin lore; a wolf had appeared, wrapped its powerful jaws around one of his legs, and began to pull him from the depths of the bloody pond. Hikaru shook his head to free his mind of those images, and the woman looked at him curiously, the expression appearing as canine as the color of her eyes.

"What are you?" he rumbled at her with dangerous quiet, and Sonika stepped back from him, too alarmed by the suddenness of the question to be offended by the wording.

"Okami," she answered in a voice barely louder than a whisper.

Hikaru thought for a moment. "Unlikely as it seems, if you actually are Okami, then perhaps what you say is true; you really would have no reason to sign me over to the Giahatio. They murdered your people and stole your land, and no sort of alliance comes of that."

Sonika swallowed nervously as came closer, still wishing she had one of her knives or throwing stars near enough for defense. However, when Hikaru stopped within an arm's length of her, he grinned tightly in an attempt to cover the frustration he felt—she was an immovable force, as was he, and he sensed that a stalemate between them could last for ages.

Remaining suspicious of her, Hikaru was sure not to get too close as he leaned in toward her. "You know what I am, do you not? You *are* aware of how easily you could be killed by *me*, aren't you? What person in their right mind offers to help a disgraced assassin rather than turn him over before he follows the nature that's been beaten into him by slaughtering them?"

Sonika looked into the sorrowful, hateful, and painfully confused depths of Hikaru's jet-black eyes, wondering yet again at the golden flash she had seen in them, not wanting to hope. "You're probably aware, but old Perenin lore likes to say that savagery and viciousness is a wolf's only nature as a top predator. I have several reasons to believe this isn't true. Is killing really *your* nature, Hikaru?"

Hikaru paused, then frowned at her before backing up and leaning against the mantle in exhaustion, trying to ignore her intense eyes. "When your husband does finally come home, I'll need to speak with him—or is that too much of a demand?"

Sonika scowled. "Are all of you military men this mouthy to medics?"

"That all depends on the medic." Hikaru struggled to not smirk at the annoyance on her face.

"Sonika?" Kulako called as the front door opened. Sonika swore under her breath as Hikaru's eyes locked on her with vicious intent.

Sonika rushed past Hikaru to try to cut Kulako off in the hall, worried that the stress of seeing another assassin would trigger something unpleasant in the minds of either her partner or her patient, even though Kulako was the only one who knew with certainty that he was dealing with another hitokiri. She wasn't quite fast enough, though, and nearly slammed into Kulako at the room's entrance.

Hikaru needed only seconds to register the red hair and small stature of the Giahatian-trained assassin before him. The Emperor had sent one of his most valued hitokiri, it seemed, and now Sonika's life was in danger as well as his own. Young as hitokiri Nightshade was, stories of his brutality in combat had reached even Hikaru's ears, but he was prepared to fight. Cowardice would mean death in an instant. He had no weapons, but thanks to his height and long limbs, he had reach. He snarled and raised his fists.

Nightshade reacted quickly as could only be expected and a dagger was in his hand as he stepped in to create a protective space between Hikaru and Sonika. The group pivoted in a half circle, and now Hikaru's back was to the empty doorway.

"Name and stripes." Kulako demanded curtly.

Hikaru grinned; the expression was much darker than when he had shown it to Sonika. "Hikaru Hinatako of Genjing. No stripes."

"Are you the deserter who killed the royal family on Iki, then?"

"I don't owe a Giahatian dog like you an explanation." Hikaru suddenly shot a glare at Sonika. "But *you* didn't tell me that your husband was Hitokiri Nightshade, of all the people or assassins. *You* didn't say how entirely fucked I was going to be the second he came home."

Sonika swallowed. "Hikaru, I told you we didn't plan on—"

"I knew I shouldn't have believed you." Hikaru snarled, and Kulako wound defensively so that he could be prepared to move both Sonika and himself out of the way in the event that Hikaru lashed out. His black eyes went back to Kulako. "Where's your contact here? I need to kill him before you get around to reporting me."

Kulako inhaled deeply and looked at Sonika, her golden eyes settling on him in a way that did not permit a debate regarding their previous conversation that day. The brand over his heart itched as if reminding him it existed, and Kulako wondered why he agreed with her. He knew he was unable to afford being caught with a fugitive in his house, and even though he'd had plenty of opportunities to write a report, he hadn't been able to bring himself to do it. Sonika had ultimately made the decision to not say a word. The Giahatio would have vehemently argued—before cutting his head off—but who was he to go against her?

After a long pause, he told Hikaru directly, "Sonika didn't lie. We have no plans of reporting you."

Hikaru narrowed his eyes doubtfully and straightened to his full height, already well over Kulako's head. The statement had caught him off guard, and his stance relaxed slightly, causing Sonika to sigh with relief.

He leveled his gaze with Kulako's. Mistrust riddled his face, and his voice held the slightest quiver of uncertainty beneath the roughness when he asked, "Why should I believe *that?*"

"Everyone who tries to get out has their reasons for it, but few are ever lucky enough to tell others what those are." Kulako touched the pendant at his throat briefly, an uncharacteristically callous expression lining his eyes. "Whatever *your* reasons are, for your sake, I hope they're good. Don't ever threaten Sonika again."

Hikaru's eyes went bright with gold and he growled lowly in the back of his throat, exposing the tip of a sharper than average canine. Kulako asserted himself in the middle of the building chaos, and Hikaru gave a final snarl before turning on his heel and disappearing into the room he'd been provided. Not long after, Sonika heard the window of the room open further, and after some awkward movements, she guessed that Hikaru had gone out through it.

Sonika squeezed Kulako's hand as she stepped up to his side. They stared after Hikaru in stunned silence for a long moment before she could at last ask, "Did you see that?"

Kulako slowly nodded. "I think so."

"Do you know what this means?" Sonika tilted her head so they could look at one another. Though she tried to contain her excitement, it had already spread to every inch of her face. "I never was the last of the Okami—we're still here."

To be continued in Book II: Keeper of the Broken

Acknowledgments

I'd like to start this off right away by saying how endlessly grateful I am toward everyone who helped me get this far. I want to turn this into a pages-long gush fest, but to save on printing costs, I'll try to keep it short.

These characters and this story have been in my heart for years. Nothing would have come of it if I hadn't had the friends who stayed up for all-night chats about world building, my best friend who has been endlessly patient with my anxious texts for her opinions regarding scenes or ideas, or Shadow Spark Publishing and the support from my beautiful colleagues there.

You also wouldn't believe the support I've found in Twitter's #WritingCommunity, where I've met so many wonderful people, including my amazing beta readers who gave me so much damn good advice. Between signing my contract, episodes of imposter syndrome, drafting, editing, and battering my favorite artist with commissions, the year leading up to publication has been an insane and amazing journey. If you've been a part of the process or have had to put up with me during it, you probably deserve a medal.

I want to thank you, too, as the reader, for spending your time with my world and characters. I can't wait to see you again for *Keeper of the Broken,* and sincerely hope I do.

Credits

Cover Design and Editing—Jessica Moon
Cover Design—Chad Moon
Editing—Susan Floyd
Formatting and Editing—Mandy Russell
Map—Jarrod Vandenberg

About the Author

Alyssa Lauseng is a fantasy writer who lives in Michigan's beautiful Upper Peninsula with her husband, two warrior princesses, and moose-dog. When not writing or momm-ing, she practices Kuk Sool Won, listens to metal, and tries to draw.

Her upcoming novel, *keeper of the fallen*, is a light adult fantasy which includes romantic themes, fighting for what is right, and having the courage to do so.

She can be found on Twitter @5FeetofRedFury and will nerd out about just about anything with you.

Printed in Great Britain
by Amazon